BREATHING IN REVERSE

a novel

DENSIE WEBB

Breathing in Reverse
Red Adept Publishing, LLC
104 Bugenfield Court
Garner, NC 27529
https://RedAdeptPublishing.com/

Cover Art by Streetlight Graphics[1]

This is a work of fiction. Names, characters, places, and incidents either are the product of the author's imagination or are used fictitiously, and any resemblance to locales, events, business establishments, or actual persons—living or dead—is entirely coincidental.

---

1. http://StreetlightGraphics.com

Dedicated to the actor, who shall remain nameless, who inspired me to tell this completely fictional story

Painless memories fade with time.
Those stained with blood
leave an indelible mark,
like a tattoo on your brain.
You can cover it up,
keep it hidden from view,
but it's there just the same.
—Lyrics by Rachael Allen

"If you don't address the wounds of the past, you continue to bleed."
–Tina Turner

Each year, there are more than three million cases of stalking in the United States.

Prologue
Mick

The night found him antsy, unwilling to give himself over to sleep and painful nightmares, so he came downstairs to the hotel bar, believing he'd made his way to the corner booth unnoticed. He was experiencing a unique brand of loneliness after weeks of non-stop traveling—another city, another luxury hotel, a series of mind-numbing press junkets to promote his latest movie. The film festival in Austin, Texas, was his final stop. He settled into the corner booth, away from curious eyes, and ordered a beer then another and another as he fixated on the photo shoot from earlier that day.

No one had told him he was going to have to strip down. When he took off his shirt, the photographer demanded loud enough for everyone in the room to hear, "Dude, where's the six-pack?"

What a dick.

But he wasn't done. "Get makeup over here *now* to cover up Snow White. I thought you'd lasered that thing," he said, pointing to the colorful tattoo on Mick's unchiseled chest.

He had become a commodity—a product you worked on, changed, improved to make it more marketable. And he'd begun to despise everything about it. But he was caught in a series of contractual traps that prevented escape.

As he nursed another beer, he sensed a body hovering. His eyes at half mast, he looked up and blinked against the backdrop of the lights over the bar. She was attractive, blond. He preferred brunettes but didn't want to face another night alone.

"Mind if I join you?" She smiled seductively and slid into the booth beside him.

"Mick Sullivan," he said, offering a handshake.

She had no visible reaction and didn't offer an introduction. He considered for a moment that she might be a high-priced hooker or that it could be a setup to get compromising photos of him that would surely provide a big payoff. But he was drunk enough to believe he'd lucked upon a woman—a hot one, no less—who didn't recognize him. She wanted to keep him company, not scream at him, grab him, touch the hem of his coat. That shit, he could get anytime.

"What'll it be?" he asked her as he gestured to the bartender.

She said nothing, but her warm hand on his thigh told him what she really wanted. If he waited much longer, he wouldn't be able to get it up, he'd fall asleep, or both. She leaned closer and smiled.

Nice teeth. Nice tits.

"Can we go up to your room?" she asked in a throaty whisper.

He was used to women wanting him. No introductions, no strings—just sex. He was famous, after all, a fact that still struck him as fucking ridiculous. But that girl seemed to want *him*, not his celluloid image.

As he stumbled out of the bar with her, he turned to the bartender. "Put it on my room."

They entered the lobby elevator, and as the doors closed, he pressed her against the mirrored wall, groped her breasts under her shirt, and sloppily kissed her. Interrupted by the ding of the doors opening, they stepped into the deserted hallway. He stumbled back then regained his balance.

"Here, you open the door. It's room... Shit... I can't remember," he said, his tongue thick with alcohol.

He fumbled in his pocket and pulled out his phone to check the room number. Unable to focus, he shoved the phone and the key card into the palm of her hand. She opened the door, and he staggered in, stripped down, and crawled into bed. He watched her undress before he closed his eyes and felt the mattress shift as she joined him. He had a vague notion of her naked body pressing against his, her tongue in his ear, her hot breath spreading across his chest.

A knock on the door jolted him awake. He'd been dreaming of earthquakes, bridges crumbling, and running to safety. Unwelcome sunlight peeked through the hotel-room curtains. He blindly felt around the bed for his cell and discovered it under his pillow—four missed calls from his handler. The hotel phone on the nightstand blinked insistently. He didn't need to listen to the messages to know they were from her, screaming, "You're late!" That had to be her at the door, pissed off and anxious to escort him to the airport and through security. Her job would be on the line.

He gingerly sat up, his head pounding out a painful rhythm. He would've flunked a Breathalyzer test, and he had no clue who was in bed with him, her hair cascading in tangles across the pillow. They were both naked, their clothes left in random piles on the floor. Blackout sex—wasn't the first time, but he swore to himself that this time would be the last.

"I'm up," he croaked.

The banging on the door continued.

"Okay, okay."

The knocking stopped. He pushed his hair away from his face and glanced at the woman next to him. She was snoring loudly. A string of saliva from her parted lips had left a puddle on the pillowcase. That familiar blend of disgust and regret made its way to the sober part of his brain. He sat up on the edge of the bed and felt the bristle of the hotel carpet on his bare feet as he lit a cigarette, inhaled deeply, and felt better for that fraction of a second as the nicotine shot through his bloodstream.

He smelled like shit—chain smoking, fast food, dried sweat, and sex. An ether of alcohol seeped through his pores. He would splash cold water on his face and rinse his mouth a couple of times with that mouthwash in the bathroom. It would have to do.

Still sitting on the edge of the bed, he pulled on his jeans. Smoke from the cigarette clenched between his teeth rose and burned his eyes. He took one last drag and dropped the stub into a half-empty beer bottle on the nightstand. Dizzy and nauseated, he clutched the headboard as he leaned over to pick up his T-shirt from the floor. His stomach heaved, and he vomited onto the carpet. Steadying himself, he stood, wiped his mouth with the back of his hand, and pulled the T-shirt over his head. The banging on the door started up again. With no time to even wash his face, he threw his things into his bag, grabbed his Nikes, his cigarettes, and his phone and walked barefoot out the door. His handler glanced into the room, and her mouth twisted in disgust as she reached inside and quietly closed the door behind them.

Chapter 1
Rachael

*I*t *was all because of an espresso machine.*

Standing on the second floor of Zabar's, a gourmet institution on the Upper West Side of Manhattan, I was lusting after a shiny new espresso machine I couldn't afford. As much as I admired it, I understood that my longing wasn't so much for the espresso machine as it was to get a place of my own, with a kitchen and a small breakfast table, where I could peacefully caffeinate myself each morning. After I lost my job at Broken Vinyl Records and escaped my toxic relationship with Conrad, I had begrudgingly moved back into my parents' home in New Jersey in a last-ditch and utterly demoralizing maneuver to save money. Day trips into the city to wander neighborhoods and window-shop were the only things keeping me sane.

My cell vibrated in my purse. I reached in and glanced at the screen—my father. I released a weighted sigh and pressed End Call. As I shoved the phone into the back pocket of my jeans, my purse fell from my shoulder and landed on the floor with a thud.

The guy standing a few feet away glanced in my direction before he turned back, slipped his Wayfarers onto his head, and leaned over to get a better look at the espresso machine on the shelf in front of him. Van Morrison's plaintive voice singing "Brand New Day" wafted from his AirPods.

All it took was a quick glance to recognize him. I knew his bio courtesy of my best friend, Jenna. She'd seen every movie he'd ever made, at least twice. His name was Michael Christopher Sullivan. He'd starred in his share of blockbusters and been on the cover of *People* several times, including a turn at being named Sexiest Man Alive. He was a player of legendary status and a favorite on the talk show circuit because of his inability—or unwillingness—to self-censor. I couldn't deny that he was ridiculously gorgeous, but I refused to participate in the cult of celebrity worship by staring. Despite my general ambivalence toward celebrities, my thoughts jumped around like a herd of hyperactive kids let loose in a bouncy castle. And I was disappointed in myself for having any kind of reaction at all. Selfies and autographs were ridiculous celebrity customs that I swore I would never, *ever* participate in. But as my mother always said, *Never say never. You'll always be wrong.*

As I repositioned my purse onto my shoulder, I sensed the words rising in my throat, and they escaped as if I were a ventriloquist's dummy. "Could I take your picture? My friend is a huge fan, and, well... she would never believe me without proof."

He looked nonplussed. He was either bored or irritated at the idea of being asked, yet again, for a selfie or—*Shit, what if it isn't him?* It wasn't like he had introduced himself.

"You are Mick Sullivan, right?"

He threw his head back and laughed, his perfectly aligned, pearly white caps on full display. "Yep. Last time I checked." He looked at me and frowned. "Just curious—what if I'd said no?"

"I'd still take your picture and lie to my friends."

He nodded in approval. "You got a phone in that... uh... duffel bag?" he asked.

I reached into my ridiculously oversized purse and skimmed the bottom and the pockets—a pack of gum, coins, Tic Tacs, that missing earring, my sunglasses, lip gloss. Loose change spilled out with a dull *clank* onto the hardwood floors. Then I remembered. I slipped my fingers into my back pocket, retrieved my phone, and handed it to him.

"It's warm," he said and followed his comment with a solicitous grin.

I was well acquainted with that entitled expression. Guys that looked like him were born locked and loaded with a full magazine of social advantage. They carried around everything they could ever need to get what they wanted in life. He clearly had everything and expected even more.

"Yeah, well…"

"What's your name?"

"Rachael. Rachael Allen."

"Come here, Rachael," he said, motioning for me to come closer, and without hesitating or asking permission, he slipped his arm around my shoulders.

I sensed it was a well-rehearsed routine he ran through often. I detected the faint scents of alcohol and tobacco and the rich aroma of new leather from that expensive-looking jacket he was wearing. *Eau de Bad Boy.* He held my phone out at arm's length, leaning over so we both fit in the frame. But instead of taking a picture, he pressed Record.

"Hi, friends of Rachael Allen! I'm Mick Sullivan, and Rachael and I met in Zabar's. Right, Rachael?"

I nodded. Then he did the unexpected—and unacceptable, from a stranger. He kissed my cheek. I disengaged and took a step back.

He stopped the video and handed the phone to me. "Here. That oughta do it."

He stood there, waiting for me to say thank you, I assumed. So I did.

"No problem. I hope *your friend* is satisfied."

I wanted to say something about his inappropriate behavior, but the rules for what constituted acceptable behavior with strangers were clearly different for the famous. Anyway, I was never going to see him again, and Jenna would be beyond excited to live vicariously through the video kiss.

He was staring at me, and the realization of why had just clicked when he said, "Sorry, but you have crazy-cool eyes."

The startling color contrast of my eyes—one seaweed green, the other violet blue—always elicited double takes or occasional comments from strangers.

"Heterochromia," I said.

"Hetero... what?"

"That's what it's called. It's a genetic fluke. Some people think it makes me look like an alien," I said. "I hated it when I was a kid."

He flashed a knowing smile. "Is that a Southern accent I detect?"

I'd tried for years to harden the soft edges of my accent, but sometimes it resurfaced when I was angry, excited... or nervous.

"Right." I glanced down at my feet and caught a side-eye glimpse of his used-to-be-white Nikes. "Born in Louisiana."

"Oh yeah? Me too!" he said.

I was more surprised by the fact that Jenna hadn't told me than the fact we had this one small thing in common. He must've worked hard to rid himself of his Southern twang.

"You should hear my mom," he said. "She sounds like Dolly Parton with a Louisiana drawl."

I was taken aback by his sharing of such personal information about his mother, but it simply confirmed his reputation for revealing too much too soon.

"Where in Louisiana?" he asked.

"Natchitoches."

"No way. When I was a kid, my mom and I used to go to the Christmas festival there every year."

The image of him as a child, strolling the riverbank with his mother, stuffing his face with funnel cake and cotton candy while watching the fireworks, was in stark contrast to the self-possessed—some might say self-absorbed—guy standing in front of me.

"Not a whole lot of Louisianians—is that even a word?—roaming the streets of Manhattan," he said then hesitated. "Hey, you think you could help me out? I wanted to buy an espresso machine, and I saw you looking at them." He glanced back at the boxes lining the shelves. "I'm not sure what the hell I should be looking for. Any suggestions?" His thick brows shot up in a question.

Maybe I'd been too quick to judge, a tic that developed after one too many encounters with assholes. Maybe he thought he was simply doing a good deed with the video and the kiss. Maybe at the end of the day, he was just a guy who was clueless in the kitchen.

When I didn't respond, he said, "Sorry, I thought you might know... uh... something." He took a step back.

"Well, I might have one suggestion. Most espresso machines can be finicky, but I've always wanted one of these," I said, pointing at the machine in front of me. "It's got tons of five-star reviews."

He looked away as though considering my suggestion and scratched his days-old beard, then he said, "Done." He took a box from the shelf and checked out the image on the side. "I hope it comes with an instruction manual." He chuckled.

I hung back as he approached the checkout counter. The cashier's bored expression shifted, but he was acting cool. He clearly wasn't about to go all fanboy over Mick Sullivan. He never made eye contact, but as soon as the transaction was complete and Mick began to walk away, the cashier whipped out his phone and snapped a picture of Mick's readily recognizable profile. In a few seconds, his whereabouts would be all over social media, and he'd be forced to change locations. I couldn't imagine how stressful it must be to constantly zigzag to avoid detection. Just the thought of living in a glass bubble like that made my teeth itch. He might have pretty much everything, but he didn't have anonymity or privacy, the two things New Yorkers valued most.

He removed a well-worn beanie from his jacket pocket, pulled it down over his head, and slipped his sunglasses back in place before turning to face me.

"Nice to meet you, Rachael Allen." He tapped the box in his arms. "And thanks for the espresso recommendation." He grinned before adding, "*Y'all* have a nice day." Then he disappeared down the stairs.

Chapter 2

I sat on the New Jersey Transit train headed for Madison, mulling over my unexpected encounter with Mick Sullivan—my photo request, the video, and his entitled intrusion of my personal space. The whole thing had been uncomfortable, but I decided it would be a fun vignette I could drag out, dust off, and display at parties.

I pulled out my phone—this time from my purse—to prescreen the video before sending it to Jenna. I slipped in my earbuds just as the conductor strolled down the aisle, barking, "Next stop, Madison!" The train was already rolling into the station.

"Oh shit!" I shoved my phone back into my purse, ran down the aisle, and jumped out onto the platform just as the doors slammed shut behind me.

A summer squall had rushed in, quickly transforming my cheap umbrella into a bright-red tulip reaching for an absent sun. The soles of my gray suede boots squished with each step. *Ruined.* Okay, so they weren't Manolo Blahniks, but they were far from free.

As I walked home from the station, I kicked off my least favorite pastime, reviewing my life's to-do list. First on the list—get my foot in the door at Houdini Records and rent a place of my own in Manhattan. But the most elusive goal was to repair my damaged relationship with my father.

I was desperate to create a new life for myself, a happier life—at least one with less drama. But after four years of college, graduate school, and an all-too-short stint of working and living on my own, I was back home, and my father's presence was a constant reminder of all the things he couldn't undo, couldn't unsay. Getting a job at Houdini Records would be an easier trick than forgiving my father. For years, I'd questioned my mother's decision to stay as she doled out forgiveness like Halloween candy and accepted his empty promises to stop drinking.

She once told me, "Honey, if it weren't for second chances, we'd all be alone."

Maybe. But she'd given him more than his fair share. I knew I could never be as forgiving.

I was already home. I reached out to open the front door.

"You're drenched. Get in here!" my mother said.

She had an irritating habit of appearing in the doorway just as I was about to walk in. I stomped my feet on the doormat, took off my soggy boots, and dropped my umbrella in the stand near the door—house rules. Maggie was wagging her stubby tail and rubbing her snout affectionately against my leg. Her little tongue peeked out from the space where her teeth used to be. I reached down to give her the head scratching she was waiting for.

"When are you going to start locking this door, Mom? You still act like we live in a small town in Louisiana."

"Oh, it's fine. This is a small town, too, you know." My mother's genteel Southern accent, curated in St. Vincentville, Louisiana, hadn't faded in the almost thirteen years we'd lived in New Jersey. It always seemed more pronounced after I'd spent the day in the city listening to New Yorkers grouse about everything from the price of strawberries at Whole Foods to the chronic lateness of the F train. "So how was your day? What did you do?"

"It was... weird. I'll fill you in at dinner."

The smell of a garlic-stuffed roast in the oven wafted into the entryway. It was Monday, so roast was the entrée du jour on the rotating menu, which hadn't changed since I was in middle school. My mouth watered, and my stomach grumbled. I hadn't gotten around to eating lunch. Having meals waiting for me was one of the few perks of moving back home.

"Oh, I put your mail in your room," my mother said as she headed toward the kitchen.

"Thanks," I mumbled.

I ran upstairs to the room I'd reluctantly reclaimed six months before. I turned and saw Maggie standing at the bottom of the stairs, looking forlorn. I retraced my steps, scooped her up, and set her on the bed. She could no longer jump up on her own, but it was still her favorite perch. Sitting at my desk, I dropped my purse on the floor and waited for my laptop to boot up.

My room looked exactly like it did when I left for college with the understanding that I would graduate, get a job, and a life, and return only for holidays and the occasional visit. The iridescent-orange bedspread reflected my teenage tastes. The furniture, IKEA white, had sent my adolescent heart aflutter. Mementos from high school still hung on my bulletin board untouched—torn tickets to football games; a dried homecoming corsage; concert stubs; my senior prom photo with Aiden, my high school boyfriend. And there was Jim's smiling face. He was the guy I'd relegated to the "friend zone" all through high school, deeming him "sweet." I sighed. *I could use a Jim right about now.* The décor might've been stuck in a depressing time warp, but redecorating would mean I expected to stay awhile.

"Rachael, dinner will be ready in an hour!"

"Okay, Mom!"

There was a tap at my door. "It's me."

My chest tightened. "Yeah, Daddy?"

Jenna had snickered the first time she heard me call my father "Daddy." It sounded childish even to me, but somehow seemed fitting. Our relationship hadn't matured along with me.

He stuck his head in the doorway, hesitating before he asked, "How were today's interviews?"

"No interviews. I was taking a break." I stared into his eyes as he stood there waiting.

He was six years sober, and I still found myself checking to see if his eyes were bloodshot. Three years of therapy and regular meetings with Adult Children of Alcoholics hadn't erased the aftereffects of his descent into hell. The demons of doubt that his drinking conjured up were still there, but I had, so far, managed to keep them on a short leash.

I turned back to my computer. "I need to check my email."

"Sure." He hesitated for half a heartbeat. Maybe he was hoping to initiate an intimate father-daughter conversation. If so, he was in for a very long wait.

I wasn't sure which of us felt the chasm more. The remnant of our relationship was a confusing mix of rage, bitterness, and compassion. I knew he was trying to make up for his absent years, the years lost in a murk of alcohol, anger, resentment, and eventually, soul-shaking regret. But his moral compass now swung in the opposite direction, and his new rigid rules and lofty expectations were tough to take. He backed away and quietly shut the door.

I turned my attention to my inbox—nothing noteworthy.

I heard Jenna downstairs, announcing her presence with the brass door knocker. "It's just me!" she yelled into the house. The sound of her footsteps preceded her as she took the stairs two at a time and entered my room breathless.

My best friend since middle school, Jenna had been the first to offer friendship when I was the new girl on the block. The moving van hadn't even finished unloading when she boldly knocked on the door, introduced herself to my parents, and asked if we could hang out. Our first adventure was to Walgreens to shoplift M&Ms. Jenna was a pro, but I was so nervous that I peed my pants a little, almost dropping my loot in front of the security guard as we speedwalked to the exit. That was my first and last foray into a life of crime. Jenna later lifted makeup, earrings, and key chains until she eventually got caught by an eagle-eyed cashier. In high school, she was voted "most likely to be found not guilty." True to her title, she managed to get off easy—a slap on the wrist and a warning.

Despite her fierce independent streak, Jenna was having her own life troubles and, like me, was back living with her parents. Our lives were once again running on parallel tracks. She plopped down on my bed, her spiky hair defying gravity.

"So how was the Big Apple?" Jenna asked. "What'd ya do? Who'd ya see? Buy anything?"

"Just wandered around, window-shopped. The usual. Didn't buy anything." I wanted to save the best for last. "Oh, but guess who I ran into?"

"Oooh, Conrad?"

"God, no."

"David?"

"Wow, you're really reaching."

"Okay, I give up."

"Does the name *Mick Sullivan* mean anything to you?"

"Pffft. Yeah, right."

I grabbed my phone, pulled up the video, and pressed Play, as the two of us huddled over the screen—conjoined twins attached at the head. If you overlooked the fact that we were several years older and supposedly somewhat wiser, it was high school déjà vu.

"Wow! Tell me everything." Jenna hit Replay. "He's so hot!"

"Down, girl," I chided.

"Rachael, dinner is almost ready! Is Jenna staying?" My mother shouted the invitation from downstairs.

When I was growing up, Jenna and I and the calorie-laden good-ies my mom baked were inseparable. My mother was a compulsive baker—the more my father drank, the more my mother baked—and the constant aroma of fresh-from-the-oven cakes, cookies, and my favorite, brownies, soothed me and assuaged my overwhelming guilt for being so incredibly grateful when my father wasn't around. I blamed him when I began to pack on pounds.

But I was all grown up and had shed the excess weight, if not the emotional baggage, long before. But my mother still baked in quantity, as though my father were still drinking and Jenna and I would be marching into the kitchen any minute to finish off the last batch of homemade chocolate chip cookies before the homecoming dance.

"Well, hello, Miss Jenna," my father said, staring at her hair. "So, it's pink this week? What's next, blue, orange, chartreuse?" He laughed and shook his head. Drunk or sober, my father had always given Jenna a pass while holding me to a far higher standard—as long as it wasn't *his* daughter.

Jenna ran her fingers through her spiked fuchsia strands. She had informed me that guys thought it was hot. But I figured it much more likely that they took it as a sign she was willing to try anything—which she was—and they were eager to be present and accounted for when she did.

We all took our assigned seats, including Jenna.

"So," my mother began as she removed her apron and passed the roast, "tell me about your day, sweetie."

"Mom, do you know who Mick Sullivan is?"

"No. Should I?"

"He was in that movie we saw a couple of months ago. *Southern—*"

"*Southern Sensibilities,*" Jenna interrupted.

"Oh, I remember. Cute movie."

"I met him today."

Her eyes opened wider. "What do you mean, you met him? You actually talked to him?"

"He was standing close to me when I was in Zabar's, and he started a conversation. Then he took a video of the two of us on my phone."

My mother was in freeze-frame. The roast-laden fork in her hand had screeched to a halt midway between the plate and her open mouth. "And why on earth would he do that?"

"Because I asked him to. It was for Jenna."

"Hot, rich, *and* generous," Jenna said.

Sitting at the head of the table, my father had been listening without comment. He had little patience for the likes of celebrities. *"A bunch of lotharios and lushes."* I had long since discovered that reformed drinkers and reformed smokers—my father was both—were an unforgiving lot.

"It was nothing, really," I said to end the exchange before my father launched into a diatribe about the inequities of society and the idiocy of unearned fame. And for good measure, he would likely toss in the evils of alcohol.

After dinner, Jenna told everyone good night and headed home, but not before making me promise to email the video to her. My mother followed me upstairs and sat on the bed next to me as we watched the ten-second video. "He kissed you? Was he nice? What did he say? You think you'll hear from him again? Maybe he can help you find a job."

I laughed out loud. "Mom, relax. It was a chance encounter with a celebrity. By the end of the week, he will have repeated this same performance at least a dozen times. He wasn't trying to pick me up. He's a famous actor. We talked for maybe five minutes, tops, and he took this video. That's it."

My father stuck his head in the doorway. "Don't stay up too late." After issuing his nightly parental instructions, he headed back downstairs.

I turned to my mother. "I guess it's slipped his mind yet again that I'm twenty-four, not twelve."

She sighed and patted my leg. "Honey, you know your father loves you."

I nodded, ashamed that my first impulse had been to jump up and slam the door in his face like I used to when I *was* twelve. God, I wanted to slam it—hard. But my mother was right. He meant well, and I was too old to throw prepubescent temper tantrums.

My mother said good night, kissed my forehead, and walked across the hall to the bedroom. I collapsed on the bed and stared at my "shocking pink" popcorn ceiling. Maggie waddled over, sniffed me a couple of times, and licked my cheek.

"Thanks, Mags. I needed that."

Getting out of there and into a place of my own in the city had to happen soon, before I reverted to a scrawny, flat-chested kid with glasses and braces, slamming the door in Daddy's face.

Chapter 3

Over the next couple of weeks, I focused my energies on finding a job. After I finished graduate school with a useless degree in psychology sprinkled with some random music-appreciation classes, I'd thought I'd finally cracked the code on my life when I scored a position as an assistant at Broken Vinyl, a small independent record label in the city, and found a great little four-hundred-and-fifty-square-foot studio in the Bronx for an exorbitant monthly rent. I couldn't have been happier. I had everything I'd dreamed of. I was working in the city at a job I loved and was actually good at, and I was in the thick of it, mixing it up with record execs, producers, and cute band members. My career path was well lit, and I could see for miles.

Music had always been my escape. I never learned to play the piano, the clarinet, or the guitar, and I couldn't even read notes, but I had an ear for music and, as it turned out, a head for the music industry. Over time, the two merged and matured into a passion. My love of music was the one decent thing that came out of my dating musician number one, Greg Bashman, the guitar-playing prick in the band he'd dubbed Choir Boys without a teardrop of irony. Good looks, bad behavior, and the bluest eyes I'd ever seen on another human being. We met in college. His song lyrics made me believe something deep and meaningful was hidden underneath that luxurious head of hair. I was wrong. His single well-mannered move was to open the door to music for me.

When I was working at Broken Vinyl, Conrad, musician number two in my rogue's gallery of ex-boyfriends, entered my life. I thought he was the angel atop my Christmas tree. He would flash that smile and wrap his arms around me like he would never let go. I thought it was real. He certainly kissed me like it was real. Made love to me like it was real. Then a nuclear bomb of a lawsuit sucked the company dry, and I landed face-first on the asphalt. When my job evaporated, so did Conrad. His parting shot was to inform me that he was going back to his old girlfriend—while we were still naked in bed. I realized, only in retrospect, of course, that aside from the sex, which was eye-popping, my bed was simply a place for him to crash, and I was his gateway to the record company where I worked.

Conrad was followed by a disastrous rebound relationship. That was when celibacy began to sound like a healthy option. And when I took the ultimate walk of shame back through my parents' front door and into my old bedroom, my fate was sealed.

I had sworn off bad boys and musicians. And definitely no more bad-boy musicians. I couldn't keep repeating the same mistake like a scratched record. I was ready to turn my life around.

Then Jenna called.

"Rachael, don't be mad."

I gripped the phone more tightly. The last time Jenna opened with that line, she confessed to posting my profile on seniormatch.com. I was deluged with emails from horny fifty-year-old men for weeks. I loved Jenna like a sister, but just like sisters, we didn't always see eye to eye. From my perspective, Jenna's idea of a practical joke sometimes bordered on mean-girl behavior.

I took a breath and closed my eyes. "What did you do?"

"You know that video of you and Mick Sullivan?"

"Uh, yeah. I vaguely recall."

She was already testing my patience.

"Well, I thought it would be fun to post it online."

I seesawed between anger at Jenna for not asking me first and relief that it wasn't something far worse.

"Rach, you still there?"

"I'm here."

"Wait till you see some of the comments. They're freakin' hilarious! Listen to this," she said as she infused the lines with overwrought drama: "'Who the hell is she? Is she trying to worm her way into his life? I bet she was lying in wait for him.' Lying in wait," Jenna repeated and exploded in laughter. When I didn't join in, she said, "Oh, come on. Lighten up. This is funny shit. Admit it."

"Jenna, I swear..."

"I'll send you the link. It's better than Comedy Central."

"Sounds like I'm the joke."

"Don't be mad," she begged, ending the conversation the same way it started.

I went online and got sucked into the comments, fascinated by the exchanges triggered by Mick Sullivan's image. Some were beyond ridiculous as voracious fans carefully examined and dissected his choice in clothes, his hair, his words, his actions, his thoughts—as if they could read his mind. A virtual army of Mick Sullivan faithfuls was out there patrolling the internet. And, apparently, they'd all watched the video—one hundred thousand hits so far. A fan with the username TwoHeartsAsOne was following the thread, commenting on most of the posts, and leaving messages clearly meant for me:

That kiss didn't mean anything. You'll never know what a real kiss from him is like.

I'm his one and only love. There is no place for you in his life. Stay away.

I won't let you come between us.

Some poor soul had taken a deep dive into an ocean of fantasy. But then I reconsidered. Maybe it was a pimply-faced thirteen-year-old girl with an overactive imagination. A rush of empathy triggered me to type a response:

Nothing to worry about. He's all yours.

Within minutes, another comment was posted:

Are you patronizing me? Don't.

I jerked back and sat straighter. That didn't sound like an insecure young girl.

I called Jenna back.

"So?" Jenna answered.

"I admit it, some are pretty funny, but I want you to take it down. Some of the comments are really sad… and more than a little creepy."

"They're all idiots. Watching them put their stupidity on display is half the fun."

According to Jenna, if you didn't know someone, they didn't really exist and therefore didn't matter—not in her world, anyway. I had always envied her me-centric attitude.

"Jen, I'm serious. I want you to take it down now, tonight."

Jenna released a weary sigh. "You big party pooper."

Early in the morning, Maggie's raspy bark downstairs woke me from a titillating dream. Conrad might've been a prick, but he made regular appearances in my dreams, leaving me wanting. I bolted upright and slid my phone from the nightstand to see the time. I threw back the covers, swung my legs off the edge of the bed, and checked the temperature of the hardwood floors like I was dipping my toes into the cold waters of the Atlantic.

"Be quiet, Mags," I mumbled as though she could still hear. "You're going to wake—"

"Rachael? What's Maggie barking at?" my mother called from her doorway.

"I don't know, Mom," I said, still hoping not to wake my father. "I was just headed downstairs to see. Go back to sleep."

I slipped on my robe and, not yet fully awake, gripped the wooden banister to steady myself as I descended the stairs. Maggie had somehow made her way down and was lying spread-eagle on the tile entryway, panting like she'd just run a doggie marathon.

"What is it, girl?" I pulled the curtain back from the glass panel next to the door to peer into the gathering light of day.

Ms. Woodrow was still trying to jog off those stubborn pounds that took up permanent residence years ago. Mr. Jester was walking his puppy—*did Maggie ever have that much energy?* Celia from next door was making out with her basketball-player boyfriend in the front seat of his car. Nothing was happening that would set off the Maggie alarm.

Maggie stood and waddled over to me, revealing a paper that had been dropped through the mail slot onto the floor in the entryway. I leaned over to pick it up, scratching Maggie's neck in the process. The folded paper fell open. The letter, written in barely legible cursive, started off:

I'm warning you. Leave him alone. I'm his woman now.

Leave who alone? Does Conrad have someone new in his life who sees me as a threat? Maybe that creepy guy at the bar, who kept hitting on me and Jenna, has a girlfriend or a wife. Maybe the note was simply dropped through the wrong mail slot. A rope of fear and paranoia twisted around my throat. *Could it have something to do with the video and those creepy comments?* I let the thought simmer for a few seconds before I quickly dismissed it as outrageous. *How could anyone track me down based on the video alone?* I stuffed the paper into my robe pocket, scooped up Maggie, headed back upstairs, and snuggled with her under the covers while sifting through all the possible nasty-note writers in my life.

Chapter 4

I dressed in my carefully coordinated interview outfit—a pale-yellow knit blouse that complemented the color contrast of my eyes and emphasized my breasts enough to say "I'm confident" without shouting "Do me!" and paired it with a black business skirt that made me feel sophisticated and camouflaged my little-boy hips. The ensemble came out of my closet only for interviews. I'd discovered while at Broken Vinyl that one major benefit of working in the music industry was the lack of a dress code, unless looking like you didn't care was a code. But it was still de rigueur to make a good first impression. My interview that day was with Sisyphus Recordings. They weren't my first choice, but working there would be a huge step in the right direction. I wasn't sure how many interviews this one would make. I'd stopped counting somewhere around eleven. My skill set wasn't the obstacle to getting another foot in the door—it was the loss of my network. Just when I had started to feel like an integral part of the music industry, my professional support system collapsed.

"So how would you describe your taste in music..." Jude, the interviewer, who couldn't have been much older than me, glanced down at my résumé then looked back up at me. "Rachael?" He kicked back in his chair and clasped his hands behind his head. He had just-messy-enough stoplight-red hair, a wispy goatee, skinny jeans, Buddy Holly glasses, a paisley shirt, and, clipped to his belt loop, a key chain that clanged restlessly each time he shifted position.

He might as well have sported a name tag that said, "Hello, My Name Is Jude, and I'm a Hipster."

"I guess I'd describe it as 'alternative light.' I tend to latch onto bands that no one's ever heard of, and within a year, you're hearing them twenty-four seven on the radio."

"For example?"

"Sure, um, Arctic Baboons, Electric Twigs, Modern Dinosaurs, Serial Killers, Trap the—"

"Excellent. So tell me what you think you would bring to Sisyphus Recordings."

"Well, as it says on my résumé"—I nodded toward the papers resting on his desk—"I worked for about a year at Broken Vinyl Records, booking studio time and writing press releases. It was an all-hands-on-deck situation, so I was involved with almost everything. I would love to be able to apply my skills here at Sisyphus."

"So were you there for Broken Vinyl's epic fail?" He leaned forward and propped his pointy elbows on his desk as his keys released a high-pitched tinkling. "What's the real story there?" he asked with barely contained glee.

I was all too aware of every last dirty detail of the lawsuit—the battling egos, the growing greed, the suffocating animosity. I also knew that Heartbreak Collective, the band that had filed the lawsuit, jumped over to Sisyphus, and Jude wanted me to spill the tea, in the hope that I would be rewarded with a job. There was just one problem—before I left, I signed a twelve-page nondisclosure agreement. I could either tell all and get a few interview points or keep my word—and my legal obligation. I took a breath, unclenched my fists, and discreetly wiped my clammy palms on my skirt as I crossed my legs.

"I'm sure you know that we signed Heartbreak Collective shortly after that," he said. "So I'm aware of some of what went down. Maybe you could shed some light on pitfalls to avoid... you know?"

Up to that point, he'd seemed somewhat interested in me, and I really needed the job. My conscience was hanging on by a thread. Maybe I didn't have the right connections, but I had intel I could offer in exchange for a job. I felt pesky red blotches forming up and down my neck. I took a breath.

"I'm afraid I was out of the loop. Everything leading up to the bankruptcy was kept quiet. It was a shock when I was let go."

The fire in his eyes went out. He leaned back in his chair again, propped his tangerine-colored Chukka boots on the edge of his desk, and took a sip of his Red Bull.

"Too bad." He sighed. "Okay, so what is it you think you can do for Sisyphus Records?" The repetition was a clear sign he'd lost interest and disengaged. The interview limped along from there, though he threw me a bone when he said, "Maybe we can offer you some freelance work, writing for our website and blog."

"That would be great!" I didn't really think it was great, but it would place me at the starting block.

The economy sucked, and good jobs were mythical creatures that everyone had heard of but no one seemed to have actually seen. Still, I was determined to find my next dream job. At least that was what I told myself as I sat on the train, once again watching the New Jersey towns fly by, longing for home to be in the opposite direction.

It was Friday, so meat loaf would be the meal of the day. I found the seven-day menu cycle either comforting or stifling, depending upon my mood. I started the fifteen-minute walk home from the train station, mulling over the interview and what I could've done, what I should've done, and how I would handle things differently next time. Maybe I should've provided Jude with a slow striptease of information, revealing just enough to keep him wanting more. I should've played up my involvement with the talent at Broken Vinyl.

I should've told him about how I discovered The Cage Kings on YouTube, tracked them down, and arranged for them to come to New York for an audition. They were signed on the spot. Or I could've shared how I'd saved the day when the guy who had the job before me double-booked studio time, leaving one of the hottest new bands with no place to record. Frantic, I'd called everyone I knew and quite a few I didn't, until I found an open studio. My boss led me in a little victory dance around the office.

Woulda, coulda, shoulda. For the time being, I was going home to rest up and start again in the morning. Something good was waiting for me out there. I just knew it. A breeze surfed through my hair, and I picked up my pace. I had unearthed fresh hope. I had read somewhere that pessimism was an illogical response to failure. Maybe, but sometimes I wondered if my bursts of optimism were an illogical response to my life.

Daylight was slipping away, casting unfamiliar shadows as I walked up to the house and glanced at my faded-green Toyota sitting in the driveway. It had been my faithful ride since high school. Though not much to look at, it was paid for—a fact for which I was increasingly grateful. As I came closer, the light shifted, and I stopped short. I blinked twice, certain I wasn't seeing clearly. Reaching out, I traced a razor-thin line that ran across the driver's door to the rear door and around to the trunk. My fingers absorbed the simple words scratched into the finish:

"Mick is mine."

Chapter 5

The sun was up, but I languished in bed, listening to the mourning doves outside my window, deliberating what my next move should be. I hadn't told my parents about the car. I simply moved it out of sight to a spot farther up the driveway, where they rarely went. Hell, I hadn't even told Jenna. I would tell them—eventually. I found myself too overwhelmed to deal with their reactions. My wandering thoughts and the melancholy sounds of the birds were interrupted by Jenna's ringtone, Beyonce's "Run the World." I dug my phone out from under the covers, cleared my throat, and sat up.

"Hey."

"Meet me at Drip." No introduction, no explanation—just Jenna speaking in an urgent tone.

Drip was the local coffee shop/bakery/bookstore where Jenna routinely dispensed drama like the strong black coffee served there.

"What's up?"

"I'd rather tell you... and show you... in person."

I sighed. Resistance was futile. "Sure. I'll be there in fifteen."

Things were seldom as dire as Jenna made them out to be. My job was to put the situation into perspective, talk her down, and make her realize the world as she knew it wasn't over. I washed my face, brushed my teeth, grabbed my faded blue jean jacket, and ran downstairs, stopping to scratch Maggie's sweet spot.

"Sorry, girl. You can't come, but I'll bring something back for you."

I pushed open the heavy wooden door to Drip, ready to surrender to the siren call of freshly ground Columbian coffee beans. The place was packed. Jenna had scored a table in a secluded corner and was hunched over her laptop.

"Hey," I said.

Jenna looked up, startled, as if I were the last person she expected to see.

"Sorry. Didn't mean to scare you." I laughed as I slung my purse over the back of a chair and plopped down. "I'm all ears."

Jenna swung the laptop around in my direction. "Read."

I glanced at the screen. "Shit. You promised you would take this down."

"I know, I know, but you need to see this before I get rid of it."

"I've already read this crap."

"Not these latest ones. Just read!" she said, nodding toward her laptop as she slumped back in the chair and tucked her hands under her armpits.

Saturday

So, go ahead, ignore me. You'll find out how wrong you are to try to take him from me.

Sunday

I know you want him. But he belongs to me. Our two souls are the same. You are nothing to him. He'll never love you.

Monday

Last chance to save yourself. Don't forget, I know where to find you.

I pushed the laptop aside, leaned in toward Jenna, and whispered, "This is insane."

"It was the 'I know where to find you' that freaked me out," she said. "You think she could really track you down?"

"Well..." I swallowed hard before speaking again. "Actually, I think she already has." I filled Jenna in on the note dropped through the mail slot and the message etched into the finish of my car.

Jenna didn't shock easily, but upon hearing my story, her jaw went slack. "I can't believe you didn't tell me. *Jesus.* Have you called the police?"

"And tell them what? 'Someone wrote some not-so-nice comments about me online'?"

"What about the car and the handwritten note?"

"There's that... but there's no proof it was the same person. Even if it is her, how the hell would she know where to find me?"

"Rachael, he said your full name in the video."

"So? I'm sure there are tons of Rachael Allens."

"Yeah, but I checked Facebook and LinkedIn, and your picture is there, along with all your info—that you live in Madison, New Jersey, and you're the only Rachael Allen in this town."

My stomach churned.

"I'm taking it down now," Jenna said but then stopped. "I think we should print this shit out first. You know, as evidence."

"Jesus," I said. "Yeah, I guess you're right."

Jenna sent a copy to me before she clicked Delete.

"Good. Maybe we can forget about all this Mick Sullivan drama and move on."

"I'm really sorry. I had no idea this was going to turn into such a big friggin' deal." She sat silently for a few seconds. "Let me get you some coffee. My treat. I'm loaded today." She pulled out a twenty-dollar bill and waved it in my direction.

The barely-old-enough-to-be-working waitress ambled over and assumed a standard bored-as-hell stance. "Can I get you anything?" She cocked her pierced eyebrow as she eyed Jenna's twenty.

How about a different life? would have been the most accurate response.

I ordered my usual sugar-free vanilla latte, and Jenna asked for a chocolate mocha frappe with extra whipped cream and a sour cream lemon scone.

"So," Jenna started a few minutes later as she wiped away a whipped-cream moustache, "what's the game plan?"

I took a sip of my latte and slapped a hand over my mouth as the scalding coffee burned my tongue. Speaking through my fingers, I said, "Game plan? Hopefully, I won't need one, now that you've *actually* taken it down."

"Well, if anything else happens, don't screw around. Call the cops!"

"I will." I paused to consider the possibility of something far worse happening then took another sip.

"Hey, where's your good-luck charm?" Jenna asked, pointing at my neck, where my hamsa always hung.

"The chain snapped in my sleep. I stuck it on the bulletin board so I wouldn't lose it."

"So let's go shopping for a new chain."

"As soon as I get some cash! Listen, I gotta go. I have to get out some résumés today." Eyeing Jenna's plate, I asked, "Can I have that last chunk of scone for Mags?"

"Sure, and scratch her for me." Jen was Maggie's second-favorite human, next to me.

I grabbed my coffee and Maggie's scone treat and hugged Jenna before leaving. Lost in thought and consumed by a creeping worry I couldn't shake, I made my way home by muscle memory alone. As I walked up the front steps of the house, I reached out to open the door and pressed on the newly polished brass handle—unlocked, as usual.

"Mom? Daddy?" I closed the door and turned back around, expecting Maggie to be at my feet. "Mags? Maggie, I've got something for you. Come here, girl!" Despite Maggie's aging ears, calling for her was a habit I found hard to break.

Has she somehow gotten out? She couldn't have gone far. I opened the front door again and walked into the yard. Mr. Jester from across the street was raking leaves.

I waved in his direction and shouted, "Hey, have you seen Maggie? I think she might have made a run for it."

"Nope, sorry, Rachael. I just came outside."

"Okay. Thanks." I turned to go back inside and headed to the kitchen. "Mags, where are you?" Panic slowly slithered in as I feared the worst.

I heard Maggie's muffled bark coming from my bedroom, and I bounded up the stairs, following the sound to my closet. I opened the closet door, and there sat Maggie, trembling. I leaned over, scooped her up, and kissed her head.

"How in the world did you get in there, girl?"

Chapter 6

My parents left early Monday morning for Baltimore to attend the funeral of a friend of my father—well, not a friend, exactly. I was pretty sure he'd been my father's sponsor once upon a time. I wondered if, in the end, alcohol was his friend's downfall. In the rare moments when I was feeling generous, I gave my father props for staying sober, but my empathy was a slippery thing. Everything that happened before his sober years pummeled any empathy and understanding I might've held onto. Neither his drinking nor his journey to sobriety had ever been a topic of conversation at home. My father wasn't big on sharing the unpleasant details of that part of his life. Sort of like I'd been reluctant to share the unpleasant details of what was happening to me. Anyway, I didn't want to burden them right before they left for a funeral. If I'd told them, they would've decided to stay put, and I would've missed out on some much-needed alone time. I knew that once I spilled everything, they would become my twin shadows. Even so, I decided I would talk to them as soon as they came home. I needed to lighten my emotional load.

A callback from Jude at Sisyphus replaced a slice of my anxiety with rich excitement. He wanted to know if I could come in that day. My butterflies fluttered. I imagined a kaleidoscope of monarchs emerging from their cocoons and trying out their wings. Ready to fly away with them, I said a little prayer to the job gods: *Please, please, please, let this be it.*

Light-headed with anticipation, I went to my closet and brought out my "second-interview outfit," which I hadn't yet had the opportunity to wear. I held it in front of me, looked at myself in the full-length mirror, and thought, *This is what I'll be wearing the day my life takes a turn for the better.* I dressed and checked the train schedule. I would have to hurry to make it on time. I left out the back door, double-checked that it was locked, jumped in my car, and headed to the train station.

"Rachael, how's it going?" Wearing white-framed glasses, the same paisley shirt, and expensive-looking red ostrich boots, Jude greeted me as if we were friends who hung out at Drip. I immediately deflated. If he was sucking up to me, that probably meant he was going to offer me something no one else was willing to take on.

"I'm good. You?" I wanted to sound as perky as possible.

"Great! Listen, I'm short on time, so I'll get straight to the point. When you were here last time, we talked about you doing some freelance writing for our blog, website, et cetera. Well, turns out we need a full-time person. It would be remote, so you can work from wherever, but you'd have benefits—health insurance, dental, 401K, paid holidays. You would come in for staff meetings once a month. Sound like something you'd be interested in?"

This was happening, and it was happening way faster than I dared hope. I tried desperately to suppress the childlike grin I felt taking over my face. "That sounds perfect. So, yes!"

"Sweet. I'm still talking salary with the powers that be, but I think you'll be pleased. My assistant will email the details and schedule you for a staff meeting."

He stood. I hadn't even warmed my seat yet, but my second interview was already done.

"Just stop by HR to fill out paperwork." He pointed in the direction of the elevator. "Go to the fourth floor. Turn right. Office is on the left. I'll let them know you're on your way." He picked up the phone, grinned, and gave me a thumbs-up.

After filling out reams of paperwork, I stepped out onto the sidewalk of Sixth Avenue and called Jenna. "I'm employed! Cue happy dance!"

"What?"

The avenue was even noisier than usual as two fire trucks and an ambulance were slowly making their way through the tangle of traffic.

I shouted into the phone, "I got a job!"

"No way. I seriously hate you. What, when, where?"

"I can barely hear you. I'm about to head to Penn Station. I'll call you when I get home and fill you in."

Dizzy from the sudden shift in fortune, I began thinking of all the questions I hadn't asked Jude but should have. *Does Sisyphus use project-management software? Would the blog be mostly business news, or would I be interviewing recording artists? How many posts and press releases would I be expected to write each week? Who would be administrating the website? Who would I answer to?*

But it was all good. *I have a real job. With benefits!* I would be living in the city as soon as I could save enough for the move, jump-starting my life again. I decided to hold off on talking to my parents about all the crap that had happened, that was happening. I wanted them to celebrate my good news, not be consumed with worry.

"**R**achael?" my mother called from the stairs.

"I'm in the kitchen. I just walked in the door."

My parents appeared, looking somber.

"How was it?" I asked in a tone that matched their expressions.

"Sad," my mother said.

My father simply shook his head, which I interpreted to mean he was thinking, *That could have been me.*

"Well, this may not be the best time, but I have some news. I got a job!"

"Oh, Rachael, that's wonderful," my mother said and came in for a hug. "Congratulations. You so deserve it."

My father, on the other hand, looked grief-stricken—not from the funeral, I thought, but from the news that I would be leaving them soon. His opportunities for relationship repair with his only daughter would become few and far between.

"Let me change and get out of these heels," my mother said. "I want to hear all about it! I have questions!" Her proud smile was the cherry on top.

"Daddy, aren't you going to say anything?"

"I'm really happy for you. It's just... we got used to you being here, and we're going to miss you."

Such a rare outpouring of sentiment from my father had me on the verge of tears.

My parents retreated to their bedroom to change out of their funeral clothes, and I headed to my room to put on my well-worn yoga pants and T-shirt. When I flicked on the light in my room, the sight halted my next breath. The word was spray-painted in black in perfect contrast to my bright-pink walls:

WHORE!

Chapter 7

I stared at the slur on my wall. I'd been struck by lightning, not twice but multiple times. I put the back of my hand to my mouth and was whimpering when my mother walked in, all smiles, clearly expecting to share in the joyful news of the next chapter in her daughter's life. I slowly turned toward her then looked back at the wall and pointed. When my mother's eyes shifted, she seemed to suffer a processing delay as she took it in. She repeatedly sucked in air as if enduring an asthma attack.

When she caught her breath, she turned to me. "Someone was in the house? Who would do this? Why would they do this?" My mother didn't wait for a response. She simply turned and yelled through the doorway, "Don, get in here!"

The three of us stood huddled together, unable to speak.

I finally broke the panic-fueled silence. "I've been meaning to tell you. I'm so sorry, but I didn't want to upset you, and then there was the funeral..."

Before I could finish my justification for why I'd kept the horrible events to myself, I spotted an envelope on my desk. I grabbed it and ripped it open. It was pages and pages of rambling about Mick, about their love, about my being the "other woman." I didn't make it past the first page.

I had to get out of my room, away from the outsized threats. My parents followed me downstairs, and we convened at the dining room table. The fear and worry in their eyes gutted me. I hated myself for not telling them sooner, but I relayed the whole sickening mess—the comments posted online, the note dropped through the mail slot, the message etched into my car, Maggie being shoved into the closet—and now this.

"Rachael, how could you not tell us? We need to call the police... now!" My mother's voice was a notch above hysteria.

My father stood tall. He was shifting into his take-control mode. "I'll call."

"No, let me splash some water on my face, and I'll call," I said. "I'm the one in this mess. I'm the one who should be handling it." Trembling and with shaky breath, I whispered to myself—or to them, I wasn't sure—"It'll be okay."

Truth be told, I felt like nothing would ever be okay again. Simply walking back upstairs to the bathroom was like trudging through mud. Every pore in my body ached with fatigue and fear. The thought of having to explain to the police how a harmless video had attracted a raving lunatic into our home—into my bedroom—was more than I could handle. But it had to be done. I went back to my bedroom, trying to avert my eyes from the wall, and sat at my desk. I picked up my phone, and as I tried to quiet the succession of explosions going off in my head, I called the police station.

A patrol car pulled up to the house within minutes of my call. My mother answered the door with me tagging close behind. She made me feel like she could shield me from harm, just as she'd done in the past.

"Hello, Ms. Allen. Hi, Rachael." One of the two officers was Matt, one of my favorite people from high school.

I might've had a bit of a crush on him back in the day, but he made no secret of the fact that he wasn't into girls—not in the way I hoped—but we ended up being friends. We went to concerts together, cried on each other's shoulders when our hearts were broken, and vowed to always be friends. But life got in the way. We hadn't been in touch for four years.

"Matt, I... I'm so glad it's you."

Without missing a beat, he walked over and put his arms around me. "Let's go sit in the living room, and you can give me the details." He knew the way. He turned to his partner. "Greg, check for signs of forced entry."

He sat next to me on the sofa, close enough that our knees touched. "Rae," he started—he was the only one who ever called me that. "I know it's hard, but tell me everything you remember about what happened tonight, and then I'll give you a ride to the station so you can talk to Detective Napoletano." He hesitated. "It's not the normal procedure, but I don't want my written report to get lost in the shuffle."

I laid my head on his shoulder and burst into sobs. When they subsided, I told him everything. His reaction was muted, but I guessed he'd heard it—or something like it—all before. When I was done, I went upstairs, printed out the comments, grabbed the note on my desk and the handwritten note that had been dropped through the mail slot, and forwarded the video to the email address Matt had given me for Napoletano.

Despite my insistence that I could handle the situation myself, my parents followed Matt and me to the station. And honestly, I was relieved they were tagging along. I wasn't emotionally equipped to deal with all this alone.

That was my first trip to the police station—on official business, anyway. My mother and I had gone to the open house a few years before, when the new headquarters was finished. The walls were shiny and new, and the smell of fresh paint permeated everything. The police chief was in attendance, offering refreshments and brochures. They even handed out trading cards for kids with the officers' photos on them, as part of the latest effort to humanize the police force. *Collect and trade until you've got 'em all!*

As I entered the station this time, the atmosphere was far less festive, the faces not as friendly. The scent of new paint had been replaced by the smell of sweat, fear, and burnt coffee.

Matt told my parents to wait, and I followed him into the detective's office. The inner sanctum was furnished with no-frills government-issue desks and metal office chairs. Fluorescent lighting cast an undead pallor on everyone.

"Rae, Detective Napoletano will help you from here. I have to finish my patrol." He turned to the man behind the desk. "Joe, this is Rachael Allen. Here's the handwritten notes and the posted messages." Matt handed him a plastic evidence bag like the ones I'd seen on cop shows, but this one had "Victim—Rachael Allen" written with a black Sharpie on the label. "Rae, you have my number now. Call me if you need anything."

"I will. Thank you, Matt."

Detective Joseph Napoletano stood. His appearance was nothing like I'd expected. My mental image had conjured up a hulking member of the Corleone family. Detective Napoletano couldn't have been more than five feet tall, with a Humpty-Dumpty body and a bald spot on the crown of his graying head that was so precise, it could have been drawn with a compass.

"Have a seat," Napoletano said in a surprising baritone. When he sat down, his feet barely grazed the floor. The trash can by his desk overflowed with evidence that his very pronounced paunch was fast-food induced. He picked up his phone and began swiping the screen. Taken aback by his lack of attention, I turned to see if Matt had lingered, but he was gone.

"So, you think your break-in has something to do with this video with the actor Mick Sullivan?" he asked with a straight face as he turned the screen toward me. I appreciated the effort it must have taken not to smirk at my claim.

I nodded. "Believe me, I know how crazy it sounds, but yeah, I do."

He snapped on a pair of latex gloves and opened the evidence bag, and we sat in silence as he scanned the first couple of pages. I imagined the writer frantic with hate, her words spilling out faster than she could write. It read like someone had thrown all their thoughts into a cement mixer, pushed the button, and dumped them out to harden without form.

"So?" I asked.

"We'll go over everything in detail to see if it provides any clues," he said as he carefully placed the pages back into the plastic bag. "But, you know, as of right now, there's no evidence for us to follow up on. Your front door was unlocked, so there was no forced entry. We can't file charges until we know who the perpetrator is."

"So that's it? That's why I came down here? For you to tell me to go home, and there's nothing you can do? She keyed my car—she was in my room, and she's basically threatening to kill me, for Chrissake!"

Other officers in the room unburied their heads from paperwork to see who was making a scene.

He leaned toward me, looking unexpectedly paternal. "Ms. Allen, I know this is scary stuff. If it's any comfort, I can tell you that personal violence in stalking cases, if that's what this is, typically happens with prior intimates, people who were in some sort of love relationship that ended badly. That would make your case a bit unusual."

Despite Napoletano's attempt to reassure me, I could feel this delusional woman breathing down my neck, waiting for the right moment to lunge at my throat.

He hesitated before he asked, "So you don't personally know Mick Sullivan? You never had a sexual encounter with him?" He shrugged. "No judgment. It happens."

"What? No! That video was the first and last time I met him." I jumped at the sound of the phone ringing on his desk.

"Excuse me." He answered, "Detective Napoletano." He nodded twice. "Thanks." He hung up and looked at me. "They didn't find any fingerprints."

Stunned by my lack of control over the events unfolding at warp speed, I said nothing because nothing I could say would help.

"Ms. Allen, we'll check into whatever leads we can find, but there's really not much to go on at this point. We'll try to send a patrol car around, and you should take every precaution you can—just in case. Have an alarm system installed that alerts the station. Always, always lock the doors and windows. Don't travel alone. And let us know right away if anything else happens." He reached into his drawer and pulled out a brochure titled "Are You Being Stalked?" and handed it to me.

It was horrifyingly clear—the police couldn't protect me.

I was on my own.

Chapter 8

My parents did their best to reassure me, but they gave off a musk of fear and anxiety that seeped into my bones. The stress of being the bullseye for someone's misguided hate and the aftershock of my fruitless trip to the police station had taken a toll on my most recent bout of optimism. I kicked off my shoes, crawled into bed fully clothed, and burrowed under the covers. Everything after that was fuzzy until I felt the warmth of the sun on my exposed toes sticking out from the sheets, signaling the start of a new day. Instead of sleep smoothing out my emotional rough edges, my jagged fear had metastasized overnight. I had to remind myself that the roiling in my gut wasn't the remnant of a nightmare. The threats were all too real. My phone blasted out Jenna's ringtone. I answered and breathlessly brought Jenna up-to-date.

"So the cops aren't going to do anything?" Jenna asked, even more outraged than usual. "This is some serious shit. You need to do *something*!"

"I've been thinking maybe I should try to contact his 'people.' You know, his agent, his manager. I just doubt they would do anything. I mean, she's not threatening *him*. Maybe they'll think I'm just another obsessed fan."

"Still, it's worth a shot," Jenna said. "I just hope she doesn't decide that getting rid of you for real is the answer to her imaginary relationship with Mick Sullivan."

I had been obsessively ruminating over the possibility already, but hearing the actual words delivered an electric shock.

I heard Jenna tapping on a computer before she said, "Okay, all that info is on IMDb. His management company, Triple Threat Talent Agency, has offices in Los Angeles and New York. His agent's name is Randy Border; his publicist, Grace Woodelson; and his manager, Samuel Stephens. I'll send you the link." Jenna took a breath. "Change of subject—what about the job?"

"God, I was so excited, but now... I don't know. Can I fill you in later?"

"Sure, but keep me posted on this stalker shit."

I hung up and began weighing the pros and cons of contacting Mick Sullivan's "people." *What are the odds they'll take me seriously?* I read somewhere that the question wasn't *if* a celebrity had stalkers, it was simply a matter of how many. Still, maybe his people needed to know that this misguided woman had him in her delusional sights even if her anger was directed at me. Or they might ignore me. Like my father always said: "If you never ask the question, the answer is always no." He'd taken to handing out pearls of wisdom like that on the regular ever since he stopped drinking.

I didn't know what I could say to convince any of them that their super-celebrity client, whom I'd met for all of five minutes, was the reason I was under attack and that they should help me. But maybe Jenna was right. It was worth a shot. I slid out of bed, walked over to the computer, and sank into the chair, my fingers hovering over the keyboard before I finally began typing:

To: Triple Threat Talent Agency

From: Rachael Allen

Subject: Mick Sullivan

This is going to sound strange, but...

I shook my head. *No, no, nooo.* My insistence that I wasn't strange would automatically put my normalcy under suspicion. I started again:

I happened to run into Mick Sullivan a few weeks ago.

Uh-uh. That sounded like we were old friends who'd bumped into each other on the street.

Either message would be deleted before they read past the first
line. I needed a different tack. I mentally cleared my throat and started over.

*A few weeks ago, your client, Mick Sullivan, was nice enough to take
a video of the two of us in Zabar's, which a friend of mine posted online without my knowledge. (I've attached the video file below.) Someone is now targeting me because of it. She started out with threatening
comments online, then she tracked me down and dropped a threatening
note through my mail slot. It has escalated since then. She keyed my car,
broke into my parents' home in New Jersey, and spray-painted the word
"whore" on my bedroom wall. I've also attached a copy of the police report. I know celebrities have obsessed fans, but this person has somehow
zeroed in on me as the obstacle to what I can only assume is an imaginary relationship with Mick Sullivan. The police say they have no clues
as to who this might be. I'm hoping that you might have some information that would help. Thank you for your time.*

Sincerely,

Rachael Allen

Madison, NJ

I cc'd four of his people and obsessively checked my inbox the
way I had while waiting for acceptance emails from universities seven
years earlier. Not a single response. The next day, I followed up with
calls, starting with a call to his manager.

"Triple Threat Talent Agency, Sam Stephens's office."

"Yes, my name is Rachael Allen. I sent Mr. Stephens an email
about threats I've been receiving connected to Mick Sullivan. I was
hoping to speak to Mr. Stephens."

"Is he expecting your call?"

"No, but—"

"If you give me your name and number, I'll pass the message on to Mr. Stephens."

"Look, I really need to speak to someone connected to Mick Sullivan. I'll resend the email with the police report, so you can see that this is serious." I started typing on my phone.

She stopped me short. "That won't be necessary, Ms. Allen. If you'll just leave your name and number, I'll pass the message on to Mr. Stephens."

I was talking to a well-programmed automaton. I recited my name and number through clenched teeth before slamming the phone on my desk. Repeated attempts to contact Mick Sullivan's agent and his publicist proved to be no more successful. Each time I called, I heard the who-the-hell-are-you tone in their voices, and I felt a gnarl of anger and frustration twisting in my gut.

Three more days passed with no word from anyone. I googled Triple Threat Talent Agency again—Sixth Avenue and Fifty-third Street. I would have to take my outreach to the next level—I would show up at Samuel Stephens's office and plant myself in the lobby until someone agreed to speak with me. *What's the worst that could happen?* I had visions of a pumped-up security guy "escorting" me back through the revolving doors and tossing me out onto Sixth Avenue.

S tanding outside the building on the corner of Fifty-third Street and Sixth Avenue, I looked up at its dizzying height and leaned against the granite wall. I took several deep calming breaths to shore up my courage before entering the lobby. In an incredible stroke of luck, the security guard's back was turned, and he was whisper shouting an argument into his cell. I scurried onto the elevator, waited for the doors to close, and prayed I wouldn't be discovered via the lobby's security cameras before I reached the seventh floor. Looking both ways before I stepped off the elevator, I headed for Triple

Threat. *Made it.* But I was facing a buzzer and another camera mounted above to door. *Shit!* I hesitated before turning the doorknob, fully expecting it to be locked. Like magic, the door opened, and I cautiously entered. The walls of the office were lined with awards and plaques, life-size movie posters, and black-and-white images of larger-than-life movie icons James Dean, Marlon Brando, Jack Nicholson, and Meryl Streep—along with an image of Mick Sullivan, of course. Radiohead was being piped in through the ceiling.

Startled by my sudden appearance, the receptionist demanded, "How did you get in here?"

"The door was unlocked."

She frowned. Sam Stephens's receptionist looked like a fresh college alumnus, with a cascade of auburn hair and an air of earnest determination. Her desk was buried in thick documents held together with jumbo binder clips and sprinkled with rainbow-colored Post-it notes. Four more lines on her phone lit up. She ignored them and cleared her throat. "How can I help you?"

"My name is Rachael Allen. I've been trying to get in touch with Mr. Stephens."

"Do you have an appointment?" Her face was unreadable, but I knew she was aware that no appointment was on the books.

Before I could respond, she said, "Excuse me," and answered one of the blinking lights. "Triple Threat Talent Agency, Sam Stephens's office... Yes... Of course... Yes, he's in, and he has the contract on his desk... I'll tell him... We'll see you then." She turned to me once again. "I'm sorry. You were saying?"

I stood straighter. "I've called and emailed about a situation in connection with Mick Sullivan, but I haven't gotten a response. It's extremely important that I speak with Mr. Stephens. Can you please see if he can spare five minutes?" I wanted to sound confident and concerned but feared I was coming across as desperate and demented.

She held her index finger up as she answered the phone again in a singsongy voice. "Triple Threat Talent Agency, Sam Stephens's office." She listened for a few seconds before she threw her head back in laughter. "That's a good one... No, it's okay... Yes, I'll forward the email to you." She hung up and scribbled something down before looking at me again.

I took a galvanizing breath. "Look, I realize that it's your job to screen everyone who comes in here, but I have to speak to someone who might know something about this crazy woman who's stalking me!" In a move that surprised even me, I pounded my clenched fists on her desk. I'd taken a long leap beyond worrying what people might think. The girl's eyes bugged out, and she shifted back in her chair as she reached for the phone.

"What? Are you calling security?" I couldn't decide if I should make a run for it or snatch the phone from her hand.

She shifted her eyes toward the door and back to me. Maybe she had one of those panic buttons under her desk, and security had arrived to drag me away. *Is my imagined scene of a pumped-up security guy "escorting" me out of the building about to play out?* I couldn't force myself to turn and look.

"Hey, Kristen, is he in?" The breezy, matter-of-fact voice was unmistakable.

I slowly turned around. The three of us were frozen in place like Goebel figurines, cheeks flushed, mouths agape in surprise.

Mick hesitated for a second, his brow furrowed in concentration and maybe a dash of concern, before he said, "I remember you! Zabar's, right?"

"You know her?" Kristin was gobsmacked.

"Yeah, well, no, not really. Um, we met a few weeks ago." He cocked his head as he took in the situation.

"So, what, are you stalking me now?" He let out an uncomfortable laugh.

"No!"

My story came rushing out like water from a busted pipe. It felt good to release the pressure. When I got to the reason I was standing in Sam Stephens's office, arguing with his receptionist, Mick shook his head and rubbed the sandpaper stubble on his chin.

He turned toward Kristen. "Is anyone with him?"

"No, but..."

He turned toward me. "Hang tight." He strode to the door and tapped twice before opening it.

Someone inside said, "Hey, my man. What the hell are you doing here? I wasn't expecting you until this afternoon."

The door closed behind him, and I was stranded with Kristen. She shrugged, apparently as clueless as I was, then resumed answering the phone, which had been ringing nonstop.

I was unsure of what to do—stay, go, hover—then the office door opened and Mick stuck his head out. "You wanna come in here for a minute?"

Kristen glanced at me and flashed a tight smile before Mick ushered me in.

Sam Stephens was seated behind an oversized mahogany desk. The desktop was clean and polished, not a single stray paper clip in sight. He ejected himself from his chair. He was even taller than the celebrity he represented. He bestowed me with a too-white-to-be-real smile and reached out to shake my hand, revealing a pair of well-developed biceps beneath his crisp mauve shirt. He looked like a celebrity himself.

"Hello, Ms. Allen. Sorry for the wait." He gestured toward the two plush leather chairs angled in front of his desk. "Please, have a seat."

I lowered myself into the chair closest to the door, clutching my purse like a security blanket. Mick sank into the chair next to me. I'd desperately wanted this meeting, but now that I was there, it felt surreal. No need for anyone to escort me out—I wanted to make a run for it on my own.

"So, Mick tells me we've got a bit of a problem."

I have a problem. Me. Not "we."

He paused, signaling it was my turn to talk. Everything seemed to be happening in slow motion, but my mind was racing, my thoughts stumbling over one another in an effort to be first out of my mouth.

"Well, I don't know how much you know, but—"

"Mick filled me in," he interrupted as he leaned forward, grabbed a pen, and distractedly examined it. "Usually, it's some psycho who's sure Mick, or whoever they're focused on, is their soul mate and they start harassing them. Strange that she's only targeting you."

The skepticism in his voice was hard to miss.

"Sam, who the hell knows what goes through the mind of someone like that," Mick said. "I'm just thinking there must be something we could do to offer her protection from this wacko. I mean, I'm the one who took that video."

"But you didn't post it online," he snapped, shooting me a look of disdain.

"Neither did I, actually," I said, steeling myself for a dreaded confrontation. "A friend posted it without my knowledge. That's when everything started."

Stephenson sighed, his patience clearly stretched thin. "Well, Mick, what is it exactly you think we can do to help Ms. Allen?"

"Not sure." He shrugged. "But I thought maybe you, Randy, and Grace could put your heads together and come up with some ideas."

"Then I'll handle it from here. There's no reason for you to be involved beyond this point."

Mick's face flushed, and his lips thinned. He shifted restlessly in his seat. "Sam, I'm telling you for the last time, I don't need you running interference for me. I thought maybe you would've dealt with something like this before. I'm not trying to dump this in your lap."

Just when I was certain they'd forgotten I was there, Mick turned toward me. His charm-the-pants-off-you persona was gone. He looked me in the eye, and in a voice so low I could barely hear, he asked, "Has she hurt you?"

"Not physically..." I fought back tears as I pictured the epithet spray-painted on my bedroom wall.

"I expect crap like this to happen to me, but I never thought it would affect people I don't even know." He took a deep breath and drummed his fingers on the arm of his chair. "Look, Sam and I will talk with my lawyers, and we'll follow up with you."

My heart sank, an anchor dropped into the depths of the ocean. My initial expectation was spot-on. I would never hear from any of them again.

I had barely finished the thought when Mick turned to me, and a reassuring, if grim, smile spread across his face. "That's a promise, Rachael."

Chapter 9

If anything positive had come out of the stalker situation, it was that my mother started locking all the doors and windows and obsessively checking to make sure they were secure. But each time the phone rang, each time there was a knock on the door, each time mail dropped through the mail slot, it triggered my fight-or-flight response. The constant state of hypervigilance was sapping my energy.

The weekend passed with no written threats and no word from Mick's people. Monday morning, I received a postal notification to pick up a package. I often had to go to the post office to collect packages that wouldn't fit in the mail slot, so I dutifully drove to the local post office, waited in line, and gave the notice to the woman behind the counter. But when I was handed a padded envelope, my throat closed. I managed to eke out a thank-you.

My mailing address on the front of the package was scrawled in colored markers, with a crude drawing on the back that looked like a tiny headstone with my initials on it. I scanned the room, profiling every woman standing in line. *Is she here, waiting to watch me open it?* But none of the women fit my conjured image of a stalker. *But what is a stalker supposed to look like?* I speedwalked out the door, ran to my car, locked the doors, and started the engine, preparing for a quick getaway in case I'd been followed. I looked to my left, to my right, and out the back windshield. A couple of guys were talking on their cell phones and getting into their cars, but no women were in sight. I ripped open the envelope. The smell of urine wafted up, and I grimaced as I shook out the contents and stared. *What the fuck?* A positive pregnancy test lay on the front seat along with a note, "Mick and I are meant to be. You're nothing. NOTHING! Stay away or you'll be sorry, bitch!!!!"

A snippet of hair was taped to the paper with arrows pointing to it and the word "proof" scrawled above it in all caps. *Proof of what? Is it* her *hair? Is it supposed to be Mick's hair—another dimension of her delusion?* Thoroughly shaken, I sat in the parking lot, watching the steady stream of people coming and going, until my heart rate slowed and my breathing steadied.

Just as I turned the key in the ignition, my phone rang. Mick's lawyer was on the other end. "Meet us at Mick's manager's office in midtown at eleven tomorrow," he said. He rattled off the address—then silence.

"Hello?"

He'd hung up. *A preview of what I can expect from a meeting? He said "us." Will there be an entire Mick Sullivan entourage sitting at a conference table, staring me down?* Still, Mick Sullivan's celebrity status meant he had serious connections. No one cared if Rachael Allen was being stalked. But Mick Sullivan has a psycho stalker? That was front-page, tabloid-worthy news.

I went home, and an hour later, my phone rang again. "Change of plans, Ms. Allen," the lawyer said. "We'll send a car at ten." His tone suggested he wasn't happy about the shifted schedule, but he wasn't requesting an RSVP—I was expected to be accommodating.

I called Jenna and brought her up-to-date.

"Wow," she said. "I know I said it was worth a shot, but I guess I'm shocked it's actually happening. Text me as soon it's over." She paused. "Will *he* be there?"

"I doubt it. He's got people who handle that stuff." Despite Mick's pushback when Stephens attempted to take him out of the conversation, I was certain his role in the whole thing was done. Over dinner, I told my parents about the next day's meeting. Their reaction was muted, but they made up for it when they marched into my room later that night.

"Be careful what you say tomorrow. You never know when things might come back to haunt you," my mother warned, and she clicked her tongue in disapproval at the callousness of these people she'd never met.

"You need to bring a lawyer." My father laid down his edict with such conviction that if I hadn't known better, I would have thought this was a situation he dealt with on a daily basis. "I'll call Howard Samuelson. We've worked with him on several claim lawsuits. Maybe he can come with you or at least give you some pointers on how to handle this."

And maybe when I'm forty, you'll start treating me like an adult.

"Daddy, seriously? I'm not on trial. Don't call Mr. Samuelson. I don't want to make a bigger deal out of this than it already is."

"Well, you steer clear of that actor." He spewed the word "actor" as though he'd said "motherfucker."

I danced around sleep for hours. I didn't know what to expect from the next day's meeting, but I ran through every possible scenario in the dark until I was exhausted and finally dozed off.

In the morning, I tiptoed downstairs, fixed myself toast and coffee and carried it back to my room, a practice my mother forbade: *"Nasty crumbs. They bring roaches, you know."* But my parents were sleeping in. Not only could I eat breakfast in my room in peace, I would sidestep their last-minute briefing and my father's well-intentioned but horribly misguided concerns about lecherous Hollywood actors.

I sipped my coffee while I watched the video on my phone, desperately searching for a clue to what might have set off the stalker. Mick Sullivan surely took selfies with women all the time. That's what famous people did. *But why is this woman targeting me?* There was nothing special about me that would trigger irrational jealousy. Maybe it was the kiss. Maybe that woman couldn't stop imagining what it would feel like to be kissed by him, to be with him. Maybe she'd gotten as close to him as I had, and it triggered something—something that was bleeding over into my life.

Dressed in jeans, an emerald-green T-shirt, and black ankle boots, I went outside, stood on the front steps, and waited. I was eager to get this thing, whatever it was, underway. The car pulled into the driveway at ten sharp. The driver's broken English and thick Eastern European accent made conversation difficult, so I rode to the city with nothing but the jarring sounds of rap in an unfamiliar language throbbing through the back speakers. The highway scenery of New Jersey transitioned from lush green to air-polluting factories as we passed toll after toll, drove through the tunnel, navigated lower Manhattan, and crossed the Brooklyn Bridge. After half an hour of spinning the hamster wheel in my head, we pulled up to a homey brownstone building on a quiet tree-lined street in Brooklyn. It was a world away from Sam Stephens's office in midtown Manhattan.

The driver pointed at the front door. "Go to door. Press buzzer," he said. "You call to me after. I make busy to then." And he handed me a business card. Igor was his name.

"Thanks." I stuffed the card in my pocket. Even though I'd done everything I could to get Mick's people involved, I wondered if this was a mistake. *Am I making things worse? Will they think I'm crying wolf and then, if the situation escalates, ignore my pleas for help?* Despite my insistence to my father that I wouldn't be on trial, I felt like I was about to take the witness stand in my own defense. I stepped out of the car, and the driver sped off. I was alone, staring at the ornate double doors at the top of the stoop.

Up and down the street, crepe myrtle, dogwood, and red maple were exploding in bursts of purple, white, and crimson, standing their ground in the stubborn patches of grass carved out near the curb. People were sitting on their stoops, visiting with neighbors, walking dogs, and pushing babies in strollers. I lifted my chin, walked up the steps, and peered inside the front windows to see who or what lay in wait for me, but the curtains were shut tight. I pressed the buzzer.

A woman's voice crackled over the speaker. "Yes?"

I cleared my throat. "This is Rachael Allen... I have an appointment?"

At the crisp buzz and decisive click of the lock, I pushed open the thick wooden door and stepped into the vestibule. A very blond thirty-something woman wearing a slip of a skirt and balancing impressively on spiked heels greeted me. The woman's flawless paper-white skin was a stunning contrast to the flash of bright-red lipstick applied to her perfectly plumped lips. She was as well scripted for the scene as I was miscast.

"Hello, Rachael. I'm Grace Woodelson, Mick's publicist."

She offered me a firm handshake. Her nails were immaculately manicured. I glanced at my own nails, which rarely came within sniffing distance of nail polish.

"Come in."

I stepped onto a plush rug that resembled a Picasso in his blue period, layers upon layers of blues with only occasional sparks of reds and yellows. It must have cost a fortune. My mother's admonitions rang in my ears. *Did I wipe my shoes outside?*

Grace ushered me through the grand interior double doors to the right of the vestibule. Four other people were waiting for me in a room that must have been designated as the parlor in the 1800s, but it had been renovated and was bright and modern. The work of a high-priced designer, no doubt. Only the original etched-glass-panel pocket doors into the dining room and the cast-iron fireplace mantel remained. The overall effect was Scandinavian sleek. Despite my initial impression of the room's clean architectural lines, a thin layer of dust had settled everywhere, unemptied trash cans sat in corners, and makeshift ashtrays overflowed with cigarette butts. Newspapers and magazines were spread out on tables, and shirts, jeans, and jackets hung over the backs of chairs.

"I understand you've met Sam," Grace said as she began introductions.

He gave an unenthusiastic nod in my direction.

She went on, "This is Steven Edelman, Mick's lawyer. Randy Border, his agent. Angela Broderick, my assistant." Not one of them looked pleased to meet me.

The group was seated on an übermodern sofa and matching love seat. Not a hair was out of place, and their clothes must've cost more than I made in a year at Broken Vinyl. Even if I couldn't afford them, I knew Dolce & Gabbana, Vera Wang, and Prada when I saw them.

"Have a seat, Rachael." Grace pointed at the chair that completed the seating arrangement.

I sat.

"We all know why we're here, but maybe you can start from the beginning so we're all on the same page. Angela will be taking notes."

I really was on trial, and Angela was the court stenographer. The anger that fueled my trip to Sam Stephens's office was nowhere to be found. I felt uncomfortably vulnerable and a bit nauseated.

"Could I get some water, please?"

Grace's assistant jumped up. She was a perky waif of a girl I had already pegged as someone who was using the job as a way station before moving on to bigger and better things in the film industry. "I'll get it for you," she said as she ran to the kitchen and returned pronto with an ice-cold bottle of Fiji water.

"Thank you." A couple of sips and one deep breath later, I asked, "So, where do you want me to start?"

"From the beginning," the lawyer droned, his voice the equivalent of an eye roll.

I looked around the room once more. "Is this someone's office?" I blurted.

"It's Mick's place," Grace said, as though I were dim-witted.

I had to remove myself from the scene and regroup, if only for a minute. "Could I use the restroom?"

Grace exhaled, clearly put out, and pointed. "Around the corner and to the left."

The muffled whispers I heard as I walked away only heightened the sensation of being caught in a trap—first by the stalker and now by Mick Sullivan's entourage. A mild sense of relief washed over me as I turned the corner. If the place had a back way out, I would've taken it. But I could see the back door led to a garden and a privacy fence. There was no escape. I leaned against the wall and closed my eyes.

"Are you okay?"

A cigarette dangled from his lips. He was wearing a worn and wrinkled Dead Kennedys T-shirt and what I thought were the same ripped jeans he'd worn that day at Zabar's. He looked every bit the bad boy he was made out to be in the tabloids.

"I was just looking for the bathroom."

"With your eyes closed?" He grinned.

I managed an obligatory smile. I pushed away from the wall and threw my shoulders back. "I needed to step away. If your entourage is trying to intimidate me, they're succeeding."

He cocked his head in empathy. "Don't let the Gang of Five get to you." He glanced around the corner to where they were, leaned in toward me, and lowered his voice. "To tell you the truth, they used to intimidate me until it dawned on me that *they* work for *me*, instead of the other way around. But you have to understand—if I make a crappy movie or, like with this stalker, someone wants to hurt me or someone connected to me, it hits them where they feel it most, their bank accounts." He slid his vibrating cell phone from his back pocket, glanced at it, and put it back.

"Come on." He nodded toward the living room. "I was about to join the meeting. Don't want you to be chum for the sharks."

I was shocked and relieved at his offer to run interference for me. He motioned with a wave of his hand toward the parlor, and he escorted me with his palm on my lower back. I tensed. Like the kiss in Zabar's, it was another indication he had no concept of personal space. I sped up, and his hand slipped away.

We reentered the room, where the "gang" was impatiently waiting for my return. Their furrowed brows clearly indicated they weren't happy about Mick joining us. But he must have laid down the law beforehand, because they said nothing.

"So, Rachael," his lawyer began before I could even sit down. "What was your intent when you took the video?"

"My intent? I... I just wanted a picture."

"*Jesus*, Steve. I already told you the video was my idea," Mick interjected. His phone had been buzzing nonstop. He pulled out a pair of oversized black-rimmed glasses from his jacket pocket, put them on, and glanced at his phone. They made him look oddly collegiate as he pushed them up on the bridge of his nose and his lashes bumped up against the lenses.

"So why did you post it online?" His lawyer wasn't going to let it go.

"Actually, I didn't. I—"

Mick removed his glasses and slipped his phone into his back pocket before he said, "*Shit*, does anybody listen to anything I say? She didn't post it. A friend of hers did that." He turned to me. "Right?" he asked with the slightest shade of doubt in his voice.

"I didn't know anything about it until she told me," I said.

They all shook their heads in synchronized rhythm.

"Guys, it's like all you need is a spotlight and thick German accents. I thought we were here to help her, not interrogate her." Mick bristled. "So can we cut the accusatory shit? It was totally innocent. This whole thing has just spun out of control."

The lawyer sat back and let me tell the story again, uninterrupted this time, as Angela took notes. When I was done, he stood and spoke first. "Rachael, we appreciate you coming here and filling us in on the details. We'll talk it over and see if we can't agree on the best way to proceed."

I looked up at his towering figure. "But the messages are getting more bizarre and threatening, and after that woman came into my house, into my room, I'm worried for my safety and the safety of my parents."

"Well," he said, frowning, as though he'd already given the matter a tremendous amount of thought, "first we need to determine if this woman has pushed the limits enough to classify her actions as stalking and to obtain a restraining order against her... and, of course, that's possible only if we can find out who she is. Have there been any phone calls?"

"No."

"If she calls, record it. The court will want to have proof of all contact from her."

Court? Maybe I should have brought a lawyer after all.

"Guys, guys," Mick said, shaking his head, "is this the best we can do—tell her what she's probably already heard from the police? There must be something concrete we can offer—move her out of her house, put her up someplace else, get a security patrol, a bodyguard."

The lawyer pursed his lips, grabbed Mick by the arm, pulled him aside, and whispered just loud enough for me to overhear. "We've met with her. She's expressed her concerns and explained the situation. We're not liable here."

Mick drew an exasperated breath. He abruptly turned and announced to the group, "Meeting adjourned. Thanks for all your help."

They all stood and reached into their pockets and purses for their phones and mumbled something about calls to make, people to meet, flights to catch. They were on to the next projects on their lists.

Grace broke away from her phone and ordered Angela, "Call the car service for Rachael."

Mick jumped in. "That's okay. You guys go ahead."

"Mick!" his lawyer shouted.

"Steve, chill!" His brows were deeply furrowed, forming an angry unibrow. "Thanks for coming. Now, go home. Seriously! I think I can handle it from here."

Sam gave Mick's lawyer an I-told-you-so look, and they reluctantly filed out of the room and headed for the front door but not before each one of them shot me a look that said, *"Tread carefully. You're trespassing on exclusive private property."*

Mick followed them, and Sam leaned over to him, patted him on the back, and whispered, "Call me if you need anything."

"I'm fine, Sam," he said, shrugging off Sam's hand.

One by one, they disappeared around the corner to the vestibule, and I heard the front door close.

I was alone with the reason I was being stalked.

Chapter 10

"Well, that was fun," Mick mumbled to himself as he returned from seeing everyone off. He lingered in the doorway for a moment before collapsing in a chair next to the sofa, where I was sitting.

I stared at my white-knuckled fists in my lap as I once again flipped through the countless scenarios for how this surreal stalking situation might end—none of them good.

He leaned forward, rested his elbows on his thighs, and said, "I know my whole entourage seems weird. I guess I've gotten so used to all this shit I forget how over-the-top it must seem to someone not in the business. Sorry they weren't exactly helpful."

I shook my head. "I'm not sure what I expected, but... I thought I'd somehow walk away feeling safer." I looked him in the eye. "But I don't."

He sat back in his chair and ran his fingers through his hair in a futile attempt at containment. His fidgety silence broke when he said, "Listen, I think I might have an idea."

I was reluctantly hopeful. "Oh?"

"How about I hire a bodyguard for you?"

I imagined a guy built like a bison sitting next to me on the train and tagging along with me and Jenna for a sugar-free vanilla latte at Drip. "No, that would be too weird." I forced a strained laugh.

"Then why don't you let me put you and your family up in a hotel?"

"Thanks, but... no. I'll just go home and wait to hear from your lawyer." Determined to make a dignified exit, I quickly stood and slung my purse over my shoulder. "I really appreciate you going to all this effort to bring everyone together, but..."

When he stood, I was forced to look up at him.

"Maybe this is crazy," he said. "I'm sure my lawyer will think it is, but you could stay here if you want. I'm leaving for LA, and I won't be back for a while. In fact, this place is vacant most of the time. I doubt this wack job even knows where it is. If she did, she would have been here already." He gestured toward the ceiling. "The top floor is a separate apartment. I have bars on the windows, a high-tech security system, surveillance cameras outside, and the security firm sends a car around every hour or so to check on things."

I stared at him, expecting him to throw his head back in laughter and bark out, *"Just kidding!"* But he wasn't laughing. I fell back onto the sofa, my purse still on my shoulder. This super celebrity was standing in front of me, offering to let me stay in his beautiful home. The idea was outrageous. "Why would you do that? You don't even know me."

"Look, this whole thing is really my fault, and I don't want to be responsible for something happening to you or your family."

My parents... Oh my God, my parents.

As if he'd jumped inside my head, he added, "Your parents could come too."

I laughed. "Sorry, but *that* would *never* happen."

"Then let me set you all up in a hotel until this shit blows over." He paused. "You can pack a few things and move tonight if you want. I'm catching the red-eye back to LA."

"I... I really can't," I said. *Would I be refusing his thoughtful offer if he wasn't famous, crazy rich, and alarmingly attractive?* Jenna would surely have me committed for cutting off my connection with him.

"Why not?" he asked, clearly surprised by my refusal.

I couldn't think of a reason I felt comfortable saying out loud, and I couldn't decide which of his options would make me feel safest.

He shrugged. "Okay, your call." He hadn't moved. "You look like you could use a drink. How about a glass of wine before you head back?"

Before I could respond, he strode toward the kitchen. I finally caught the back of his Dead Kennedys T-shirt, which read Too Drunk to Fuck. He returned with a bottle of wine and a couple of mismatched glasses. He filled both to the rim.

"Cheers." He chugged his wine as if it were an ice-cold glass of lemonade on a sweltering August day then refilled it. His phone vibrated repeatedly, but he ignored it.

"Do you mind if I ask you a question?" I asked.

"Sure, go for it. Not sure if I'll answer, though," he said, grinning.

"Why *did* you take that video with me in Zabar's? What if I had been the crazy one? Do you do that a lot? I mean, don't take this the wrong way, but looking back, it doesn't seem like a very smart move."

"Yeah, Gracie is always getting pissed at me for doing the wrong thing, saying the wrong thing." His expression hardened, and he refilled his glass. "It's like I'm expected to ask permission from my lawyer and my manager before I take a piss. I'm so fucking sick of being told what to do. Sometimes, you just have to do what feels right, you know?" He stopped talking and smiled, seemingly amused by his own intensity. "I guess I've gotten tired of having to justify the way I live my life to everyone. Anyway, you seemed nice. And, no, I don't make a habit of taking videos with random strangers." He paused. "If I'm being honest, I wanted to get a closer look at those eyes."

His smile told me he was well aware of the effect his words would have.

"Has this stalker thing ever happened before?" I asked in a not-so-subtle attempt to change the subject.

"That's two questions." He grinned. "So, yeah, I mean, nothing like this, but I get strange letters and naked photos from overly zealous fans all the time. I've even gotten some dick pics." He laughed. "Just this week, I got, like, a dozen greeting cards, all with the same postmark and similar handwriting. All that shit goes through the clearinghouse that collects my fan mail. They automatically flag anything that seems questionable. The handwritten messages said stuff like"—he switched his voice to a lusty whisper drenched in drama—"'Our future together means everything to me' and 'I can't wait to be in your arms and feel you inside of me again.' Or some shit like that."

I felt the blood rush to my face.

"Sorry," he said. "TMI?"

He left it at that, lit a cigarette, and took a gulp of wine. He scooted forward on the chair and turned back to me. "At least let me arrange to get a good security system installed in your parents' house."

His insistent offer of help was reassuring even if it was unlikely to happen.

"That's incredibly nice of you," I said. "I'll tell my parents you offered, but my dad's not great at accepting help with anything—from anyone."

"Look, I'm not taking no for an answer. Give me their address, and I'll take care of it. And I'll make arrangements for a security patrol." He sat back, nodded to himself, and took a drag of his cigarette. Evidently, in his mind, it was a done deal. After a brief pause, he asked, seemingly out of nowhere, "So, what do you do, Rachael?"

"Do?"

"Yeah." He laughed. "You know, for a living?"

"Oh, I actually just got hired at Sisyphus Records."

"No shit? They're great. I know a couple of artists who signed with them. Heard really good things."

"I'm super excited. My last job was at a much smaller record company, but I was laid off when they went bankrupt. That's why I'm staying with my parents right now."

"Was it Broken Vinyl?"

"Yeah, you knew about that? It was awful."

"I follow the ups and downs of the music industry. I'm a bit of an amateur musician myself. I write and play the guitar, and I try to work on it as much as I can, but there never seems to be enough time," he said, sounding wistful. He took a sip of his wine and another drag before changing the subject once again.

"So, after all this, did 'your friend' appreciate the video?"

He was leapfrogging from one topic to the next, extending the conversation.

"I can't believe you remember that. But, yeah, Jenna went berserk."

"Jenna?"

"Yeah, my friend's a huge fan. She was so excited she—"

"So it really was for a friend?"

"Well, yeah. Did you think it was my cover story?"

"It happens." He shrugged. "'It's for my sister, my girlfriend, my boss.' I've heard it all."

"I don't want you to get the wrong idea. Jenna is a major fan, but she's not a stalker."

"Good to know."

He stood and stretched his slim frame. He finished off the last of the bottle and headed to the dining room for more, checking off the last item on my bad-boy checklist—drinks too much.

As he walked back into the room with a fresh bottle, my cell phone rang. I took it from my purse and glanced at the screen. "Sorry, it's my dad. They're probably anxious to know what happened."

I stood, wandered over by the window, and braced myself before answering. "Daddy?"

"Is your meeting over?"

"Yeah, I was just about to leave."

"So?" he demanded. "Are they going to take care of the situation?"

"Well, not exactly. They—"

"Then what the hell was this meeting for? I told you to bring a lawyer!"

I was certain his booming voice was projecting into the room. I cupped my hand over the speaker and lowered my voice. "Can we just talk when I get home?"

My head was throbbing with a swell of aggravation, as it always did when he got like that, which was often. "Daddy, I gotta go. My cab is here." I hung up, already weary from the "conversation" awaiting me at home.

Mick grinned at me as I walked back. "Was that Darth Vader on the phone?"

"Sorry about that," I said.

He took a gulp of his wine, and his voice dropped. "Just be glad he cares."

A loaded response, but I let it lie.

My father's over-the-top reaction had me rethinking my options. I swallowed hard and took a deep breath before saying, "You know, if your offer still stands, maybe staying here isn't such a bad idea after all."

"Yep. The offer is still good."

"I don't think your lawyer or your publicist will be too happy, though."

He seemed amused at the prospect. "Steve is going to have an aneurysm. I'm sure he'll get hung up on something to do with liability—one of the top ten words in his vocabulary. He'll probably want you to sign a liability waiver and a nondisclosure agreement or something."

Another nondisclosure agreement. I guess what happens in Mick Sullivan's place stays in Mick Sullivan's place.

He snuffed his cigarette out in the ashtray on the coffee table and cracked his knuckles.

"I'll need to deal with my parents. My dad isn't really a fan of celebrities—on principle. No offense."

He gave me a thumbs-up. "Hey, I like him already. I'll talk to your dad if you think it would make him feel better about this arrangement."

"Thanks," I said, knowing that conversation would have to wait until hell actually froze over.

"Okay. Someone will be in touch about the alarm system, and I'll have a hotel reservation made for your family—and you—in case, you know, you should change your mind. I've gotta head out soon, but I'll leave the keys in the lockbox. What's your number? I'll text you the passcode."

I had Mick Sullivan's personal cell phone number and would soon have the key to his house. All this was creating another strange chapter in my already incredibly bizarre story.

Chapter 11

My driver, Igor, pulled into the driveway of my parents' home, and I steeled myself for their knee-jerk reaction to my rash decision. As I looked in the window to the living room, where they were watching TV, I felt as though my time in Brooklyn, meeting Mick Sullivan's entourage, and sharing a drink and a conversation with him were all part of a dimming dream rather than actual events. I suddenly felt foolish. *What if Mick's generosity was fueled by a mixture of alcohol and guilt? What if by the time I arrive, he's sobered up enough to realize his offer was ridiculous? What if when I walk up the stoop, packed bags in hand, I'm met by his lawyer offering a few choice words of warning?*

My second-guessing felt like when I was ten years old and standing on the high diving board, about to jump in but deciding at the last moment that I just couldn't do it. But then I thought about the stalker, who'd let me know she was gearing up to take her threats to the next level. If that happened, there would be no second-guessing.

My thoughts were broken when Igor said, "I wait," as he put the car in park and turned up the music.

"I won't be long," I said.

The key was in my hand, positioned at the lock, when my mother opened the door. The aroma of lemon Pledge and freshly baked chocolate chip cookies permeated the air. It was a stark contrast to Mick's place, where the air was filled with the smell of tobacco, wine, and the unexpected scent of Ivory soap each time he came close. As I stepped inside, my father approached the entryway.

"I want to know exactly what they told you."

He left my mother and me at the door and parked himself in his BarcaLounger. We followed him into the living room and took our usual seats.

"Daddy, you would've been amazed at his brownstone. From the outside, it's historically preserved, but it's totally modern on the inside." I'd decided to appeal to his interests as a way to ease into what was going to be an incredibly uncomfortable conversation.

He once had dreams of becoming an architect, before life got in the way, and he ended up making his living selling insurance policies to people who couldn't afford them and probably didn't need them.

"I'm sure it's great." He didn't even take a breath. "So, they aren't going to do anything?"

"Well, they weren't able to come up with anything for now."

Ensconced in his ersatz throne, he stiffened, his thin veneer of tolerance buckling.

I cleared my throat and shifted in my seat. *You're an adult, Rachael. Act like one.*

"He offered to let me stay in his building in a separate apartment upstairs. He won't be there. The building has a high-tech alarm system, and there's a security firm that patrols the place on a regular basis." I paused for a second or two before reiterating, "He's leaving later tonight for Los Angeles. He won't be there."

"He's giving you the keys to his home?" my mother asked, wide-eyed.

Before I could answer, my father blurted, "Rachael, you can't be serious."

"I'll only have access to the apartment upstairs, and I actually think I might be safer there until the police can track down whoever's doing this. There's no evidence that she's been at his place."

They looked at each other before my mother spoke up. "Rachael, honey, have you really thought this through?"

"I know it sounds crazy, but I have to get some peace of mind, and I think I'll feel safer there." I wasn't about to tell them that staying there also allowed me to sidestep the added burden of their concern and my father's overwrought lectures. "At least for now."

My father's jaw muscles relaxed as he mulled it over.

"And it will be easier to go to my meetings in the city with Sisyphus," I hastily added.

My father sat back in his chair and gripped the arms as if readying himself for a rough landing. "For how long?"

"Just until the police can find out who's doing this."

"I don't like it."

My mother reached out, patted his arm, and whispered, "Don, if she would feel safer there, I think that's her decision. Don't you?"

As if the decision were his to make and he'd come to the conclusion on his own, he said, "Well, I'm not crazy about the idea, but I think maybe it's for the best. At least for the time being."

My mother continued to work at lowering the setting on my father's tension. "Maybe we should check into a hotel for a day or two while we get a security system installed," my mother suggested.

"Oh," I said, excited to offer my father a consolation prize, "he actually said he would pay for a hotel for as long as you want and for getting the security system installed too."

"That won't be necessary. I think we can manage to pay for everything ourselves," he said with a grimace.

"He told me to insist. He said it would make him feel better about everything."

"Make *him* feel better?" he shouted. "It's *my* family that's in danger here. I don't give a damn how he feels!"

"Your father and I will talk about this later, Rachael," my mother said in an effort to further soothe my father's tender ego.

"But could you please take the hotel room?" I begged. "It would make *me* feel better."

My father was thinking it over but too proud to give in.

"Well, I'm going to go pack a few things." I stood, waiting for them to throw obstacles in my path. When neither of them spoke up, I retreated to the stairs.

With no time frame in mind—*Maybe the police will track the stalker down in a week? A month? Six months?*—I crammed as much as would fit into my overnight case and tossed clothes, my iPad, my phone charger, and a book I hadn't cracked open yet into my suitcase. I checked the bathroom countertop, the drawers, and the closet. I stuck my head out of the bedroom doorway and called, "Daddy, I'm going to need some help up here!"

I heard his leaden footsteps on the stairs and braced myself for a follow-up lecture now that he would have me alone without my mother there to run interference. He hesitated in the doorway, and I stopped fiddling with the broken zipper on my suitcase.

"Daddy, it'll be okay. I really think this is the best thing for me right now."

"Well, you're going to do what you want anyway. You always do." He sighed. "Just the one suitcase?"

"Yeah," I said. "I can carry the overnight."

He picked up my suitcase, paused in the doorway, and turned to look at me, his eyes dark with concern.

"Daddy, I promise I'll be fine."

He opened his mouth as if to say something but gave a single nod and abruptly turned and headed downstairs.

Chapter 12

Though living in Mick's building wasn't anything like I'd envisioned my new life in New York would be, I settled into something resembling a normal routine and was living by my own house rules since my current "landlord" didn't seem to have any. Navigating the surreal detour my life had taken was not easy. I would be going about my day and it would just hit me, how unreal it all was, how uncertain my future. The looming threat of a deeply deluded woman had followed me to Brooklyn like a stubborn shadow.

Daily phone calls with Jenna and my mother provided support, but the last time I'd called Jenna, she got on my last nerve with her adolescent focus on Mick Sullivan, the celebrity. He was still just a beautiful fantasy to her, a digital image, not a flesh-and-blood guy who was trying to help keep me safe.

"Jenna, I get it. I do. But from what I can tell, he's nothing like he's made out to be in the media. He seems—I don't know—nice."

"Nice? That sounds boring," she said, laughing.

Alone at my computer, I was going over notes from my interview earlier in the day with the lead singer of Tar Pit, the latest "it" band to sign with Sisyphus. As I was trying to figure out how to make the guy sound like he wasn't a complete megalomaniac, my email dinged. The message contained only two sentences: *He loves ME!! Soon you'll be gone and I'll be the most important person in his life again.*

My chest tightened. I prayed my parents were turning on the alarm system that my father had begrudgingly allowed Mick to arrange for them—and that they were still locking the doors. As expected, my father had refused Mick's offer to pay for a hotel room for them.

I closed my eyes and took a calming breath before calling the Brooklyn Police Department and asking for the detective assigned to the case when I left New Jersey for Brooklyn.

"Detective Melnitsky here."

"Detective? This is Rachael Allen."

"I'm sorry, who?"

My anger and frustration rose to a crescendo, but I managed to keep my voice calm. "The Mick Sullivan stalking case?"

"Oh, yeah, yeah. What can I do for you, Ms. Allen?"

"I got another threatening message today in an email, and you told me to let you know if I did."

"It's really not necessary to call. Just forward it to me. I'll take a look and let you know if it's traceable."

I hesitated to ask since I was certain that I already knew the answer. "Is there anything new at all?"

"Nope. No luck tracking her down—she's evidently using public computers. Mr. Sullivan was getting calls on his cell before he changed the number, but she'd been calling from burner phones before that anyway."

I felt sick. I hung up and forwarded the emailed threat to Melnitsky while trying to remind myself that despite the latest message and the NYPD's lackadaisical approach, I felt safe—most of the time. The security system's elaborate control panel would warn me of an intruder, and the security firm drove by several times a day, just as Mick promised. Sometimes, the guys even double-parked the patrol car, got out, and knocked on the door to check on me. I was already on a first-name basis with them——Tony and George. Tony, the cute one with the thick black hair and an even thicker Brooklyn accent, always asked, his face full of hope, "Is the big guy here today?" I couldn't decide whether he had a girlfriend pressing him for information or if he wanted to check Mick out for himself. George was a transplant from Buffalo with a flat accent, a receding hairline, and a wife and three kids. He rolled his eyes each time Tony asked if Mick was there.

Mick stayed in touch from the west coast, emailing and texting me daily to make sure all was well. Despite my irritation at Jenna's stubborn perception of him, I was experiencing my own disconnect between his celebrity persona and the very real guy texting me.

Any word from our stalker friend?

Friend?

That was sarcasm, in case you didn't pick up on that. I suck at subtle texting :-)

I was enjoying the light exchange after dealing with the aggravating call with Melnitsky, and I didn't want to bring things down.

Quiet so far.

Whew! Good to know.

I was surprised anew each time he called in response to my texts when I couldn't figure out how to use the remote, reset the alarm, or adjust the thermostat. And he filled me in on where to get the best bagels, who had the tangiest gelato, the freshest falafel, the warmest baguettes, the greatest selection of beer on tap, and which newsstand always had the Sunday edition of *The New York Times* first on Saturday night.

Your recs were amazing! Getting to know Brooklyn. TY!

Glad to be of service. Brooklyn IS the best borough. When all this is over, you should think about finding a place there instead of the city.

The perks of Brooklyn and my regular contact with Mick were choked by the fact that I was still being harassed by a woman who thought I was in some sort of competition for Mick's affections. The whole situation was as ludicrous as it was frightening. But I wasn't in some low-budget stalker film where the person being stalked was yanked to safety at the last minute before the credits rolled. An undeniable chance existed that my real-life circumstances wouldn't have such a happy ending.

My cell rang, and I jumped. The constant adrenaline spikes left me dry mouthed and depleted. I didn't recognize the number and hesitated but thought it might be a callback from someone I needed to interview. "Hello?"

"Rachael? This is Heloise from next door. Michael thought you might like to join me for tea. Is now a good time?"

He'd briefed me on his neighbor: "She's a nice lady, but don't let appearances fool you. She's led a crazy life. If she invites you over for tea, say yes and ask questions. She loves to talk. Oh, and she doesn't know who I am... you know... what I do, and I'd like to keep it that way. I don't want her to treat me any different—not that she would."

A server of tea and a lover of cats, who proudly claimed every one of her eighty years, Heloise didn't believe in television. "Rots your brain." She never went to the movies and didn't subscribe to any of the streaming services. "Colossal waste of money." She preferred to spend her hours listening to music and reading.

Mick was just the sweet young man next door she sometimes invited over for tea and cake. She said she thought he could use a little fattening up.

I sat in Heloise's living room in the middle of the afternoon, watching her expertly pin her waist-length alabaster hair into a tight, neat bun. The curtains were drawn, as they always were, and Billie Holiday's whiskey voice crooned in the background. The room was a few degrees too warm, and the aroma of soiled kitty litter stung my nostrils as I sipped stale Lipton tea from a rose-petaled teacup.

"So, are you Michael's new girlfriend?" Heloise smiled at me as a tabby jumped onto her lap and purred. She picked up her teacup, leaned back in the burgundy Queen Anne chair and crossed her legs, moving as surely as someone twenty years younger. She said, "You're the first one who's stayed long enough for me to invite over for tea."

Mick had also warned me that Heloise had a penchant for asking pointed questions and speaking the truth.

"I'm just an acquaintance. He's letting me stay here while I look for an apartment in the city." *It isn't that far from the truth.*

"Oh? Well, good luck. Finding apartments in the city is like digging for hidden treasure with a teaspoon. So I guess you'll be there alone a lot. I know Michael travels for work. But I've never been completely clear on what it is he does for a living."

I hesitated. "He's a musician." I figured I might as well lump him in with other bad-boy musicians who'd paraded through my life.

Heloise mulled that over for a second before she said, "Yes, I can see that. You know, he's a nice-looking boy—if he'd do something with that hair."

I took another sip of the awful brew to hide my grin.

His tousled hair was his trademark.

"I had a relationship with a musician once," Heloise said, sounding nostalgic. "It's a hard, hard life. Wasn't for me." She sighed and gave a dismissive wave of her hand. "That was a long time ago." The tabby curled up in her lap was startled by her sudden movement, jumped down, and made his way to the nearest litter box. My nose was becoming desensitized to the aroma.

"Do you have a boyfriend, Rachael?"

"No. Still looking, I guess. Met a few toads, but no Prince Charming."

"Well, there are plenty more where they came from. And you're so young... What, twenty-six, twenty-seven?"

"Twenty-four. Twenty-five in a couple of months."

"Oh, sweetheart, you've got all the time in the world. Enjoy it. Anyway, you'll learn soon enough, if you haven't already, that handsome or not, men are all pretty much the same in one respect." She smiled, leaned in, and lowered her voice. "In bed, I mean. At least, from what I can recall."

Sex with Conrad flashed across my brain. I have to respectfully disagree with Heloise, I thought. After some gentle prompting, Heloise segued into a few of her most memorable romantic trysts—the Israeli soldier she met in Tel Aviv, the Romanian designer she dated in New York, the very American cartoonist she lived with in Connecticut, and the Tunisian woman she hooked up with in Sfax.

"I never quite figured out what she did for a living, to have such a lavish lifestyle." She laid out the gory details of her stint as a WAC nurse during the Vietnam War. "Spent most of my time in Saigon at the hospital, treating wounded and dying—mostly dying—soldiers. The girls weren't supposed to carry guns back then, but the boys taught us, and I still have an army-issue .45 automatic one of them gave me. I was a good shot."

She'd never married, never had kids, said she never felt the need. She had her memories, and she nurtured them, doted on them, and exaggerated them, as if they were her children. That was the first of several tea parties with Heloise, in which she served up the tales of her life one at a time like Godiva chocolates—rich, sometimes dark, and always leaving me with a taste for more.

Knowing I had a friend next door comforted me even if that friend was an octogenarian with a tendency to speak her mind and ask pointed questions.

Chapter 13

Mick returned to New York sooner than expected. The invitation he extended that night was even more unexpected.

Want to come downstairs and join me for a beer?

Really? I thought. Despite our friendly texts, I had assumed we would stay in our designated spaces and rarely, if ever, cross paths. Not bothering to change clothes or freshen my makeup, I simply looked forward to the company of someone born in the same half-century as me. I knocked on his door, and when he opened it, the shock of recognition jarred me. With our casual texting back and forth, it was easy to forget who was on the other end.

"Hey, Rachael, come on in."

I had just lowered myself onto the sofa when his phone dinged. He pulled it from his back pocket and read a text. He rolled his eyes and clicked his tongue as he threw his head back, exhaled, and stared at the ceiling for a second or two. Seeming sincere, he said, "I'm really sorry, but I have to meet someone in the city."

I, on the other hand, was one hundred percent insincere when I mumbled, "Sure, no problem," and I retreated to my apartment upstairs, alone.

The next day, he texted an invitation to join him downstairs for drinks—plural—and followed that up with:

I've attempted to create something resembling chili. Brave enough to taste?

After running the brush through my hair and dabbing on lip gloss, I squeezed into my favorite pair of jeans and a white V-neck T-shirt, went downstairs, and knocked on his door.

"Yeah?" he called. Music blared in the background.

"It's Rachael."

He didn't answer right away.

"From upstairs?"

I heard him stomp to the door before he opened it then turned and walked barefoot back into the room. "Come on in. I was in the middle of a scavenger hunt for a T-shirt. *Shit*. I know it's here. Somewhere." He wore a dress shirt that was missing a button. He took three lanky steps over to the fireplace, where a collection of discarded clothes was draped over the back of a chair.

"Ah, here it is!" His back was turned to me as he pulled a shirt over his head, not bothering to unbutton it. He grabbed something from the pile, put it on, and turned around to reveal a threadbare gray T-shirt that said, *Sex, Drugs & Smooth Jazz*.

"Better. So, what'll it be, Rachael? Beer, wine… Diet Coke?" When he smiled, his face bore little resemblance to the cinematic heartthrob image familiar to millions. It was warmer, more open.

"Wine sounds good."

"Awesome… I've got a case of some stuff I haven't tried yet."

Unsure whether to stay put or follow, I hesitated before trailing behind him. Like the rest of his place, the kitchen was sleek and modern—Sub-Zero fridge, Viking stove, Miele dishwasher. All were pristine, barely used except for the huge double stainless-steel sink overflowing with dirty dishes. A pot of chili bubbled. It was about to spill over and christen his stove.

"I think your chili might be about to pop."

"Shit." He turned it down, stirred, and lifted the spoon. "Wanna taste? Don't worry. I was kidding earlier. I got the recipe from my mom. It's good." He held the spoon out for me.

"Oh wow, that is good! What's your secret?"

"A little dash of sugar. It works, right?"

I spotted the espresso machine from Zabar's on the counter—the reason I was there in the first place. That and one psycho stalker. He pulled a bottle of red from a case on the floor and scanned the label.

"Looks impressive, but I don't know shit about wine. As far as I'm concerned, there's red wine and there's white." He followed my gaze to the espresso machine. Smiling, he added, "About as much as I know about espresso machines. How about you?"

"I actually learned a little about wines when I worked as a waitress."

He handed me the bottle.

"This is supposed to be really good," I said.

"So let's see if it lives up to the hype. The wine glasses are in the cabinet to the left of the fridge."

He pulled the cork with a resounding pop as I grabbed two wineglasses from a cabinet stocked with mismatched stemware, and I placed them on the counter. He filled the glasses three-quarters full.

"Cheers!" He clinked his glass against mine and took the bottle. "Not so sure red wine pairs well with chili." He laughed. "So let's do wine first." He nodded for me to go first, and we walked to the parlor and settled on opposite ends of the sofa. "So..." He took a breath. "What have I missed in Brooklyn?"

I hesitated. I could have told him about the email over the phone, but that had felt like something that should be communicated in person. Still, I found myself avoiding the subject. "Not much. Jenna calls me every day, actually sometimes two or three times a day." I laughed. "I think she's hoping one of these times you'll be home and talk to her."

He stopped and took another drink. "Think you can get her on the phone now?"

"Right now?" I worried she would blurt something outrageous, like *"Wanna hook up? I can be there in an hour."* She lacked a filter even under more normal circumstances.

"Are you sure?" I asked, hoping to dissuade him.

"Totally. Call her and just hand me the phone."

I knew it would make her week. Hell, it would make her year. I dialed Jenna's number.

"Jenn, hey, it's me."

Mick was motioning for me to hand him the phone. I laid it on the sofa between us and put it on speaker.

"Jenna?" he said. "Hi, this is Mick Sullivan."

Silence.

"Rachael says you've enjoyed my movies." He turned to me and grinned like talking to Jenna was the most fun he'd had all week.

"Uh, yeah."

I wasn't used to Jenna being at a loss for words. But it didn't last long for her to regroup. "So, what do you think of our girl, Rachael?"

"Shit, Jen."

He turned to look at me, his eyes roaming from head to toe. "She's good." The subtle deepening of his voice when he said "good" twisted my stomach. He picked up the phone, pointed it in my direction, and snapped a picture.

"What are you doing?" I asked.

"I'm sending your friend proof."

"Proof of what?"

"That you're as good as I say you are."

"Are *you* as good as they say you are?" Jenna blurted.

"Okay that's it. Jen, he was just about to leave. I'll call you later."

"Don't do anything I wouldn't—" But I hung up before she had a chance to finish.

"I think I like your friend."

"Don't forget," I reminded him, "she's the one responsible for this whole shit show."

"True. But it hasn't all been shit."

I wasn't sure how to react to that comment, so I took a sip of wine before taking a conversational one-eighty, filling him in on the threatening email and Detective Melnitsky's less-than-helpful response.

As soon as I wrapped up my story, he leapt off the sofa, nearly spilling the contents of his glass, and started pacing. "What the fuck? I'm calling him tomorrow—or maybe I'll just show up at the station. That oughta get his attention."

Clearly, he was aware of the power his presence would wield. In the beginning, I'd reached out to him exactly because of that power. But after my conversation with Melnitsky, I was afraid that him showing up unannounced might backfire. Any resentment of his celebrity, his wealth, his perceived expectation of special treatment, wouldn't help my case.

He sat back down, and his shoulders slumped.

"Sorry. *Shit.* You know what? On second thought, maybe not. My cousin is a cop, and rescuing privileged people is not exactly high on his priority list."

He took a drink. "But do you still feel safe here? Would you rather be in a hotel now or maybe a different apartment?"

"It was just an email. If it's okay, I think I'd like to stay."

"Stay as long as you like, but if anything happens..."

He reached for a blue box on the side table next to the sofa, pulled out a cigarette rolled in yellow paper, and dug in his pocket for a lighter. "Want one?" he asked as he offered the box of Gitanes Maïs to me. "I picked up this habit about a year ago when I was filming in Paris. There are only a few places in the city where I can buy them." He shook his head and pursed his lips. "Jesus, did that sound pretentious, or what?"

"Maybe just a little." I chuckled. "But sure, I'll take one," I heard myself say. I slipped one from the box and leaned in to let him light it for me. That first familiar drag made me dizzy. I took another drag, fascinated by the smoke escaping my lips as I exhaled. It triggered memories of postsex smokes with Conrad. I quit right after he dumped me. I snuffed the cigarette out in the nearest ashtray.

"Not a fan?" he asked.

"Yeah, sorry."

After my first glass of wine and his second—or was it his third?—he retreated to the kitchen and returned with two bowls of chili on a tray and some saltines. He set it on the coffee table, handed me a bowl and a spoon, and sat next to me on the sofa. "Bon appétit," he said as he grabbed his bowl and propped his feet on the table.

He took a bite, jerked to his feet, dropped the bowl back onto the tray, and began fanning his mouth. "Whoa! Too hot! Don't eat it. I shouldn't have added that last shake of cayenne pepper. *Fuck*, I ruined it." He hurried to the kitchen and returned with two glasses of ice water. "Top Chef, I'm not. Next time, we'll order in."

His "next time" comment did not go unnoticed.

Once he doused the fire in his mouth, he changed the music, and I recognized the tune after only a couple of beats.

"This is that band you told me about," he said, closing his eyes and bobbing his head to the beat. He gave me a thumbs-up. "I've got one I want you to listen to after this. Oh man, this is the best part. Do you hear those horns?"

Do I hear them? I can feel them in my toes. "Yeah, I love it."

"You know, Bob Marley once said, 'When the music hits you, you feel no pain.' That's what it does for me."

Is he in pain? If he was, he kept it well hidden. We listened to song after song and began waxing nostalgic about gumbo, boiled crawfish, and hot, humid Louisiana nights punctuated with fireflies sending SOS signals into the darkness. And we swapped stories of our quirky Southern relatives, like his bass-fishing Uncle Otis, who never caught a thing.

"Aunt Clara usually found him the next morning, passed out, wearing nothing—and I mean nothing—but a wife-beater, the boat bobbing in the water, still tied to the dock." His laugh faded, and he took a breath. "I can laugh about it now, but... anyway, that was a long time ago."

There it was again, a suggestion of sadness.

I told him about my basket-toting Aunt Gladys, who would sneak into the pecan orchards down on Highway 1 in the dead of night and climb over the fence to pilfer what she needed so that she could make her blue-ribbon pecan tassies.

His face lit up. "God, I could eat a dozen of those! I'm salivating just thinking about it!"

Sometime well past midnight, he broke out another bottle, poured himself a glass, and began to open up about his life, what it was like to be Mick Sullivan. "I never expected to be handed such outrageous amounts of money—or fame." He confessed that he was blindsided by all the rock-star adulation that popped up overnight, and he claimed he'd had no previous life experience to prepare him for the onslaught.

"When I was in middle school, my mom was the only female who thought I was good-looking." He shrugged. "And most of the kids thought I was gay. I mean, I was in the drama club in a small town in Louisiana. They used to call it 'the drag club.' Didn't get much better when we moved to California. I wasn't into sports, I couldn't surf, I burn if I stay out in the sun longer than fifteen minutes, and I was a straight-A student. I had a tough time even scoring a date for the senior prom."

"I find that hard to believe." I'd always figured he was born popular.

"Oh, believe it. I honestly don't know what other people see now when they look at me." He was starting to slur his words. "When I look in the mirror, I see Neanderthal brows, a boxer's misaligned nose, and hair that, no matter what I do, looks like I've just come in from a violent windstorm. I mean, seriously, my features are so off-kilter I have to be shot from the left or I look like I have some sort of facial deformity."

He was, I realized, reluctantly handsome.

Still, he admitted that once the fame kicked in, "There was a time when I thought the party didn't start until I got there." But, he said, the novelty wore thin almost as quickly as it developed. "It's like my life took on a Fellini-like quality, and I was—I am—the freaky main attraction."

"Well, from the outside, it seems like an incredible life."

"Yeah, I guess so. Sometimes, it feels like I'm living vicariously through my own life." He chuckled and raised his empty glass in a toast. "I'm officially a card-carrying member of the 'famous club.'"

He was on a roll, revealing more about himself than he probably wanted to and saying things he might regret in the morning.

"The thing about fame," he continued, "is that if you embrace it, you're an egomaniacal prick. If you push it away, you're an ungrateful bastard." He stopped and gazed into his empty wine glass like he was reading tea leaves. "As long as I remember where I came from, I'll be okay." He paused for a beat. "And where I parked my car. I can never remember that."

That took me a second or two, but I laughed, almost spewing my wine.

When a new song started, he jumped up and said, "Shhh, listen." It was a song by the Playground Warriors, a little-known indie group he'd recently discovered. The music was a sort of acoustic-reggae-surf-rock stew he said he found irresistible, and he seemed invested in the notion that I find it just as appealing. He was singing along full-tilt with perfect pitch.

"Come on, sing with me."

"Forget it! I even embarrass myself when I sing in the shower."

"I seriously doubt that... though that's an image I won't soon forget," he said, cocking a half smile. "Whatever, so dance with me. Let loose a little."

He refilled my glass to almost overflowing, took a sip to prevent it from spilling, and wiped his mouth on his sleeve before handing it back to me.

"Think of it as liquid courage." He cranked up the volume to an earsplitting level.

I took a sip, and he held out his hand to help me off the sofa. We jumped around the room in time to the beat, and he slipped his arm around my waist to dip me once, twice in an exaggerated dance move. I stumbled, but he caught me, and for a second, just for a split second, I thought I sensed something pass between us.

It was a druglike rush, and like a drug rush, it wasn't natural—it wasn't real. I had to remind myself that it was easy to be led into a state of euphoria by someone whose job it was to make others feel good. High on wine that was way beyond my meager budget, booty dancing Beyoncé-style—Jenna would be proud—after midnight with a guy who was light-years out of my league, I closed my eyes to insulate myself from the ridiculous reality. The last time I'd let loose like that or drunk that much, I was seventeen, stoned, and about to lose my virginity.

When the song hit its last note, we collapsed together on the sofa, laughing to the point of breathlessness. That was the first time in a long time that disappointment and fear weren't my primary emotions. He reached over and gave my knee a squeeze. Startled by his touch, I looked at him, but nothing in his face indicated that it meant anything more than an affable pat on the back.

"You're a rock star, Rachael!"

Our laughter was interrupted by the ringing of his phone. He sighed, grabbed it, and looked at the name. "Sorry, I need to take this." He stood and wandered into the next room.

"Hey, Mom. What's up?... Everything's good. Just busy. What are you doing up? Insomnia again?... Geez, no, I'm not drunk," he whispered. "I'm just really tired. Mom, seriously? Not now. Can we talk about this later? Look, let me call you back tomorrow." His voice softened. "Yeah, me too. Get some rest. I'm fine. Really. I'll talk to you tomorrow. Bye."

He returned, sat on the sofa, exhaled slowly, and fidgeted with his phone. I wanted to ask if everything was okay, but then he would know I'd eavesdropped. Before I could say anything, he stood. "I think I'm going to have to call it a night. Got an early morning."

Right then, he wasn't Mick Sullivan, hot Hollywood celebrity, he was just a guy who looked like he could really use a hug. We walked to the door together. I was in that nanosecond before reaching out to give and maybe receive a comforting hug when he leaned against the door and flatly said, "Good night, Rachael."

Chapter 14

I woke to a text from Mick: *I'm taking off. Not sure when I'll be back. Stay safe.* He was gone again. I couldn't quite put my finger on how that made me feel—maybe surprised he was informing me of his departure or maybe disappointed that he was gone.

My "full-time" gig with Sisyphus Recordings was more sporadic than expected. With chunks of free time on my hands, no help from the police, and no new information from the investigative firm Mick had hired and was undoubtedly paying an astronomical hourly rate, I decided to do some stalking research of my own. I googled "celebrity stalkers," which brought up several hundred if not thousands of hits. None of the cases turned out well for the famous stalkees. John Lennon was shot assassination-style outside his apartment in New York by Mark David Chapman in a deluded attempt to impress the actress Jodie Foster. Theresa Saldana, who played in *The Godfather*, was stabbed ten times, also by an obsessed fan. She survived—barely. And one disturbed woman thought Leonardo DiCaprio was the father of her child, whom she insisted was Jesus. Yes, *that* Jesus. A few Google searches for "female stalkers" and "celebrity murders" turned up more—much more.

I discovered letters from obsessed fans, shockingly similar to the ones Mick and I had received. And I learned that a restraining order, my last hope for protection—if they ever found out who she was—could have the opposite of the intended effect, triggering violent attacks that spilled over to family members and friends.

Despite the horror stories, celebrity stalkers were actually the least likely to harm the object of their obsession. That's what Google said, anyway. And just as Detective Napoletano told me, physical violence was most common among stalkers who'd been in a relationship with the victim—ex-boyfriends, -lovers, -wives, or -husbands. Mick's lawyer had assured me that while a stalker's obsession could be intense, it was usually short-lived. *But what the hell does he know?* I read about cases where the stalking lasted for years, even decades. Not surprisingly, most stalkers were men, but the bad news for me was that female stalkers were the most persistent.

That was enough—more than enough. I shut my laptop but couldn't shut out the vivid images of these deluded "lovers," whose brain circuitry had somehow rewired itself to convince them that their fantasies were real. Nothing could dissuade them from their version of the truth. Sometimes, even after murdering their fantasy lover, they held firm to their belief of an intimate relationship like a religious conviction. Rather than walking away feeling better equipped to deal with the situation, I was even more confused and anxious about how everything might play out.

As I scrolled through romantic comedies on Netflix to distract myself from what I'd learned, the extension in my apartment rang. I answered without thinking—a reflex conditioned by years of answering the landline my parents stubbornly refused to disconnect.

"Hello?"

"Is Mickey there?"

Mickey? He doesn't seem like a Mickey. "No. Sorry. Can I take a message?"

"This is his momma. I'd call his cell phone, but I'll be damned if I didn't delete all my contacts from my phone. This is the only number I can remember. Do you know when he'll be in?"

She did, indeed, sound like Dolly Parton with a Louisiana drawl.

"No, ma'am." I figured I'd better drag my Southern manners out of mothballs.

"Who are you, hon?"

"Rachael Allen. I'm a friend of Mick's."

"Friend or girlfriend? You can tell me, sweetheart."

"Just a friend."

"That boy. I swear. Last time I called, some girl answered the phone. Pretty sure I woke her up. She wasn't very nice. He's sure had his share of 'girlfriends.'" She paused. "He'd probably have a conniption fit if he knew I was talking about him to one of his friends. He can get awful touchy sometimes. Well, I called last night, and he said we could talk today. Guess he forgot. Anyway, I thought for sure he said he was going to be in Brooklyn this week. If you talk to him, just tell him I called, would you? And if you really want to embarrass the dickens out of him, tell him his momma loves him."

"Yes, ma'am. I will."

His mother let out a full-throated laugh. It had a familiar ring to it.

"Thanks, hon."

I had just gotten an intimate look at Mick via a two-minute conversation with his mother. Her drawl brought back thick Louisiana summer nights, complete with mothers calling their tired, sweaty kids to come inside at sunset and cicadas serenading the scene with their high-pitched castanets.

No wonder Mick felt so real.

He felt like home.

Chapter 15

My cell dinged with an incoming email from Jude with the specifics for the next day's staff meeting. It wasn't an RSVP invitation but a "your presence is required" invite. It would be my first encounter with the whole crew, and my nerves tingled—stage fright without the stage.

Up until that point, I'd been just a faceless freelancer to them, a byline on a blog. *Is Jude going to introduce me to everyone? Will I be seen as an interloper, or will I be welcomed as a new member of the team? If I tell them I'm living with Mick Sullivan, would that sway their opinions in my favor, earn me special treatment?* As that joke of a thought meandered across my brain, I knew my living situation wasn't something I would be sharing with my new coworkers—or Jude.

The next day, as I waited for the F train to the city, I compulsively scanned the platform. *Am I being stupid to think I can carry on with my life as if everything is normal? Is she here, watching my every move but lost in the sea of people jostling for space?* Every woman who glanced my way was suspect. I leaned over to peer down the dark subway tunnel. *Nothing.* My paranoia swelled along with the growing crowd until the tunnel lit up, and I felt the rumbling of the train's approach. My hair danced in the whoosh of hot air that carried the caustic scent of diesel fuel. I stepped closer to the edge of the platform to be one of the first into "my" car—every New Yorker knows the exact car to ride in that will bring them to the closest exit stairs at their stop. The tips of my shoes overlapped the yellow line on the platform. It wouldn't take much of a push to send me crashing onto the tracks and into the path of the incoming train. I surveilled the crowd, stepping closer, shrinking the space between myself and the edge, and I clutched my purse to my chest. I caught a glimpse of a blond twenty-something woman looking my way, her eyes lingering longer than I would've expected from random people-watching curiosity. She slowly pushed her way through the crowd in my direction. She was getting closer. I was boxed in by people who weren't about to give up their priority positions. When the train came to a full stop in front of me, I considered waiting for the next one, but I was swept into the car by the force of the crowd's forward movement—cattle prodded into a squeeze chute.

Once inside, I grabbed a pole to steady myself just as the train lurched into motion. The *ding-dong* signaled the closing of the doors, and the skunky scent of weed filled the air around me, an early-morning coping mechanism for New Yorkers under pressure. I put my hand over my nose and turned away. *There she is.* Right behind me. My stomach curdled, and my saliva thickened. I swallowed hard. My anxiety quadrupled. She was scrolling on her phone. *An attempt to feign disinterest?* In a role reversal, I found myself staring at her. Her doe eyes carefully shifted up in my direction, and we made eye contact. I gasped and abruptly turned back around. *Is my life about to change in an ordinary instant? Am I going to be a subway statistic?* I glanced back over my shoulder, but she'd simply returned to staring at her phone. *I'll get off at the next stop and walk. I'll be a little late for the meeting, but at least I'll be alive.* I was so deep in my own head that I didn't hear the announcement for the next stop or the opening of the doors.

She jumped off the train before I even had a chance to take a single step. My knees buckled in relief, and I talked myself down from the ledge of fear I'd been perched on. My paranoia had taken over, almost ruining a really important day for me. I must have looked as drained as I felt because a guy with a well-worn leather briefcase, a warm smile, and a middle-aged paunch offered his seat. I took it with gratitude.

I got off at Rockefeller Center and walked the three blocks to the office building as I tried to meditate away the residual effects of my unwarranted fear of the woman on the train. Normally, I loved the sounds of the city and the energy they imbued. But that day, the cacophony siphoned my energy rather than enhancing it. With my hand on the revolving door to the lobby, I took a deep breath and walked in, doing my best to act like I belonged there. If I acted like I did, maybe I would feel it. I showed my newly minted ID to the security guard, signed in, and headed to the elevators. The doors to the one closest to me opened like magic. *A good sign.* I stepped in and realized I'd somehow scored a private ride. *Another good sign.* The doors were about to shut when someone wedged a purse between them. *She* stepped in and smiled at me. I was too stunned to react.

As the doors glided to a close, she turned to me. "Are you Rachael?"

Visions of *Psycho* danced in my head. *Am I about to be stabbed to death? A gun would make too much noise. But maybe she has a silencer. Maybe I watch too many crime documentaries.*

My thoughts were flying fast and furious when she said, "I'm Gabi, Jude's assistant. I thought I recognized you on the subway—from your photo on the blog. He said you were coming to the meeting today." The doors opened. "Oh, we're here. Just follow me."

I was high with relief. She kept talking, turning toward me every few words. "I thought I was going to be late. I always get off at an earlier stop for coffee. Of all the coffee shops in the city, it's my favorite—Boast the Roast—have you been there?"

I shook my head. I hadn't said a word. She must've thought me socially awkward at best or terribly rude at worst. I followed her to the conference room and was relieved to see a small group of smiling faces. Jude welcomed me and introduced me to everyone.

"Rachael is doing a fabulous job with the press releases, bios, and promo materials," he said.

I nodded in appreciation and sat in the only empty seat. Gabi brought me coffee.

I finally spoke my first words. "Thanks, Gabi." I was going to have to work at not having a visceral reaction every time Gabi looked my way.

Jude stood to address the group. As much as I wanted, no, *needed* to focus on what he was saying, my adrenaline hangover was making concentration impossible. Thank God, Gabi was taking notes that would be emailed to us all. I'd anxiously awaited that meeting, but I just wanted to get back to Brooklyn, lock the doors, and set the alarm.

I skipped the subway and took an Uber home.

Chapter 16

A week passed before Mick returned, and he jokingly called up the stairs as he opened the door, "Honey, I'm home!" His baritone voice was familiar by then, and I welcomed the sound of it. When I met him at the door, he set down his luggage and began tapping on his phone. "I'm sending you a playlist of some new tunes I thought you might like."

It felt like musical foreplay.

"Let me wash off the plane smell, and maybe you can come down?"

When he opened his apartment door, he greeted me with an ice-cold bottle of his favorite brand of imported beer. It struck me that I actually knew what his favorite brand of beer was. Off-the-beaten-path music played in the background.

We settled on the couch. I took a swig of my beer before sharing with him what I'd discovered in my stalker research. I was hoping he would tell me that those famous cases were outliers, that everything would be okay, that my staying at his place, the alarm system at my parents' home, the security guards, the private detective, were all simply done in an abundance of caution—that everything would blow over, and that I was safe.

"Threats just come with the territory," he said. "I wish you hadn't done that. It'll just freak you out even more." He huffed a tired breath. "Maybe let's talk about something else. How was your meeting?"

I was stunned he remembered. "It was good, but..." I relayed the whole incident on the subway and in the elevator and watched deep lines form in his forehead.

"Jesus, that must have been scary as shit. But... you took the subway? Seriously? Bad idea."

"A mistake I won't make again. I got an Uber for the trip back."

"Good."

We later stumbled onto the topic of past relationships, and he was trying to explain why having women flock to him like ants at a picnic was not all it was cracked up to be.

He looked off into space, as though carefully considering his words. "What's something you want but wish you didn't have to work for? Something you think would make you feel better about yourself?"

"An apartment?" I wasn't sure what he was probing for.

"Okay, but more like something where the feeling is temporary."

I thought about my last indulgent shopping spree, when I spent more than I could possibly afford. I'd felt so good as I checked out my reflection, turning this way and that, reveling in how those pants made me look slimmer, taller, how that top with the low-cut V-neck made me feel sexier. Then a shopping hangover set in when the bill came.

"Clothes?"

He chuckled. "Okay. Imagine you could go shopping whenever you wanted, buy more clothes than you could ever possibly wear. At first, it's a rush. It's fun, it's great, it's awesome! It makes you feel better—about yourself, about everything. Then the newness of it wears off, and... That's a terrible analogy, but you get the idea," he said. "All I'm saying is the feel-good effect from all that attention didn't last. None of those women wanted to be with me—I mean *me*," he said, pounding his fist against his chest. "They just wanted to have sex with a celebrity and then blab to their friends." He took a breath. "My relationships with women were different *before*."

I knew he meant before he became *the* Mick Sullivan.

He frowned and took a swig of his beer. He leaned forward, his elbows resting on his thighs. "You ever been in love? I mean, like, really in love?" he asked.

Oh, so we're going there. I shrugged. I'd confused lust with love before. Only in retrospect had I understood the difference. "No, I don't think so."

"You would know, believe me," he said.

Her name was Lauren. His voice dipped when he said her name. She broke his heart in the "before."

"We met at an audition in LA. Dated for about two months before we moved in together. I was still struggling, dragging my ass to audition after audition, when she dumped me for this blue-eyed pretty boy who was getting parts. He looked like a fucking mannequin," he said as he worked on peeling the label from his beer bottle. "And then she had the balls to call me after my first big movie came out. Wanted to start up again. Said she loved me. It was total bullshit." He laughed unconvincingly. But he bounced back, spicing up the conversation with tidbits about some of his celebrity "acquaintances" that, up until then, I'd only read about in the tabloids while in line at the supermarket checkout.

I wasn't naive enough to think that he didn't have a history of past lovers, one-night stands, and what-the-hell-was-I-thinking mistakes. *Doesn't everyone?* Mick's history just seemed overstuffed, overindulgent, and bloated next to my anorexic love life. In the spirit of sharing, I began to spill about my own what-the-hell-was-I-thinking relationship with Conrad. I left out the specifics of the scene where Conrad informed me that he and his ex were getting back together.

"He was your typical asshole. I guess. I was a little slow on the uptake. I mean, sometimes he seemed desperate for me, you know? He'd call in the middle of the night. 'I need to be with you.' It felt so good to be wanted, and I always said yes. He'd come over, and then after a little heavy breathing, he couldn't wait to leave."

"Sounds like a grade A dick. What the hell were you doing with him?" He excused himself to the kitchen to get another beer. "Do you want one?"

I was certain my story had bored him. Hell, it bored me. When he came back, he handed me a cold beer. I reached out to take it, but he wasn't letting go. I looked up.

"I hope you know you deserve better than that," he said.

He released his grip, sat on the sofa, propped his legs on the coffee table, and took a swig of his beer, acting as though he hadn't just looked me in the eye and said what he said. I was unsure if I should take it as a criticism or a compliment. Either way, I felt compelled to explain myself.

"Yeah, I have this habit of getting involved with guys who are incapable of caring about anyone but themselves, and I somehow fail to see it until it's too late. I really need..." I took a second to think of exactly what I needed. "I need to find someone who can provide an emotional safety net, I guess. Something I didn't have growing up. Anyway, it's a habit I'm trying really hard to break. I made a promise to myself: no more bad boys, especially bad-boy musicians."

He didn't respond right away. "Yeah, they're the worst," he mumbled before chugging the rest of his beer.

His statement about what he thought I deserved was still rumbling in my head when he stood and dug through his carry-on bag, looking for the next day's shooting schedule. The tiny silver necklace that was a fixture around his neck swayed with each movement, reflecting the dim light from the floor lamp over the sofa. I would've needed a magnifying glass to read its inscription.

"That's a beautiful necklace. What does it say?"

He straightened and grasped it to stop the swinging motion. "It's the Ten Commandments in Hebrew. It was my old man's. Got it at his bar mitzvah. My real name, at least the name on my birth certificate, is Michael Abrams. Sullivan is my mom's name, O'Sullivan, actually."

"Michael Abrams." I said it out loud, trying out the sound of it.

He chuckled. "Yeah, I like Sullivan better too. Anyway, his being Jewish didn't go over so well with my mother's very Irish Catholic family, and they refused to help her when he walked out on us. I think this is literally the only thing he left behind. One of the best days of my life was when I finally scored enough money to buy my mom a house with central air and a dishwasher, the only two things on her wish list."

I felt my face redden, and I swept my hair behind my ears. "Oh, I'm sorry."

"Don't be. He was an asswipe." He shrugged. "I guess this represents what he was before he went to shit, maybe even what he could have been. I was only five when he walked out on us, so I don't remember much about him." He stopped and closed his fingers in a fist around the necklace as if it were an amulet meant to protect him from harm.

"Can I see?"

He was holding the necklace out, and I stepped closer, but I was distracted by the reddish-brown stubble on his chin, the tuft of chest hair peeking out from his T-shirt, the small freckle on his neck.

"I can't read Hebrew," he announced, throwing off a weighted blanket of lust that had enveloped me without warning.

I let go of the necklace, stepped back, smiled weakly, and sat down.

"It meant something to my mom, so it means something to me. I'm always losing shit, but somehow I've managed to hang on to this."

"Oh, by the way, I spoke to your mother today." I was happy to shift my thoughts in another direction.

He jumped back as if stuck by a taser. "My mother?"

The balance between us had suddenly shifted.

"What did she say?"

"She accidentally wiped all her contacts from her phone, so she was calling the landline. Sorry for answering. It's a habit from staying with my parents. They have a landline and use it regularly." I hesitated. "Your mom seems sweet. She asked if I was one of your many girlfriends."

He grimaced and ran his fingers through his hair as if to comb away that last exchange.

"Jesus Christ. Thanks, Mom."

I couldn't help but smile at his embarrassment.

After a blur of more music and more conversation, I said good night and retreated to my apartment upstairs. I crawled into bed and closed my eyes. My skin was buzzing, my head swimming with unsolicited images of him.

That's when I heard it—erratic footsteps making their way up the stairs. I stopped breathing. The footsteps hesitated, climbed another stair, then retreated. My eyelids fluttered, and I lapsed into an exhausted slumber just as the morning light peeked through the blinds.

The next afternoon, I woke with the putrid taste of overindulgence on my tongue and a relentless pounding in my right temple. I climbed out of bed and was headed to the bathroom when I spotted a note slipped under my door. I picked it up, and a key fell out. The note said:

Thanks for listening to me ramble last night. Here's the key to the main floor. Make yourself at home. And help yourself to the wine and the garden out back. Oh, and can you bring in the mail and put it in my place? Mi casa es su casa. Looking forward to next time. Mick

Chapter 17

The key Mick left for me and his request to collect his mail were surprising acts of faith on his part. In the past, he'd just let the mail pile up until his return. It was usually nothing but junk and a few magazines that he said always ended up in the trash unread. His bills were paid by his accountant, and anything else of importance went to his lawyer, his manager, or his agent. He'd told me that all his fan mail went to a clearinghouse in Los Angeles.

When I stepped into the vestibule later that day, the mail looked like the usual, with one major exception. Mick's face was staring up at me from the pile, splashed across the cover of *Essentials* magazine. His image triggered a strange sensation of familiarity, the result of our last encounter. He was decked out in designer threads and looking like, well, like a movie star. It was a much-needed dose of reality. He might come across as down-to-earth, but he was super rich and überfamous—smiling-on-the-cover-of-a-national-magazine famous. The gulf between our lifestyles loomed large. I picked the magazine up, along with the rest of the mail, opened the door to his apartment, and glanced at the cover once more before I set it all on a side table.

That night, after wrapping up work and going over Gabi's minutes, I showered, grabbed his key and my book, and headed downstairs to his place to take him up on his offer to make myself at home. As I opened the door, it occurred to me once again that the sleek modern décor, like the image of him on the magazine cover, was so not him. The mess he'd created made the place uniquely his. I was tempted to tidy up, almost tying my hands behind my back to suppress the urge, but aside from washing the dirty dishes in the sink and putting them away, I talked myself out of it.

My hair was still damp, and I was in my standard loungewear, baggy sweats and an oversized T-shirt with a faded LSU logo from my alma mater. I gave myself permission to indulge in a glass of wine from the pricey stuff Mick had offered, before settling on his sofa and opening my book. Reading Stephen King seemed ill-advised, but I was too deep into the tome to put it aside.

My eyes were on the page, but my mind shifted elsewhere, imagining the stalker making a midnight visit, hovering over my bed while I slept. No threatening emails had come recently, no break-ins at my parents' home in New Jersey, but fear had become a part of me. I could suppress it for only so long. I stared at the page, unable to concentrate as I reread the same paragraph half a dozen times. I marked my place in the book, set the wine glass on the table, and began making the rounds to triple-check the alarm and the locks. I was in the kitchen when the shrill sound of the front door buzzer shattered my frayed nerves. My stomach lurched, and I gulped air.

The buzzer went off again, more insistent. Hesitating for a few seconds more, I walked in fits and starts to the intercom as I debated. *Maybe I should ignore it. Maybe they'll go away.* But whoever was at the front door was even more emphatic, pushing the buzzer, stopping and starting again.

I approached the monitor and pressed the button.

"Mick?" I exhaled.

"Thank God you're there," he said, waving at the camera.

He looked tired, but he was flashing that smile. Taking one last look at the monitor, I buzzed the door open.

As I walked to the front door to greet him, I became hyperaware that my wet hair was haphazardly clipped on top of my head and my face was naked, scrubbed clean. My T-shirt and sweats suddenly seemed far grungier than they had moments before. But then his image on the magazine cover popped into my head, and I laughed at myself for thinking my appearance mattered.

I opened the door, and he stepped in, dragging his rolling duffel bag behind him. "Hey, Rachael. For a second, I thought you were going to leave me standing out there on the stoop all night."

He was disheveled, just shy of slovenly. But beneath all that, he was still arrestingly gorgeous. I would've had to be blind not to appreciate it.

He set his bag down, closed and locked the door, and gave me a hug that lingered for half a beat longer than expected. I had an overpowering urge to open the door and shove him back outside until whatever I'd just felt dissipated. He took half a step back, and his eyes fell to my mouth, a motion so fleeting that I doubted my perception.

"Sorry if I scared you. I tried calling your cell before I left, but it went straight to voice mail. I would've called the landline, but unlike my mom, I can never remember the number. I really need to put it in my contacts," he said.

"What are you doing here? You just left this morning."

"I had barely walked into my apartment in LA when I got a call that shooting was pushed up to tomorrow here in New York. Something about location availability. So I had to catch a flight and come back. I've spent the last eight hours in airports, airplanes, and taxis. Didn't even realize I'd forgotten my keys until I was getting out of the cab here. Anyway, sorry for the unannounced appearance."

"Are you kidding? This is your place, not mine."

He looked around as though he was checking to see if the coast was clear.

"As you can see, I wasn't expecting company."

He took a step back and cocked his head. "I think you look kinda cute like that." He shoved his hands in his pockets and glanced furtively at me. He opened his mouth again, as though he was going to say something else, but fell silent.

I headed back to the sofa to grab my book and held it against my braless chest. "I'll leave you to it. I was getting ready to call it a night anyway," I lied. "Oh, and I've stocked the fridge if you're hungry."

Before I could take a step, he pleaded, "Stay awhile. I've been fending off autograph seekers, paparazzi, and strange people who think they know me or want to be my best friend most of the day. I would really appreciate a normal conversation."

I flushed, thinking back to when I bugged him for his picture.

"How about a drink?" he offered. "I think I've got some brandy in the kitchen. Unless you drank it all," he said with a wink.

Oh, what the hell. After all, he'd just gotten there, and he was being his usual warm, friendly self. A friend was what I needed—that and a nightcap might've been the prescription for a good night's sleep. He disappeared into the kitchen.

I heard cabinets open and close and things being shuffled around before he reentered the room with a bottle stuffed under his arm like a football. In his hands, he held two juice glasses decorated with faded images of oranges and lemons.

"I don't think I've seen the bottom of that sink in two years," he said. "Remind me to call a service. There's no reason for you to play housemaid."

He strode over to the sofa. "Here," he said as he handed me a juice glass. "I don't have any brandy snifters lying around. But it'll taste the same. I promise."

He pulled the cork with about as much fanfare as if he'd popped the top of a Bud Light and poured the liquid gold into my glass. He poured a glass for himself, set the bottle on the table, and plopped down next to me on the sofa. The faintest hint of Gitanes tobacco and Ivory soap surrounded him.

I took a sip. Mick took a gulp.

"Wow, this is really good."

"It was a gift from my agent. Hennessy Paradis Cognac. A thousand bucks a bottle, if you can believe it."

I couldn't hide my shock.

"Yeah, I know. Randy's insane."

There was that smile again. I wondered how many women had succumbed.

I held my juice glass with both hands as I took another sip. An awkward silence filled the space between us, and I wondered why he'd even invited me to stay. He leaned forward to refill his glass, sat back, and stared at the copper liquid. That was my cue. It really was time to call it a night. After one final sip, I scooted to the edge of the sofa and hesitated before setting my glass, still half full, on the table. The brandy was warming me in all the wrong places.

I turned to face him. "Thanks for the drink, but I'm really pretty tired. And you've got a busy day ahead. What time do you have to be on the set?"

"Seven a.m. Me and the bags under my eyes!"

"You should get your beauty sleep, then," I said, rattling off the stupid cliché to prevent my encroaching feelings from making themselves known—to either of us.

We stood in unison, but instead of walking me to the door, as he'd always done before, he turned to me, reached out, and gently rested his hands on my shoulders. Being at eye level with the Ten Commandments felt like an admonition, though I wasn't quite sure which commandment would apply.

He skimmed his thumb across the hollow of my cheek, lifted my face up to his, and leaned in to me in slow motion as he whispered, "Rachael..."

But instead of meeting him halfway, I jerked my head away. His almost kiss landed squarely on my ear.

Straightening, his hands dropped, his arms limp at his sides. He backed up a step. "Sorry. I thought..." He glanced down at the floor before looking back up at me.

That flash of vulnerability, if that's what it was, made me regret my decision to stop him in his tracks. But I couldn't let myself jump down the Mick Sullivan rabbit hole. Even if he was actually interested in me, he was an actor-musician with a penchant for alcohol—and women. I couldn't subject myself to those emotionally lethal character flaws and repeat my self-destructive relationship merry-go-round. But then I thought maybe I was really jumping the gun. He had simply wanted to kiss me.

"Mick, look," I said, shifting my weight from foot to foot as I kicked off my improvised rationalization, "you've gone out of your way to be nice to me under these bizarre circumstances. You didn't have to do all this, and I'm grateful. Seriously. And I don't think it's a secret that I've enjoyed your company." My heart beat an erratic rhythm that I was certain he could hear. I managed a weak laugh and took a breath. "But I really think we should just stay friends. I think it's best—for both of us, given the circumstances."

"Friends?" Frustration flushed his face. He crossed his arms, hugging himself, and shrugged. "Look, I know I'm made out to be some sort of man whore in the tabloids, sleeping with every woman I meet—'anything with a pussy and a pulse' as one smart-ass blogger put it." He hesitated. "But that reputation pushes away the women I really want to be with... like now."

Believing him would be too risky. I didn't trust my gut telling me that he might be one of the good ones, and if he wasn't, I didn't have the emotional reserve to deal with another heartbreak. I said nothing and looked away.

"I feel like I've gotten to know you through all this weird shit that's been happening, and I like you." He shook his head. "That sounds so lame. I more than like you." He paused. "I thought it was mutual."

And he smiled. He wielded it like a weapon intended to deliver the final blow with laser-like accuracy. He must've sensed my resistance dissolving because he stepped closer. "I think maybe we should stop pretending that we're just going to be friends, don't you?" As I was frantically rushing through a mental list of the pros and cons of letting this happen, he said, "I really want to kiss you."

Without having made a conscious decision, I wrapped my arms around his neck. He slipped his hands onto my hips and pulled me close. His kiss was soft and warm yet intense, a rich blend of brandy and French tobacco. He pressed his lips against mine with a startling urgency, and I was plunging down that first breathtaking drop on a roller coaster.

Downstairs in his bedroom, I was barely breathing, convinced that if I made a sudden move, the scene might fade to black. He yanked his T-shirt over his head, revealing a small tattoo on his chest. I smiled, tracing the colorful image of Snow White with my fingers.

"A drunken dare a few years ago," he mumbled.

I reached back and lowered my sweats just until the small white-ink dandelion tattoo on my hip came into view. "A dare I made to myself."

He outlined the scattering dandelion seeds blowing in the imaginary wind. "What did you wish for, Rachael Allen?"

"I can't even remember," I lied.

The light from the streetlamp shone through the bars in the window, and I could see the dark line of hair that ran down his abdomen to the band of his low-slung jeans. I felt my expression change, taking on the same look of desire reflected on his face.

"You okay?" he whispered.

"Just nervous."

"There's no reason to be nervous. It's just me, here, with you." He hesitated then chuckled. "Maybe you're expecting more than I can deliver." But I sensed a serious undertone. It was a recurring theme in his life—people wanting more from him than he was either willing or able to give.

He slowly pulled my baggy T-shirt over my head and kissed my bare breasts before sliding his hands down to my waist, my hips, my thighs. He knelt in front of me, and his stubble rubbed against my skin as he gradually lowered my sweats, kissing my thighs along the way. I nudged him to standing, and I took his face in my hands, raised myself on my toes, and kissed him the way he had kissed me. I hesitated for a second before unzipping his jeans, and he stepped out of them.

The room was dark, but the blinds were open. He reached behind me to turn the slats up, and pale ribbons of light filtered into the room. In a single move, he swept a pile of clothes from the bed onto the floor.

"You know," he said, his words little more than a whisper, "I've been thinking about this—about us—for a while."

"Me too," I confessed as I gently pushed him onto the bed and straddled him.

He was there with me, about to be inside of me. I was acutely aware of every part of him, skin to skin. And he was responding to my every touch, kissing me like he wanted to be loved. I closed my eyes. Still, a needling question stung. *Am I making an already messy situation even more complicated?* But my worries were quickly lost in a dense fog of lust. His breath quickened, his movements became more insistent, and he rolled me over.

His face was inches from mine, and the chain around his neck grazed my cheek as he leaned in to whisper in my ear, "Tell me what you like, what you want."

I didn't hesitate. "I want you."

He reached into the nightstand and pulled out a foil packet and kissed me again before he ripped it open. He scooped one hand behind my waist to pull me even closer, and I wrapped my legs around him. I let myself believe that what was happening between us was real, and the stalker was relegated to a recurring nightmare that faded into the background when I was fully awake.

Like I was right then.

Chapter 18

I opened my eyes and raised my head off the pillow to glance over at the digital clock on the nightstand. It looked like something from a SkyMall catalogue. Six fifteen in the morning—still dark out. I reached up to touch my swollen lips. The taste of Mick lingered. He was sprawled across the bed, facedown, the twisted sheets barely covering his body. He roused and rolled over to face me, and I grabbed the sheet to cover myself—a ridiculous nod to modesty after the night before.

"Good morning," he said, his voice gravelly. He seemed relaxed, one hand behind his head, like he woke up every morning to find me naked in his bed. "Come here," he said as he pulled me next to him.

"I thought you said you had to be there at seven."

"Yeah, but we have time. I checked the call sheet, and I'm not first up today." He smiled as he slipped my hand under the sheets and down his warm skin.

Mick had insisted he was just like any other guy. And he was right, at least in one respect. Every guy I'd ever been with wanted a repeat a.m. performance of the night before. In a futile attempt to suppress my feelings, the voices in my head recited the mental mantra, *"It means nothing, it means nothing, it means nothing."* But the moment he drew me close, uttering my name in a moan, and his hands once again slid down my body, I knew that was a lie.

We were lying together, our bodies intertwined, my head buried in his chest, as I absorbed his heartbeat, memorizing its rhythm. I didn't want to move. I glanced at the clock again—already seven o'clock.

"Shouldn't you be going?"

He opened one eye. "Why don't you come with me today?"

"To the set? Are you serious?"

He arched a single brow. "Sure, why not?"

"I mean, it wouldn't be weird?"

"I'll introduce you around. I have to warn you, though, it can be boring. There's a lot of standing around, waiting. You can bring your book, and lunch is free," he joked.

I'd wandered past movies being shot on location on the streets of New York and stopped to gawk, but I never expected to be on the inside looking out.

"Then, shouldn't *we* be going?"

"Yeah, I guess, but *Jesus*, I'm beat. What time was it when we finally called it quits last night? Two, three?"

He rolled away, sat on the edge of the bed, and turned to face me. His tousled hair gave new meaning to the term *bedhead*. It was a jumbled mess, just waiting for someone to come along and put everything in place.

"You know, Rachael..." He took a deep breath. "You're not at all what I expected. You've got a little wild streak hidden in there. Sort of took me by surprise."

I felt my face redden.

"See? You're blushing!" he teased. "It's a clever cover."

He leaned back down and kissed my cheek, then swept his hair away from his face, and headed to the bathroom. As he closed the door, my cell rang. I grabbed my T-shirt from the floor, shook it out, slipped it on, and snatched my phone from the nightstand to glance at the screen. It was Jenna. I ran upstairs, out of earshot, and glanced around the living room. The bottle of brandy and the juice glasses—props from the scene of the night before—were strewn across the table. The call had gone to voice mail. I sat on the sofa and listened.

"It's me. Call me just as soon as you get this message." Jenna's monotone belied the urgency of her words. "You're not going to be happy."

My muddled thoughts turned to my parents. A sour sensation in my stomach made its way to my throat as I hit speed dial.

"Jen, what happened? Are my parents okay?"

"They're fine. Sorry. I didn't mean to panic you, but are you sitting down?"

"Just spit it out," I said, my heart pounding.

"I know you slept with Mick last night."

Confusion trumped panic. I briefly considered the possibility that my thoughts had somehow been transmitted over the state line to Jenna. They were, after all, incredibly intense.

"What? How could you possibly know that?"

"Rachael," she said, almost in a whisper, "there's a video of Mick and a woman standing together naked next to a bed. It's shot through a window. It's definitely him, and, well, the woman's back is to the window, but I can tell it's you."

"What the hell?" The realization hit me. *Those few minutes before Mick closed the blinds.* "Shit. Oh shit!"

"So, what are you going to do?"

"Do? What can I do? I'll just tell him. He has a whole team of people who'll want to know before it goes viral. *Shit.* Listen, I've gotta go. He's going to be out of the shower soon, and I need to tell him before he leaves for work."

"Work?"

"Yeah. That's why he's here. He's shooting a movie in the city to-day. He showed up last night, and—I don't know—one thing led to another, and before I knew it, we were naked in his bedroom."

"It'll be fine, Rachael. Take deep breaths."

I hung up and slumped onto the sofa. *Will Mick be freaked out? Or is this just another day in the life of a celebrity? What if Jude sees it? What if my parents see it?* I ran back down to the bedroom. He was still in the shower. After a quick Google search on my phone, a link to a video on Twitter popped up as the first hit. I hesitated, but I had to see it for myself. The video lasted mere seconds, but there we were, standing in front of the window, passionately kissing, his hands all over me, then the crystal-clear shot of him reaching behind me to close the blinds. I felt the blood drain from my face.

"Porn so early in the morning?" Mick laughed. He was standing behind me, wrapped in a towel, peering over my shoulder. "Last night wasn't enough?"

I turned to face him.

"What's wrong?"

"Mick, this isn't porn. It's you and me from last night."

"What? Let me see that."

He snatched the phone from my hand and hit Replay, and there we were, just as naked as the first time.

"Jesus Christ! The paps all carry around night vision cameras now?" He paused as he processed the news.

"You don't think it might have been the stalker?" I asked.

"Could be, but it's not likely she would have such sophisticated video equipment. How did you find out about this so fast?"

"Jenna called while you were in the shower."

He sank onto the bed next to me. The scent of toothpaste and chamomile conditioner surrounded him. He grabbed a cigarette from the box on the nightstand and lit up, inhaling deeply. He pressed a thumb hard into his temple.

His cell rang, and he glanced at the screen. "It's Grace. She's already seen it."

"Hey, Gracie... Yeah, I just this second saw it... It was last night... Don't get your knickers all in a twist... No, she doesn't have a publicist... No, I'm not going to tell you... It's nobody's fucking business... Look, I gotta go. I'm already late... Later."

"What did she say?"

"Oh, she's foaming at the mouth to find out who the girl in the video is. I know how her brain works. She's thinking if it was an actress, she could make it out to be some grand love affair and generate publicity for us both." He rolled his eyes. "Rach, I'm really sorry. You seem to be getting sucked deeper and deeper into my insane life. I hate this shit. I guess the only thing I haven't been photographed doing now is taking a piss. I'm sure that's inevitable at some point." He chortled under his breath. "Getting involved with me seems to carry some unique risks, doesn't it?"

"Oh, let's see..." I said. "There's a nutjob out there who wants to rip my heart out and eat it for breakfast, she keyed my car, she broke into my parents' house, and now I have a sex video online."

"Well, we weren't actually having sex... yet." He raised a single eyebrow.

"I'm glad you think this is funny." I hesitated for a breath. "Maybe this is just another day at the office for you, but last night was..." I flushed at the heated memory and felt the words rising up in my throat. "It was a mistake."

He stiffened. "You don't really mean that... do you?"

I answered with false conviction, "I wouldn't have said it if I didn't mean it."

Hurt swept across his face, and something shook loose inside me.

"I... I'm sorry. I honestly don't know what I mean."

He cupped my chin in his hand. "Look at me. I don't believe there are mistakes. There's only what you decide to do and what not to do."

"Well, I don't agree," I said. "Some things are definitely mistakes. Believe me, I've made my share. And I don't want this to be one of them. It's... just everything— the situation, the way you live. I'm not sure where I fit in—or if I even want to."

"Rach, come on, I think you have me confused with that celebrity jerk-off, Mick What's-His-Face."

Collecting myself once again, I said, "Anyway, you're the one who's going to have to deal with the fallout from the video. I'm just some mystery girl right now."

"Yeah, and I'm thinking we should keep it that way. If Jenna's already seen it, the paps will be on it. They may be hiding outside, waiting for us to leave together."

His phone rang again. "I'm sure this is someone on the set. Crap! I'm so late."

"Hey," he answered and paced, running his fingers through his hair, leaving an anxious trail of water droplets on the floor. "Sorry. It's been a weird morning. I'm heading out now... What?... Well, that's just great... Yeah, yeah, I know... Very funny... Okay. I'll be there in forty-five."

He tossed the phone on the bed, clasped his hands behind his head, and heaved a sigh. "It's already making its way through the cast and crew, and they're getting a big yuk out of it. Even more reason for you to stay here. I'll try to be back by seven or eight tonight, and we can talk more then."

His phone rang again—his car was waiting out front. He picked up a pair of rumpled jeans and a T-shirt from the floor, put them on, shoved his bare feet into a pair of well-worn Nikes, and tugged a baseball cap over his still-wet hair.

"I really have to go. You okay?"

I sat on the edge of the bed, trying to process everything that had happened, that was happening. "No."

He walked over, sat next to me, and pressed his lips hard against mine. I snapped my head back.

"What's wrong?" he asked, his eyebrows angled in surprise at my reaction, the same as the night before when he first tried to kiss me.

"My lips. They're sore."

"Sorry about that." He chuckled and kissed my forehead.

Though I'd been unsure about going to the set with him, now that the option was off the table, I realized that not only was I looking forward to it, I was depending on it for a much-needed distraction. Now, I would have the whole day alone to ruminate over the wisdom of the previous night's activities and to obsess over the video.

"Just be sure everything's locked up and the alarm is set. I'll tell Grace to call the security firm and have them come by more often today, and I'll check in with you as often as I can."

After one last gentle kiss, he left for his other world, the one as alien to me as a round trip to Mars, and I was left to ponder whether being with Mick Sullivan was really worth all the collateral damage.

Chapter 19

I desperately needed to distract myself from the constant mental replay of the night before and its unknown consequences. Based on my history with men who carried far less baggage, there would be emotional repercussions. One thing I knew for sure—living in Mick's building was going to feel different and would present its own set of quandaries. *Will I be sleeping in his bed every night, or will it be a by-invitation-only situation?* I had no intention of repeating the same mistake I made with Conrad—being a convenient bed warmer.

My head was swirling. Staying busy would stop me from teetering back and forth between thinking it had been the best night of my life and the worst decision I'd ever made—on top of the incessant worry about whether the stalker might see it and act on her warped fantasies.

With a concerted effort, I managed to shift my focus onto my work and kicked off the day by doing interviews with the two new members of Intact Heart, a band that had imploded over creative differences and were in the process of reinventing themselves. The guys might've been experienced musicians, but they were clearly inexperienced at giving interviews, and they revealed way more than they should have. They took a no-filter approach, much like Mick. *Jude will love it.* After the interviews were done, I finished the blog post and hit Send ahead of the next day's deadline. My stomach rumbled, and I glanced at my phone—already one-thirty. I went downstairs to Mick's apartment, and as I was leaning into his refrigerator and considering my options, the door to the building creaked open. I jerked upright and held my breath as I cocked my head to listen more intently. I ran to the video monitor and caught a glimpse of the door closing. A hot flash of fear gripped my chest. I had the keypad on my phone open, ready to call 911, when a text popped up:

I'm here. Busy?

Dizzy with relief, I opened his apartment door before he had a chance to slide his key in.

His eyebrows shot up in surprise. "Oh, you're here," he said before smiling warmly.

"I was getting some lunch." I took a hitched breath. "You scared the shit out of me. What happened? I thought you weren't coming until tonight."

"Another production glitch. They need to get their shit together. Aren't you glad I'm here?"

He pulled me close, and I collapsed into his chest and exhaled. "I am."

We ordered pho, and between slurps of noodles, he said, "I've got some good news. At least, I hope you'll think it's good news."

"Oh?"

"I may be here for at least another week, shooting. Think you can deal?" He grinned.

"I think I can manage." I tried not to reveal the warm thrill I felt, but despite being happy about the news, I couldn't help but wonder if our budding relationship would blossom or slowly wilt over a full week together in the midst of the ongoing threat to our safety.

That night, we made love. It wasn't the frenzy of limbs and lips that the previous night had been, but it was still intense—just slower, sweeter. I nestled against his back, he pulled my hand to his chest, and we drifted off to sleep.

At two in the morning, he jerked upright, screaming, "No!" his eyes wide with terror, beads of sweat gathering on his chest. My heart pounded. Once I was conscious enough to realize we weren't about to be bludgeoned to death at the hands of the stalker, I gently massaged his back and reassured him that it was just a dream. He fell back onto the pillow, and his breathing gradually returned to a slow, steady rhythm. In the morning, he claimed no memory of it.

His recurring nightmares came in startling contrast to the evenings before we fell asleep, when we lay in bed in the dark, talking, touching, and getting to know more about each other outside our shared tales of growing up in Louisiana and the bizarre circumstances that had brought us together.

"So," I said, "what was your path to all this insane success?" I grimaced. "Geez, I sound like I'm interviewing you for the blog."

"Yeah, little bit." He chuckled then sighed. "It was a shit ton of luck."

"Oh, come on. I've seen your movies. You know you're good."

"Yeah? I'll lay money that you haven't seen my humiliating first film. Very few people have. I won't even let my mom watch it."

"Maybe I've seen it. What's it called?"

He bit his lip as he shook his head. Even in the darkened bedroom, I could tell he was blushing. "*Twice Is Not Enough*."

"You're right. Haven't seen that one. Do you have it? Can I watch?"

"No freakin' way."

"So I'll just watch it on streaming."

"Nope. You won't find it anywhere. It's that bad."

"But you have it here?"

His silence answered my question.

"Come on. Pretty please."

"You may run for the hills after you see this." He shook his head before he stood, put the DVD in, and grabbed the remote from atop the TV. "You sure you're ready for this?"

"Yes."

"You're one hundred percent sure?" He was standing, naked, in front of the TV, remote in hand.

I laughed. "Yes!"

He jumped back in bed and pressed Play.

As soon as the film started, I could clearly see that *Twice Is Not Enough* was a microbudget film.

"Check me out trying to fake a British accent."

"Righto, it's bloody awful," I said in a bad imitation of his bad imitation.

"Obviously, there was no budget for a dialect coach." He set the remote on the bed and stuck his fingers in his ears.

I slapped my hand over my mouth to stifle a giggle. He looked as uncomfortable on the screen as he was watching it.

We were only a few minutes into the movie when he said, "Okay, that's enough." He reached for the remote.

I snatched it off the bed. "I want to watch. When was this? You were a baby!"

"Seventeen, I think. No, eighteen. God, I was so fucking stupid. I was pumped that I had been cast in a 'real' movie, but I didn't know what the fuck I was doing. It got circulated at school, and the kids were merciless."

He let me watch for another five minutes before he insisted on stopping.

"Happy now? Enough about my pathetic beginnings as an actor." He pulled a cigarette from the pack on the nightstand and lit it. "I've been meaning to ask you—I haven't seen you smoke since that one night. Did you quit?"

"I quit a while ago."

He frowned in confusion. "So why?"

I shrugged. "It's just that, you know, the famous Mick Sullivan was offering me a cigarette, and I couldn't say no."

"Seriously? You see?" he said, clearly exasperated. "This is what happens. I never know if someone is being real with me." After two puffs, he snuffed out the cigarette in the ashtray.

"But you know this is the real me now," I said.

He lifted up the sheet and said, "Yep, you're real, alright."

He kissed me, and once again, I dissolved into his touch.

Later, he went upstairs and brought down a bottle of wine and two glasses.

We clicked glasses in a toast.

"L'chaim," he said.

"Tell me about your family," I said, wanting to know more about his past in order to put his present into perspective.

"My mom's a character and a half, which you might have picked up on."

"So tell me a mom story."

"I've got plenty." He frowned and pursed his lips. "Oh, I know. Once, she went to my school after work to confront my teacher about the unfair treatment of her 'gifted' son. Without time to go home and shower after clocking out from her twelve-hour shift at the chicken-packing factory, she walked into the classroom, smelling of rancid chicken fat and leaving a dusting of feathers behind. I was mortified, sure I would never get over the embarrassment, but now, when I think about the expression on Ms. Sercy's face, wrinkling her nose at my mom, I think it's one of my favorite childhood memories." He paused, looking as content as I'd ever seen him.

"It seems like you and your mom are really close."

"Yeah, she's my one-person support group."

"And your dad?"

"Like I told you, he left when I was a kid, and I don't really like to think about him and what he did to my mom, to us."

Clearly, he didn't want me to dig any deeper. He switched to stories about his rarefied world, details he hadn't shared before about actors he'd worked with—the good, the bad, and the ugly—all the juicy behind-the-scenes stuff that Jenna would die for, like the time his costar went missing during a night shoot in Central Park. "We literally had a search party of cast and crew out looking for him. It was about two a.m. when one of the PAs yelled, 'Over here!' And there was Peter Ash, all six-foot-four of him, buck naked, the soles of his feet covered in mud. He was shit-faced and hugging a tree like it was keeping him from floating away. Thank God there were no paps around at that hour. Talk about a money shot."

I couldn't help but laugh.

"I got him dressed and took him to my trailer to sleep it off instead of dragging him through the hotel lobby in that condition. Several hours later, he woke up, showered, dressed, and he was ready to shoot. Claimed he didn't remember a thing. That's confidential, of course."

"Of course. But tell me more."

"That shit's boring. Tell me more about you, about your parents. All I know about your dad is that he sounds like Darth Vader."

"My father put us through hell for a while. He drank, and my mom just dealt with it, but he's really trying hard to be a better person."

Mick's expression shifted. I couldn't tell if he was disappointed or empathetic. Either way, I wasn't ready to open up about the extent of my father's drinking or my stint with Adult Children of Alcoholics. We both seemed to be holding back, but that didn't stop me from opening my Pandora's box of horrible memories. *Like the time he...* I slammed the lid shut before the memory sent me spiraling.

Mick was in midconversation.

"I wish I could take you to the Fourth Avenue Pub, where I used to hang."

I wasn't sure what I'd missed while my mind wandered. "Oh yeah?"

"It used to be my favorite dive bar. We would have drunk PBR, made out in the corner booth. A couple of old farts would've stared and maybe drooled a little, but no one would've really given a shit." He took a breath. "But the reality is, if we tried to do that now, you'd see us next week on the cover of some tabloid saying I was cheating on a fictional girlfriend. The bloggers would claim you were a hooker giving me a hand job under the table."

"Sounds awesome."

"Maybe one of these days..." he said and pulled me close.

I prayed that "one of these days" would become more than just a collection of wishful words.

Chapter 20

After a sleepy kiss and a promise that he would text me before he opened the door next time, Mick was gone by six. I dozed off again. When I finally climbed out of bed, I went upstairs to my apartment, washed my face, brushed my teeth, and looked at myself in the mirror. *Who* are *you?* If I could take an aerial view of my current life circumstances, the edges would blur, making it seem less complicated but no less strange.

I was starting to go a little stir crazy, and I craved one of those bagels Mick told me about after I first moved in. I dressed and convinced myself that I could safely make it to the bagel place and back that early in the morning. Maybe stalkers slept in.

As I went down the stairs, I spotted mail on the floor of the vestibule. Surprised to see mail delivered so early, I picked up the single envelope lying on the rug. It was hand addressed to Mick with no postage and no return address. I recognized that barely legible handwriting. It felt threatening on its own. I turned it over. The back was sealed with a lipstick kiss. Holding it up to the light, I could make out a handwritten note inside.

The floorboards creaked, and I flinched. Rather than registering as the comforting sounds of a two-hundred-year-old brownstone settling with the years, the sound had a sinister tone. *The stalker knows where Mick's place is. Does she know I'm here? Did she try to open the door?* Gripping the envelope, I felt infected by this woman's deluded obsession. I imagined her slipping her fingers through the mail slot and trying to peer inside. I closed my eyes and shook my head, an

Etch A Sketch effort to wipe clean all thoughts of what she might've done, what she *had* done.

My hands trembled as I put the key in the lock of Mick's apartment. I set the envelope on the coffee table and went from room to room, once again double-checking every window and every door, making sure everything was secure. I called Mick. It went directly to voice mail. This latest communication was not something I wanted to relay to him in a voice message or a text. I debated whether to call Detective Melnitsky. *And tell him what? "Come over right away! Mick just received a letter through the mail slot"?* I was done calling the police and being dismissed out of hand. I decided I would send Melnitsky an email to fill him in even though he likely wouldn't react with anywhere near the same degree of alarm that I was experiencing. In fact, he would probably view it as unworthy of his attention.

I was tempted to rip open the envelope and read the note, but I wasn't ready to deal with the ugly words that were no doubt scrawled across the page. I was pacing the room when I thought, *The security footage!* I scrambled down the stairs to the basement, where the security video system was housed. The scent of damp cement, cigarettes, and stale beer permeated the air. I'd been too distracted the last time I was down there to notice that Mick's office resembled a cross between a guy's dorm room and a recording studio, or that it smelled like a bar. Tossed on the floor next to a well-worn sofa were framed black-and-white photos of him. He was wearing that "I dare you not to want me" expression, the one he evidently assumed for photographs.

I walked over to the bookcase, where the security monitors sat next to his eclectic book collection, which included a Salvador Dali biography, Anne Rice novels, and a volume of *Astronomy for Dummies*. I was definitely going to ask him more about his reading habits. Next to a row of books was the instruction manual he'd left for me. I carried it to his desk, which was covered in a blanket of papers and sheet music, all held in place by a few empty beer bottles that doubled as ashtrays, along with an orange lava lamp perilously perched on the edge. I sat and flipped through the pages of the manual, trying to find no-brainer instructions for accessing the video footage. It was written in poorly translated English, and I was short on patience. I tossed the manual on top of his other papers and tried to recall Mick's verbal instructions. He'd made it seem so easy, but standing in front of the control panel, I felt like I was being asked to pilot a Boeing 777 after a single lesson. Afraid I might erase the footage or, worse, damage his expensive equipment, I decided to wait until he came home that night to check out the surveillance video.

I went upstairs to my apartment, dead-bolted the door, and locked the bathroom before jumping into the shower for the second time that morning in an attempt to wash away the creeping sense of dread. I stayed under the steamy spray until my skin was blotchy, my fingertips wrinkled. Going to the bagel shop was out of the question. I could have ordered in, but even that might pose a risk. Calmer, I ate leftover Chinese takeout for breakfast. I called my mother and Jenna just to hear their reassuring voices, but I didn't mention the letter. I felt as if I were speaking a different language, making it impossible to communicate. They lived in a different universe, one free of panic and fear. I didn't know if I would ever live there again.

Mick wouldn't be home for several hours, and I started to rethink my decision not to call the police. *So what if they think I'm being paranoid?* Better to be thought paranoid than to be the subject of the next day's headline: "Young Woman Found Stabbed to Death in Mick Sullivan's Home!" I called Melnitsky, but he was out. I left a message then another and another.

The hours dragged by. I couldn't concentrate. Whispered threats drifted up from the letter downstairs. My obsessive checking of the locks and the alarm was out of control. I called the security company to ask that they come by even more often. By the time Mick texted me that he was on his way, I was caught in a rat's-nest tangle of exposed nerves.

When he walked in, he looked so happy to see me. I hated to spoil the moment, but just thinking about what I was about to tell him made the blood drain from my lips.

"What's wrong?" he asked, his question punctuated with concern.

I picked up the letter from the table. The lipstick-stained envelope emanated the lunatic's dark energy as I handed it to Mick. "It was dropped through the mail slot this morning."

"What is it?"

"I didn't open it. I was afraid of what it might say."

He took his glasses from his shirt pocket and slipped them on. As he ripped open the envelope and unfolded the letter, a photo fell out and onto the floor. I picked it up and stared at it in disbelief. The woman in the photograph was naked, spread-eagle like she was advertising her services. She was clearly pregnant, which took her crazy obsession to a whole other level. I silently handed it to him. His expression morphed from curiosity to alarm.

"What the fuck is this, pregnant porn?" He collapsed on the sofa, photo and letter in hand. "Shit, I can't see her face."

"What does the letter say?"

He read silently.

"Out loud. I want to hear it."

"You sure? It's some crazy shit."

"Read it."

"'Mick, love of my life, you don't understand what a huge mistake you're making. How can you abandon your one true love? Abandon your child? We have a life together, a wonderful future. I know you've been led astray by another woman, but I'm willing to forgive you if you just come back to me. I can't be without you. I WON'T be without you. I'll follow you to the ends of the universe.

KNOW THAT! I have to make you realize that the three of us are meant to be a happy family. It's written in the stars. I've been patient, but my patience is wearing thin. I'm sending this photograph to remind you of what you've been missing. I'll be watching, listening, and planning our future. Love you forever and a day! We will be together soon!'"

Our mutual silence was thick with alarm.

"Mick, there's something else I should have told you."

He frowned, and his nostrils flared.

"Just before I left New Jersey, I got a package from her. There was a positive pregnancy test in it—and a weird snip of hair taped to an equally weird note. None of it made sense then."

"What the fuck?" He leaned forward, his elbows on his knees. "Maybe DNA from the hair would help find her. Where is it?"

I couldn't believe what I was about to say. "I threw the note away."

"Why?" he asked, clearly agitated.

"It was freaking me out. I just crumpled it up and tossed it. I wasn't thinking."

"I guess you threw away the pregnancy test too?"

"Actually, it fell under the seat of my car, and I never tried to dig it out. It's probably still there."

"Okay, well, that's something."

I hesitated. "There's one more thing."

"Shit, Rachael, just spit it all out."

I swallowed hard. "You see that necklace she's wearing?"

"I wasn't really looking at her jewelry."

"It's mine," I said. "At least, the charm on the chain is mine. She must have taken it from my room when she broke in."

He stared at the photo. "So what's the deal? Is she more obsessed with you or me?" He pressed his palm against his forehead. "We need to give this to the detective here in Brooklyn. What's his name?"

"Melnitsky."

"Yeah—and to Steve."

He yanked his phone from his pocket in a white-knuckled grip. "You should have told me." He jerked his head up. "Wait, what about the surveillance video? Did you look at it? Can you see her face?"

"I couldn't figure out how to work it. I was waiting for you."

He slipped his glasses atop his head, stood, and started toward the basement stairs. Stopping midstep, he turned toward me and huffed an exhausted breath. "Maybe they can finally track her down from the video, and we can get a restraining order." He clicked his tongue in disgust. "She actually believes that the baby is mine. God, what a shit show."

The surveillance video was no help. She might have been mentally deranged, but she wasn't stupid. She'd worn a hoodie that concealed her face and lowered her head as she slipped the envelope through the mail slot. I felt nauseated watching her bend over to peer through the opening, just as I'd imagined.

"Do you think she knows I'm here?" I asked, fearing the answer.

"The note doesn't say anything, but I was certain she didn't know where this place was, so we can't be sure."

Mick wrapped his arms around me and kissed my head. "Let's call Melnitsky. This is way too close for comfort."

He grabbed a beer from the kitchen before sitting on the sofa to make the call. The detective answered on the first ring.

"Detective Melnitsky? This is Mick Sullivan... Yeah, I'm fine. Thanks. Listen, we've had more contact from the stalker... Sure, hold on." He turned to me. "Rach, hand me the note."

Maybe he'd just gotten lucky with Melnitsky answering the phone, but Mick proceeded to read it to Melnitsky without interruption. Maybe most cops lacked empathy for the rich and famous, but Mick was clearly getting a more attentive response than I was able to wrest from the detective. He told him about the photo, the necklace, the hair, and the pregnancy test.

"But can't you get DNA from the pregnancy test?" Mick's frown deepened, and he kept running his fingers through his hair. "Wait a sec." He put the call on speakerphone so that I could hear.

"Well," Melnitsky began before clearing his throat, "urine does contain small amounts of DNA, but not nearly as much as blood or saliva, and DNA from urine deteriorates more quickly, making it difficult to extract enough and to get reliable results. There would be so little DNA on a pregnancy test stick it wouldn't be worth the effort. But you said there was a hair sample?"

I jumped in. "Yeah, but I... I threw it away. It was taped to a crazy note. She labeled it as 'proof,' but I have no idea what it's supposed to be proof of."

"That might have helped us to identify her." After a pause, Melnitsky asked, "Anything else?"

The muscles in Mick's jaw tensed. "As of right this second? No."

When he ended the call, he patted the space next to him on the sofa. I sat, and he pulled my legs onto his lap and began massaging my bare feet. "I'm so, so sorry about all of this, Rach. If I could somehow jump back in time and make none of this happen, I would." He leaned forward and looked at me with such intensity that I felt an inexplicable urge to cry. "But then I wouldn't have met you."

Chapter 21

Mick's extended presence allowed me to temporarily push thoughts of the stalker into a closet and bar the door. I desperately wanted to focus on what was happening between us as much as humanly possible during the precious time we had left together. He would soon be headed back to the other coast, and I would be alone to wrestle with my fear and my feelings about Mick.

"What's that monstrous book you've been reading?" He nodded toward my tome on the night stand while stifling a yawn. He'd walked in the door after midnight and was beat.

"It's actually about monsters."

"What kind of monsters?"

"Vampires, but not sexy, sparkly vampires. These are the vampires of your worst nightmares. I saw your Anne Rice novels downstairs. When I'm done, we should compare vampire notes." I made ridiculous blood-sucking noises.

"Never would have guessed you'd be into something like that. You're just full of surprises." He smiled and came around to my side of the bed to stand in front of me. "How about you surprise me some more?"

"I thought you were tired."

"I'm not *that* tired."

He lowered me onto the bed and was nuzzling my neck when the sound of metal scraping on the slate tiles out front stopped us mid-kiss.

"Did you hear that?" we whispered in unison.

He jumped out of bed and peered through the blinds. "There's someone out there," he said, pulling on his jeans.

"Is it a woman?" I choked on my words.

"I can't tell," he said as he sprinted to the bedroom door.

"Mick, no, wait!"

He was already opening the gate that led to the front of the building. I heard his bare feet pounding the sidewalk as he screamed, "Hey, bitch! I'm calling the police!" I peeked through the blinds just as Mick walked back in, carrying a huge flower arrangement set on a metal easel. Amid my fluttering confusion, it registered that the flowers were lovely—lavender roses, white carnations, and color-coordinated ribbons.

"There's a card," he said, sounding far more upset than you would expect from someone receiving flowers under normal circumstances. He set the easel down and read the card. "Mick, my love..." His voice cracked, and he swiped his nose with the back of his hand as he shuffled his bare feet on the hardwood floor. He continued, "This is for her. I'll take care of everything, and then we can be together. Forever."

Fear rearranged his features into something almost unrecognizable. "Rachael, it's a fucking funeral wreath. She knows you're here."

Chapter 22

The next morning, Bruce, the bodyguard, reported for duty. Mick had made late-night calls and pulled favors to arrange round-the-clock protection for me on short notice. He refused to take no for an answer, and I was in no position to argue. The guy was armed with a pistol and a taser, but from the looks of him, he wouldn't need to resort to either. And, yes, he was built like a bison. Mick always had bodyguards who accompanied him through airports and in and out of venues when he made appearances. This wasn't anything new for him, but it was disconcerting for me, as if I were living someone else's life.

Bruce would accompany me for any trip—to pick up coffee and a bagel or to go to the cleaners, the corner bodega for groceries, or the city for a meeting. Surreal though the situation was, Bruce's presence did make me feel safe—*safer*, anyway. Mick had asked me once more if I wanted to leave, to go back to New Jersey or to a hotel or to have him rent an apartment for me.

"Bruce would come with you," he said, as though that would persuade me to agree to his Plan B.

The last thing I wanted to do was sit in a room all day by myself with Bruce stationed outside my door. Going home to New Jersey would leave me feeling adrift—not to mention that I would again have to deal with my father's disapproval on a daily basis. My only real peace of mind came when Mick was with me. He'd become my safe harbor. No, I was staying put.

Later that day, I got a surprise call from Houdini Records. I'd all but given up on hearing back. They wanted me to come in for an interview the next day. Bruce would tag along.

Mick didn't bother to wake me before he left that morning. He'd said he wanted me to rest, to be prepared to put my best foot forward for the interview. That was sweet, but I wasn't even sure I had a best foot anymore. Something woke me up, and wiping drool from my mouth, I grabbed my phone. It was a text from Mick.

Break a leg today. Let me know. That was followed by kiss emojis and a leg.

Mick had stuffed the funeral wreath in the trash bin, but it was bulky, and the top wouldn't close, so I was forced to look at the lavender roses sneering at me until trash day. We reported it to the police, of course, but sending flowers wasn't a chargeable offense. And the card was only vaguely threatening. "I'll take care of everything" was open to interpretation. Melnitsky said they would try to track the source, but there were probably hundreds of florists in the five Boroughs. The stalker had surely paid cash, and she'd hand-delivered the flowers to Mick's door, making the order virtually impossible to trace.

Bruce had arranged for a trusted driver, and the three of us headed into the city. I stared out the window as the quiet Brooklyn neighborhood gave way to Manhattan's kinetic energy. I leaned forward and tapped Bruce on the shoulder, and he pulled his mirrored sunglasses off and turned to face me from the front seat.

"Listen, I'm going to need you to be discreet. My having a bodyguard doesn't exactly shout, 'Hire that girl!' If I do get hired, I'll try to explain later, when the moment's right."

"Yes, ma'am. 'Discreet' is my middle name."

He'd been ma'aming me from the moment we were introduced. "Please don't do that. How about saying, 'Sure thing' or 'Cool,' or maybe just nod in my direction, but please don't call me ma'am."

"Yes, ma'am—uh, sorry. Military for seven years. Hard habit to break." He slipped his sunglasses back on and turned to face the front, sitting ramrod straight.

When the car stopped in front of Houdini's building, Bruce instructed me to stay put while he came around to open my door. He scanned the area Secret Service style. The driver left to find a place to park, and Bruce and I walked through the revolving doors and headed toward the elevators.

"Hey, wait, you need to sign in." The security guy at the front desk was about to give us grief. "Who do you have an appointment with?"

"Clarissa Hardin at Houdini Records."

"Both of you?"

"I'm her agent," Bruce said, without hesitation. "Ms. Hardin is expecting us. We're here to discuss the terms of Ms. Allen's new contract."

Is this what he considers being discreet?

He did a three-sixty scan of the lobby. "Nice place," he said coolly.

I, on the other hand, was bug-eyed over the dizzyingly gorgeous decor, from the gargantuan chandelier in the shape of a tangled vine to the mosaic Moroccan floor tile and the tasseled cushions on the stairs, in case anyone wanted to take a seat before continuing to the top.

Our driver's licenses were checked, and we signed in and were given visitor passes. We headed to the elevator bank for the fifteenth floor. Bruce pressed the button, and as we stood watching the digital display, I shifted my focus to him.

"My agent?" I smiled.

"I can be your personal assistant, your manager, or your publicist, if you prefer." He didn't seem to fit the profile for any of the titles, but his ploy had worked.

"Agent it is."

My "agent" sat in the waiting room while I worked at putting my best foot forward in Ms. Hardin's office. She was younger than I'd expected and far friendlier. Reed thin and at least six feet tall in flats, she had an impressive presence along with a firm handshake, but she put me at ease from the get-go. "Ms. Allen, so glad we were able to find a time we were both available. Have a seat. Do you mind if we just jump right in? I'm afraid I've got back-to-back meetings today."

"Of course."

The interview started with the standard questions: "Why do you want to work at Houdini?" "Tell me about your relevant experience." "Where do you see yourself in five years?" But then it turned into an easy conversation about neighborhoods in the city and our Southern roots. She'd grown up in Alabama, but like me, her accent had flattened over time. Our common Southern background made her even less intimidating and gave me the presence of mind to properly promote myself by sharing all the successes I'd forgotten to mention in my interview with Jude.

Hardin excused herself to answer a call, and my phone dinged. *Shit.* I'd forgotten to silence it. She had her back to me, so I used the opportunity to glance at my screen. Detective Melnitsky had messaged me. *Crap.* The only time he ever called was to return my calls, and I hadn't called him. *Does he have good news or bad? Has he ID'd her?* I had to fight my obsessive need to read the text before Hardin turned back around.

She ended her call. "Sorry about that. Where were we?" She gave my résumé one last cursory glance and said, "I think that does it. Thank you so much for coming in, Rachael. This was a pleasure. We'll be in touch for sure."

"We'll be in touch" was a kiss-off. But the "for sure" she tacked on at the end gave me real hope. For a blessed second or two, I was filled with excitement, unencumbered by stalker stress. I waited until

we got back in the car before I pulled out my phone and read Melnitsky's text.

We've got a fingerprint match. Call me.

Chapter 23

"Her name is Brenda Benton," Melnitsky said when I called him back.

I was giddy with relief. They knew who she was. They would be able to track her down and arrest her. Mick and I could finally relax and maybe see what our relationship would be without the sword of Damocles hanging over our heads.

"How did you find her?"

"She left a fingerprint on the card with the funeral wreath. Does the name mean anything to you?" he asked.

My mind raced to make a mental match with the name Melnitsky had revealed.

"No. Did you ask Mick?"

"Yeah. Nothing."

"So are you going to arrest her?"

He sighed. "We've run her through the system, and she has a record, but it's minor offenses."

"But what she's doing to us isn't a minor offense!"

"True, but her trail ends about two years ago. She could've changed her name, gotten a new driver's license and passport."

"Seriously? So what happens now?"

"We keep looking. I'm sorry, Ms. Allen," he said with the first indication of true empathy.

It was dawn on Mick's last day in Brooklyn, and I was on edge, unable to fall back asleep. My optimism over my Houdini interview was dwarfed by my anxiety due to the stalker's preparation for my funeral, Melnitsky's non-news, and Mick's imminent departure. I sat up in bed, hugging my knees to my chest. The two-way radio strapped to Bruce's collar crackled outside our window.

Mick was sleeping soundly, his eyes darting back and forth beneath his eyelids, making up for his restless night. He'd been running on fumes all week, working all day and staying up with me to talk and make love until the early-morning hours. He would wake up for first call between six and eight and moan and grumble about getting up, asking, "Think they'd notice if I took a mental health day?" And the routine repeated itself.

As the week wound down, I knew he would be heading back to LA then to some remote location with crappy cell service, and I felt the pressure building. Having him with me while knowing he would be leaving was like that delicious feeling of being high but knowing a hangover was around the corner. *Is this really how I want my life to go? All the uncertainty? The extreme highs and lows? The danger?*

Unable to be still any longer, I quietly slid out of bed and glanced at his sleeping form once more before going upstairs to make coffee. I settled on a bar stool next to the kitchen island and took that first glorious sip. It soothed my exposed nerves.

"Rach?" he called from downstairs.

"I'm in the kitchen!"

I heard him padding up the stairs, and I wiped away tears with the backs of my hands in a futile attempt to hide my tangled feelings. He stopped when he reached the top. He'd slipped on his jeans, but he was barefoot and shirtless, still groggy, his eyes puffy, squinting against the kitchen lights. Even so, his appearance triggered a familiar ache in the pit of my stomach.

"Why did you get out of bed so early?"

I forced a broken smile. "I couldn't sleep."

"What's the matter?"

"Nothing," I lied.

He looked at me and blinked twice. "You're crying."

The coffee mug in my hands became the sole focus of my attention. I hadn't noticed before that it was logoed with an image from his latest movie. "You're leaving tomorrow," I mumbled.

"I know you're scared, but you'll have a bodyguard out there, plus the regular patrol. I don't think she'll be coming back once she sees there's a guard at the door."

Of course I was scared. But he didn't understand the full spectrum of my fears. What happened to my promise to never again let a guy be the focus of my world and fill me with such stupid hope? Yet there I was, holding the pieces of that broken promise and wondering how to glue it back together while being scared to death that I might not even live to know if I could.

Before I summoned the nerve to open up about what had really triggered my tears, he asked, "Why don't you come with me? Bring your laptop. You can work from the hotel while I'm on location if you want, or you can stay in my apartment in LA."

"I don't think so. Jenna's coming over for a couple of days, and Houdini sent me an email to schedule a second interview, so I'd better stay here."

"Well, if you change your mind..." He kissed my forehead.

His phone buzzed, and Grace's face popped up on the screen. I stepped out of view.

"Hey, Gracie, how's it hanging? It's, like, four in the morning there. What are you—Whoa, what's with the brown hair? Being a blonde wasn't working for you anymore?"

"Charming as always, I see," she said.

"I just need to get used to it," he said. He glanced at me.

"Are you not alone?" she asked.

As I headed downstairs, I heard him say, "Okay, I am now."

When the conversation was done, he came down to the bedroom and said, "How about we get dressed and go get the paper? There won't be many people out this early on a Sunday morning, and we can buy stuff for me to make you some of my famous banana pancakes. Pancakes, scrambled eggs, chili, and ramen noodles—that's the sum total of my culinary skills. But they're killer pancakes." He was acting as if everything were normal and banana pancakes were the cure for what was ailing me.

"What did Grace want, or is that none of my business?"

"Just some shit about an article in the trades that mentioned me. It's nothing."

We hadn't stepped outside the protective cocoon of his apartment or even much from his bedroom during the previous week. Given the circumstances, the idea of the two of us on a morning outing struck me as adventurous—well, the two of us plus one beefy bodyguard.

We threw on some clothes, and Mick donned his beanie-and-sunglasses disguise. After checking to see if the coast was clear of early-bird paparazzi and crazy stalkers, Bruce nodded that we were good to go, and we stepped out onto the stoop. I felt like I was breaking the rules, like when I was fifteen and sneaked out of the house in the middle of the night with a boy my parents hated. And it filled me with the same breathless exhilaration.

Mick slung his arm around my shoulders and kissed me. "Ready?" he asked, as if we were about to storm a castle.

The morning sun hadn't yet broken through the clouds, and the streets were uncharacteristically quiet. It felt peaceful. As I breathed in the fresh air, my obsessive worrying over my fate and our future together felt like a bad dream best forgotten.

When we arrived at the bodega, Bruce hung outside, arms crossed, eyes darting back and forth. We were the only customers in the store. The cashier, who was listening to a melancholy Middle Eastern tune, glanced up from his newspaper but, uninterested, went back to reading. Mick gathered the ingredients for pancakes as I wandered over to the newsstand. Stacks of freshly delivered papers sat on the floor, still bound in plastic cord, waiting for the old-school Sunday *New York Times* devotees to arrive. I spotted a stack of tabloids pushed into the corner. As I glanced at the front-page photo, my throat tightened. Right there on the cover, next to the shots of celebrity babies and celebrity cellulite, was a crystal-clear shot of me and Mick. A digitally enhanced image of our very private moment.

"Rach, you want anything?"

I cleared my throat. "Um, yeah. Can you hand me some scissors?"

The cashier came over and handed me a pair of scissors to cut the cord wrapped around the stack, and with shaking hands, I pulled a paper from the top of the pile. The cover line, hidden before, blared "More Exclusive Photos of Mick Sullivan and Mystery Woman Inside!"

I brought the tabloid to the checkout and set it facedown on the counter. The cashier turned it over to scan it, glanced at the cover, then looked at Mick. One more time, just to be sure. Mick grabbed the paper and held it at arm's length. He threw some money onto the counter, took my hand, and pulled me outside, leaving our pancake ingredients behind. I felt exposed, vulnerable, even with Bruce hovering, and for some reason, guilty.

Mick handed it to me. "Is this what I think it is? I don't have my glasses."

I flipped through the pictures and groaned. My back was to the window, and our bodies were mostly blurred, but his face was painfully clear.

"Yes," I croaked.

"Shit!" he said between clenched teeth.

His cell rang. "It's Grace. *Jesus!* She knew this was coming."

"Hey, Grace... Yep. I have it in my hand... No. Yeah. It's Rachael." He looked over at me. "Grace, look, I don't see how it would have helped anything to tell you it was her... No... She's standing right here... Grace, can you shut up for a minute? I'm leaving tomorrow, and Rachael is going to be here alone. If you're going to be in New York, can you just check in and make sure she's okay? You know... with everything that's been happening..."

I waved my arms and shook my head, mouthing at him, *No!*

It's okay, he mouthed back. Then he stepped away and whispered into the phone, "Gracie, please... Thanks. Later."

"You knew? Why didn't you tell me?"

"I just didn't want you to get any more upset. It's nothing. Really."

"So what did she say?"

"Not much. She just wanted to be prepared for the onslaught. I mean, the video is already out there, but... I don't know, she's trying to turn it to my advantage—'Any publicity is good publicity.' That sort of thing. Whatever."

He retrieved the pancake ingredients before we headed back. On our way home, with Bruce leading the way, Heloise popped her head out as we passed her building.

"I'm glad I spotted the two of you. I was out for a walk, and I saw this package on your stoop. I buzzed, and when you didn't answer, I thought I'd hold it for safekeeping. It's addressed to you, Rachael. Looks like it was hand delivered, no postage mark." She was holding a package neatly wrapped in brown paper.

As Mick ran up the steps to retrieve it, I caught a glimpse of the fresh terror etched on his face.

"So, when are you going to join us for tea?" she asked him. "Rachael's come over a few times now."

"Just been busy. I have to leave again tomorrow morning. Next time, I promise. Thanks again for collecting the package." He turned to go down the stairs but then stopped to face her again. "You didn't see who left this, did you?"

"No, sorry."

She turned toward me. "Call me if you need anything."

Mick rejoined me. Once we were safely inside, he set the package on the coffee table, and we sat on opposite sides of the table, staring at it as if waiting for it to pop open like a jack-in-the-box.

"You think we should call the police again?" I asked, nervously bouncing my knees up and down.

"Screw the police. They haven't done shit so far," he said as he tore at the brown wrapping and yanked the top from the box. He stared at the contents, raked his fingers halfway through his hair, then stopped midmotion.

The look on his face scared me more than anything the box might contain. "Mick, what is it?"

He hesitated before tilting it in my direction. I unlocked my eyes from his and slowly leaned in to peer inside. It was a gift basket, perfectly decorated with ribbons, bows, dried pink roses, and eucalyptus leaves. And it was filled with rat poison, razor blades, and prescription sleeping pills. A note scrawled on beautiful cream-colored stationery read:

Take your pick, bitch. Sweet dreams.

Chapter 24

Mick was anxious about leaving me alone, but he had contractual obligations and hundreds of people depending on him—other actors, crew members, the director, even the craft-service people would be impacted if he didn't show. I had to practically push him out the door. We reluctantly parted ways with promises to call, text, Zoom, and Facetime. I watched from the stoop as he blew me a kiss before he rolled up the car's tinted window, and he disappeared down the street.

The house felt different when Mick wasn't there. His absence was palpable, taking up physical space. The air I breathed, the space I occupied, seemed to shrink while the house expanded, swallowing me even more than before since the threats had escalated. A visit from Jenna was just what I needed. She would take up enough space for the two of us... and then some. Up until then, I'd been making excuses for why she shouldn't visit. The idea of having my two worlds collide threw me off balance, but I missed her, and I needed a grounding reminder of who I was, of my life before Mick happened.

Bruce knew that Jenna would be coming, but he still quizzed her and waited for me to give visual clearance.

"I come bearing cheesecake," Jenna sang into the speaker.

"I'm not letting you in unless it's from Eileen's," I teased.

"Is there any other?"

I buzzed her in and met her at the door with a needy hug before stepping back to take in the welcome sight of her.

"You look good, Jen."

"Liar. I know you're not a fan of the blue hair, but it's a phase. I'll get over it." She abruptly changed the subject. "What's the actual deal with the beefcake out there?"

"I told you. I have a bodyguard now. His name is Bruce."

"Bruce, the bodyguard?"

"Yeah, I know." I chuckled.

"Here, take this thing. It must weigh twenty pounds—exactly what you'll gain if you eat it all," she said.

I took the box from Jenna's outstretched hands and headed to the kitchen to put it in the fridge.

"You want a beer?" I called into the parlor.

"Sounds good."

I returned with our beers to find Jenna planted on the sofa, her feet propped on the coffee table, her ankles crossed.

I sat next to her and took a sip of my beer. "So, how are my parents? My mom sounds okay on the phone, but Daddy won't even talk to me. He thinks I'm flushing my life down the toilet."

"I actually had dinner with them last night. Your dad was sullen, but your mom got me alone and said to tell you she loves you, she's worried—of course—and that she'll call when your dad isn't around."

"I know she's worried. So's my dad. But you know how he is. He just can't accept me making my own decisions."

"He'll come around. But can you blame them? I'm worried too."

"It isn't unwarranted," I said as I walked over to the cabinet, where Mick had stuck the basket out of sight. "This is the latest I told you about."

"From the one who shall not be named?"

I'd called Jenna with every intention to tell her, but I couldn't make myself go into the horrifying details.

"So what was behind curtain number three?"

I handed the basket to her. She jerked to sitting and set her beer on the table. "What is this shit?" she said, digging through the basket's contents. "She is one sick puppy, and she's after *you*." Her voice dropped to a whisper. "What did the police say?"

"We didn't call them."

"What? Are you out of your friggin' mind?"

"It's not like they've been a huge help so far. She even left a funeral wreath for me out front and—"

"Wait, what? When the fuck did that happen?"

"A few days ago. That's when Mick hired the bodyguard."

For once, words escaped Jenna, and she bit her lip and shook her head in disbelief.

"There's also this." I retrieved the mail and handed the photo to Jenna.

She glanced at it and began cackling. "Oh my God! What the hell is she doing? Wait, is she pregnant? This is too warped, even for me."

Jenna examined the photo more closely. "That looks exactly like the necklace you have."

"It *is* mine. It was stuck on my bulletin board, and it's not there anymore. I asked my mom to check. I guess the stalker grabbed it when she broke in."

"So is she going apeshit over you or Mick?"

"I guess she obsessively loves him and obsessively hates me."

"But she obviously knows you're here. Aren't you scared, being here by yourself?"

"This place is like San Quentin. Nobody's getting in here."

"So, what, now you're a prisoner?" She shook her head. "This is all so bizarre. Maybe you need to cross the border and hide out in Canada or Mexico or something."

I gave her my *Seriously, Jen?* look, and she raised her hands in surrender.

"They've actually ID'd her," I said. "Her name is Brenda Benton, or at least it used to be. They haven't been able to find her. They said she could have a new identity. And she's been smart about not leaving any damning evidence, any kind of bread crumbs to follow."

Jenna took a breath and opened her mouth to say something.

In a preemptive move, I said, "Let's change the subject. Ask me about my interview at Houdini."

"Oh, yeah. How'd it go?"

"Really good. I'm super grateful to Jude for giving me the job at Sisyphus, which has been perfect, but this is Houdini Records we're talking here. If they offer me a position, I can't say no."

"Well, I'm here to tell you that's totally awesome. Maybe some of your job mojo will rub off on me." She paused, and a sly grin spread across her lips as she rubbed her palms together in anticipation. "Sooo, I'm ready for all the juicy details. I want you to tell me everything, and I do mean *everything*. And I want the deluxe-package tour of Sullivan's crib."

"Tour first," I said, stalling.

As we made our way from the parlor to the dining room and the kitchen, Jenna stopped and turned around to scan the untidy area. "He's a little piggy, isn't he?" When we reached the bedroom, she glanced at the bed. "*Shit,* Rach! I still can't believe it. You and Mick Sullivan?"

Jenna and I had always shared the details of our sex lives, right down to who touched whom where, when, and how, complete with a five-star rating system. But for the first time, it was too painfully personal to share, even with Jenna.

"Come on. Details. I want details." She was sitting lotus position on the bed, settling in.

"It was, you know... good," I said as I shrugged.

She raised a single eyebrow and cocked her head to the side.

"Jenna, you know I've told you stuff I would never tell another soul, but this is... different."

She looked desperate, as if she had been on a cleansing fast and a hot-off-the-grill cheeseburger had been waved under her nose then yanked away before she could take a bite.

"Come on, Jen, don't look at me like that."

We were silent for a few seconds before she straightened, her eyes bugging out like a squeeze toy. "Wait a minute. You have, like, real feelings for him?"

I stared at the floor.

"Oh, Rachael. I figured you'd jump him a few times, enjoy yourself, and share all the juicy details. I mean, Mick Sullivan?"

"He's not what you think."

"Jesus Christ, Rachael." Jenna shook her head in disbelief. "That certainly complicates things. I just worry that if you dive in deeper and it falls apart, you'll come up with a serious case of the bends." She bit her lip before sliding over to the edge of the bed. "I mean... He's hot, and you had hot sex. I'm an expert in that area, in case you've forgotten. I just don't want this to be another Conrad and that other guy—what was his name?" She was wagging her finger at me like a schoolmarm dispensing the day's lessons. Jenna was a world-class giver of advice she rarely followed herself. She fell in and out of love almost as often as she changed the color of her hair. She was either equator hot or Arctic cold. Her emotions had no tepid setting.

"Just be sure it's more than a fun ride on the Slip 'N Slide for him. I don't want you getting hurt again."

My phone dinged with an incoming text: *What r u doing*?

Jenna's here. Just talking.

Tell her hi.

"He says hi."

Jenna gave an unenthusiastic wave. She seemed to have already passed judgment on Mick before even meeting him.

Been thinking about you.

Me too.

Jenna rose up on her knees and made her way to the end of the bed. "What's he saying?"

Stuck in LA for a couple more weeks and then on location. Won't be back to Brooklyn for a while.

OK

Gotta run. They're calling me back. Be good. Let you know when I'm done here. Bye.

I looked at Jenna, pleading with her to take my side.

"Let me guess—he said he was thinking about you."

"You saw it!"

"No." Jenna laughed. "I just know the routine."

"He said he's going to be stuck in LA for a while."

"Stuck in between some bleached blonde's legs?"

"Jesus, Jenna!"

"Sorry. That's it. Not another word from me."

"Look, I know you're concerned—and not just about my safety but my feelings—and I appreciate it. Really." I took a breath and steeled myself. "But I have to see where this is going. If I end up getting hurt, you have my permission to say, 'I warned you.' Deal?" I didn't know how to tell Jenna the truth—that my feelings for him were like quicksand, and the more I struggled against them, the deeper I got sucked in.

"And you know I'll be here if you need me. Anytime, for anything," she said.

"I know that." I reached out to give her a hug.

"So, wanna make it a sleepover?" Jenna perked up. "We can pig out on cheesecake and get drunk on some of that pricey booze you said he keeps around here. And then you'll fill me in on the five-star details. Just because I think you might be making a mind fuck of a mistake doesn't mean I don't want a blow-by-blow account." She grinned. "Pun fully intended."

Chapter 25

My second interview at Houdini sealed the deal. I was thrilled, of course. It was my dream job—the hottest record label around. But Mick wasn't there to celebrate with me, and every time I called to share the news, I got voice mail. I called my mom, but she didn't get it.

"Who did what?" she asked, seemingly clueless.

"Houdini, Mom. It's a record company."

"But I thought you already worked for a record place."

"I do, but..." I sighed. "Never mind."

The conversation limped along from there.

I'd been alone for two weeks, and silence had become my constant companion. But that day, as I returned from the corner bodega with Bruce, who'd assumed his post out front, I heard noises coming from the kitchen. I'd set the alarm before leaving for the store, even getting annoyed at myself for my increasingly obsessive-compulsive double-checking. Someone was rummaging around in the kitchen, humming, making no effort to be quiet. It couldn't have been Mick, who was on location somewhere in Wyoming, in the middle of nowhere. I gingerly set the groceries down, but before I had time to run out front to alert Bruce, footsteps headed my way from the kitchen. Frantic, I grabbed the wooden baseball bat Mick insisted I keep handy as a low-tech backup in case all the security systems in place failed. I'd refused his suggestion of a gun.

I positioned the bat. Visions of a head cracked open like a coconut, liquid oozing out, danced in my head, and I almost lost my nerve. But fired with adrenaline, I gathered my strength. So, this would be it—the tragic end to my stalking saga. The bat trembled in my grip, and I felt the blood leave my lips. The thumping of my heart grew louder as the footsteps approached.

A man strode through the pocket doors, earbuds in his ears, bobbing his head in time to a rhythm only he could hear while taking a bite out of a sandwich. His relaxed demeanor—and the fact that he was a he—caught me off guard just long enough for him to spot my aggressive stance.

He tossed the sandwich to the floor, ran toward me, and seized my hands, stopping me midswing. Everything happened so fast that I didn't have time to ask who he was and what the hell he was doing there. He was tall, taller than Mick. We grappled over the bat, me grunting with the effort, but the match was heavily weighted in his favor. I couldn't gain leverage, and he wrestled it from my hands. Operating on instinct alone, I swung my knee up and delivered a crushing blow between his legs. All those balancing poses had finally paid off, and I silently thanked Jenna for convincing me to take yoga with her.

He dropped the bat, fell to the floor, and curled into the fetal position, moaning as his face turned an odd shade of purple. I snatched the bat off the floor and backed away, prepared to deliver a decisive blow if he came at me again.

His eyes popped open, and he croaked, "Jesus! I have a key! I'm a friend of Mick's."

"What's your name?" I snapped. Keeping what I judged to be a safe distance, I gripped the bat more tightly.

"Shane. Shane Dwyer," he said between moans.

His handsome face came into focus. No, he wasn't handsome. He was pretty, even with his face distorted in pain. I'd seen him before—in a movie. And in the memory files of my conversations with Mick, I found his name. I'd almost split his head wide open with a baseball bat. I most definitely kneed him in the balls. I took a tentative step toward him.

"Oh my God. I'm so, so sorry. Are you okay?"

"Does it look like I'm okay?"

"Here, let me help you up."

I extended a hand to help him to the sofa, but he was still bent in two, huffing and puffing like a woman in the advanced stages of labor. Several awkward moments passed before I withdrew my hand and waited for him to make a move. When the color in his face faded to rose pink and his breathing eased, he got up on his knees then stood and shuffled over to the sofa. He was clearly pissed but curious.

"I know what I'm doing here. But who are you, and what the hell are you doing here—with a baseball bat?"

"I'm a friend of Mick's too. I'm staying here temporarily."

"A friend, huh?" He managed a smirk.

I chose to ignore his comment. "Mick didn't tell me anyone else had a key... and the code to the alarm."

"He probably forgot. I haven't let myself in since last year."

"Are you feeling better?"

He seemed to be sitting a little straighter and breathing a little easier.

"Can I get you a beer?"

"Yeah, maybe it'll help dull the pain."

I nodded and headed to the kitchen.

"Hey, do you know when Mick is coming into town?" he yelled into the kitchen. "I need to talk to him."

"No. Sorry. He's on location in Wyoming somewhere. Why don't you just call and ask him? The reception there is terrible, but you can give it a shot."

"You an actor?"

"No." I laughed at the thought.

"So how do you know Mick?"

"It's a long story."

As I walked back into the living room with his beer, he was patting the empty space next to him on the sofa. "I've got time." He seemed to be recovering nicely.

My cell phone rang. It was Mick.

"Hey, Rach. Everything okay there?"

"You've got company."

"Shit. I was just about to text you."

"You didn't tell me anyone else had the alarm code and a key. I almost busted his head open with that baseball bat!"

"Bruce didn't tell you he was coming?"

"Maybe he assumed I knew Shane."

Shane was hovering, motioning for me to hand over the phone.

"Here, he wants to talk to you."

Shane wandered into the dining room, talking animatedly with Mick about a script, a movie, a part, and their agent, whom they evidently shared. He was standing a couple of feet from the mirror on the wall, intently watching his own reflection, arranging his hair, and turning his head from side to side as he talked on the phone.

When he hung up, he strolled to the kitchen to get another beer as I sank into the sofa and tried to calm my still-irregular heartbeat. On his way back, he stopped and leaned against the doorframe, looking more relaxed by the minute, and took a swig.

"So, how long have you and Mick been friends?" I asked. "Are you from Louisiana?"

"Louisiana?" He scoffed. "Me? Nope. California born and raised. Mostly San Francisco. We met through Randy, our agent, about six years ago. Even shared an apartment for a while. Could barely scrape the rent together, between the two of us." He stopped and took another swig. "Did he ever tell you about the eighty-six Chevy Impala we went in together to buy?" He snorted at the memory. "It was all we could afford, but we spent more on repairs in the first six months than the car cost."

"He's told me a little about his prefame days. I get the impression he actually misses it."

"I'm not sure I buy into that line. He wasn't exactly thrilled eating ramen noodles for dinner every night back then."

That image of Mick, broke and eating cheap packaged food, fit. "Speaking of, would you like me to make you a replacement sandwich?" I stood and began cleaning up the messy aftermath of my near head bashing.

"Yeah, that would be great." He took my place on the sofa, crossed his ankle on his knee, and spread his arm across the back cushions. "I'm starving."

"Coming right up." I disappeared into the kitchen and looked at the sandwich fixings he'd left out on the counter.

Lots of young girls probably had Shane's picture hung on their walls and would happily have traded a few years of their lives to be in my place. I just wasn't one of them. My thoughts shifted to Mick and how different he was from Shane. I picked up the knife Shane had been using.

"You look happy." He was standing in the kitchen doorway.

Startled by his voice, I jerked, cut myself with the knife, and dropped it on the floor. I grabbed my finger as blood dripped all over his pastrami on rye.

"Let me see," he said as he stepped forward and held my hand, examining it. "It's a small cut, but it's gonna be a bleeder." He set his beer on the counter and ripped off a paper towel. "Here, wrap this around it and apply some pressure, like this. It'll stop after a while."

His first-aid demonstration lasted longer than necessary, and he was inching closer. I hadn't noticed before, but he had a heavy hand with the cologne.

He leaned even closer—too close. He had pinned me against the counter. "So, how much of a 'thing' are you and Mick?" he crooned. His warm beer breath in my face triggered my gag reflex.

I ducked under his arm, leaving him to deal with his bloody sandwich. "Make it yourself." And I turned to head to my apartment upstairs.

"Jesus, what's your fucking problem?" he called after me. "Anyway," he shouted, sounding as though he'd somehow been wronged, "you're not that hot!"

I heard him slide his beer off the counter and head back to the sofa sans sandwich as he mumbled a string of profanities that would've relegated my father to amateur status. Unsure what had just happened, I wondered if I'd misinterpreted his actions. Or maybe I'd somehow emitted an unintentional signal, a sound wave only dogs and horny men can hear.

My cell rang. It was Mick again.

"Hi."

"Hey, listen, I wanted to give you a heads-up—I told Shane he could stay there for a couple of nights."

Unsure how to respond, I hesitated.

"What's the matter? Is it Shane? What did he do?" He sounded panicky, his voice booming over the phone.

"Why didn't you warn me?"

A chilling sound like chalk squeaking across a blackboard filled the silence. He was grinding his teeth. "Tell me what happened."

"He was just being a sleaze, making me super uncomfortable. I'm up in the apartment, and he's downstairs."

"He's a moron. All his brains are crammed in his dick, and he has trouble thinking straight most of the time." He exhaled—an exasperated sound. "Shane has helped me out, and I owe him big-time, but he's a super dick where women are concerned. I told him you were with me. I thought if he knew, he'd leave you alone." He paused for a second. "I guess I thought wrong."

"He actually asked me how much of a 'thing' we were," I said.

"I'll call him now and tell him he's going to have to find someplace else to stay—and to leave his key. Shit... I'm really sorry."

The next morning, I woke with a start and glanced at the clock. I'd overslept. The previous day's encounter with Shane had eclipsed everything, including Jenna's return visit that morning. I bolted out of bed, dressed, brushed my teeth, clipped my hair up, grabbed my cell phone and my book, said good morning to Bruce, and planted myself on the stoop. It was one of those hot, humid, and hazy New York days that made me want to straddle a subway grate and wait for the delicious rush of hot air. But I needed to catch Jenna before she buzzed the main floor and was greeted by the blue-eyed slime bucket, who hadn't seen fit to leave just yet.

At ten fifteen, I called Jenna's cell. No answer. I left a voice mail.

At ten thirty, I sent a text: *Where R U?*

At ten forty-five, I called Jenna's house. Her parents said she'd left on time. Maybe the trains were delayed.

At eleven, I made another call and sent another text message.

Has Jenna been mugged? Has she gotten stuck on the subway? Run over by a cab? It was almost noon, and still no Jenna.

Bruce was patrolling up and down the block. I'd told him to expect her. "Bruce, have you seen my friend Jenna?"

"Yeah, she went in a couple of hours ago."

Confused, I glanced into the parlor. The reason for Jenna's delayed arrival was right there in the window, making out with her, whispering in her ear, copping one last feel.

Jenna looked ecstatic.

Chapter 26

Shane ignored Mick's request to leave right away. He finally took off, but only after sleeping with Jenna twice more. She spent more time downstairs with Shane over the next couple of days than she did with me. While Shane's encounters with Jenna were imperceptible blips on his radar, she was already picturing herself as his date for the Oscars.

"Shane said he would buy me a ticket to LA and show me around and help me make some connections. Can you believe it?"

I tried to put things into perspective for her, but her behavior pattern was deeply entrenched and hard to break. She couldn't see the duplicity of her advice to me about Mick and her own behavior with Shane.

"Jenna, listen to me. I don't want to burst your Shane bubble, but he's a dick. I don't think you sleeping with him was a good idea. At all."

"You're sleeping with Mick! What the hell is the difference?" she yelled at me.

The difference? Shane hid behind an uncommonly beautiful face that, if you didn't look too closely, projected a kind of childlike innocence—a well-honed specimen of misogynistic meanness. Mick had his faults, but he was nothing like Shane. Jenna just couldn't see it—not yet anyway. She left for New Jersey in a huff.

While finishing up my work for Sisyphus and the anticipation of my job at Houdini helped to overshadow my stalker paranoia, another concern was vying for my anxiety. As the days passed, the knot in my stomach tightened in direct proportion to the decreasing frequency of Mick's calls and messages. By the time I'd marked six long weeks off the calendar, our flood of communication had dwindled to a fraction of what it had been. Every time I called, either he couldn't talk, or my call would go directly to voice mail. When he first left, he was texting me several times a day. That had dropped to once a day then every couple of days, at most. And they weren't the love notes I'd become accustomed to. *Last night's shoot wrapped up at three. Dead on my feet. Any updates from the police? It snowed last night. Another delay.*

I needed a reality check. The doubts I was certain I had vanquished reappeared, cozied up next to me, and, like mean girls at school, whispered with great satisfaction in my ear, "See, I told you it wasn't real."

I thought back to how I'd so completely let down my guard in bed with him that first night. "You're not at all what I expected, Rachael." His words echoed in my head, and my insides seized with regret.

I wanted to digitize my disappointment so that if I ever got the notion that our time together actually meant something, I could play it back. On a sixty-five-inch screen. With surround sound. This was what I always did—getting involved with men who were emotionally shredded, ensuring that things were doomed from the start. Sometimes, I thought I learned nothing from all those meetings at Adult Children of Alcoholics that my mother had coerced me into attending. Maybe I needed to start going again and relearn how to counteract my self-sabotaging tendencies. But their "lessons" always ended with me blaming my father's drinking for my poor decision-making skills. I couldn't keep shifting responsibility for my bad life decisions onto him. He'd managed to turn his life around. I needed to do the same.

So I guessed I was going to celebrate my twenty-fifth birthday alone, with Jenna pissed at me and death threats from the stalker still looming. The funeral wreath and the "suicide basket" had been the cherries atop my sickening stalker sundae.

I couldn't very well tell my parents about Mick and me without huge blowback—I wasn't even sure if there was anything to tell about us anymore.

I kicked off my pity party by going down to Mick's office. It was the only room that was one hundred percent him, untouched by a decorator's hand. I needed his proxy presence to bring everything into focus. As I scanned the cluttered room, I made my way over to his desk and slumped down in his chair. I picked up a half-empty pack of cigarettes, pressed it to my nose, and inhaled the familiar ingredient of his peppery scent. It struck a particularly sharp chord of melancholy. I spotted the photos of him still propped up against the wall, the ones I'd noticed when I came down to look at the security video. That felt like a lifetime ago. I plodded over to the corner and picked one up, trying to soak up every nuance of his expression. I could almost feel the warmth of his body, his arms around me, his lips pressed to my neck, his fevered breath on my skin as he whispered my name. I closed my eyes.

"Rachael?"

I swung around, dropping the framed photo and cigarettes on the concrete floor. The glass shattered, and the cigarettes spread like Pick-Up Sticks over his image. He was standing on the stairs.

"Oh my God! You scared the crap out of me!"

"Sorry."

Now that he was there, in the flesh, I felt that starter culture of need fermenting, bubbling to the surface, and I was furious with myself for wanting him. Struggling to cling to my anger, I stood frozen in place, as much out of shock at his unexpected appearance as from the certainty that I could easily, willingly be sucked into the Mick

Sullivan vortex again. He walked over to me as casually as if he'd just gone out for the paper and come waltzing back a few minutes later.

Standing in front of me, he wrapped his arms around my shoulders and rested his chin on my head before he gently lifted my face up, kissed me hello, and whispered, "God, I missed you."

With those four words, I understood—he was a long-term affliction that would require constant monitoring and palliative care. He kissed me, I kissed him back, and with little fanfare, we christened his office.

Naked, lying on his well-worn sofa, I glanced at him, acutely aware that if he reached out for me again, I wouldn't hesitate.

"So, what are you doing here?" I asked.

"What? I can't just come to see you?"

"Please. You have to be here for something... an appearance, an interview, a meeting, a shoot?"

He laughed. "None of the above. I scored some time off, and I thought I'd surprise you."

"Oh."

"Don't sound so excited," he said with mock indignation. "I thought from the depressed look on your face when I walked in, you'd be a little more enthusiastic. Looked like my picture wasn't quite doing it for you." Grinning as he stared at the ceiling, he sounded smug. Or maybe pleased that he'd been missed?

"How about we order some takeout?" he asked as he rolled toward me, cupped my breast in his hand, and gave it a gentle squeeze and a kiss before he stood. "I'm gonna take a quick shower. Join me?"

He left his clothes piled on the floor and headed up the stairs. It struck me that he always looked relaxed and natural in the nude, as if being fully clothed were the exception rather than the rule.

After showering, I was in the bedroom, getting dressed, and Mick was shaving when the front door buzzed.

I shouted to him, "I'll get it!" and ran upstairs.

The image on the monitor indicated no paparazzi lurking in the background. It wasn't the usual delivery person—it was a woman wearing a knit cap, standing on the stoop with a bag of Chinese food in her hand. Her bicycle was parked near the curb, leaning against a tree, so I turned off the alarm and opened the door.

As she handed me the bag, she eased up onto her tiptoes, trying to look over my shoulder and peer inside.

My stomach clenched. "Thanks."

I quickly handed her a tip and slammed the door harder than intended, reset the alarm, and brought the food into the dining room, where Mick was putting plates on the table. He hated eating out of take-out cartons. It reminded him of past struggles he wanted to forget.

"Man, that smells good. I didn't realize I was so hungry. Any paps out there?"

"No, but it was weird. That wasn't the usual delivery guy. It was a woman. I don't think I ever remember them using women."

He shrugged, pushing his still-wet hair away from his face. "Did you give her a decent tip?"

"I worked as a waitress, remember?"

"So, serve me!" He sat down with chopsticks in both hands and began pounding the table.

"Where's *my* tip?" I teased.

"That comes *after* the meal." He cocked one eyebrow.

"Oh God, you remind me of Shane when you do that," I said as I let loose an exaggerated shiver.

"Sorry." He reached out to me with open arms. "Come here."

I sidled next to him, and he pulled me down on his lap. His body temperature always seemed a couple of degrees warmer than normal, and that night was no exception.

With his lips pressed to my neck, he murmured, "I really did miss you, you know. I'm sorry I didn't keep in touch much, but those twelve- and fourteen-hour days were killers. And the director was a real hard-ass about not having cell phones on the set."

We sat down to eat, and I pushed my mu shu chicken around on the plate, eating a few bites. He polished off his regular order of Mongolian lamb. When he was finished, he reached in the bag and retrieved a single fortune cookie. "Let's see what the future holds, and then I'm ready to crash."

"What, only one cookie?" I asked.

"Here, you can have the honors." And he presented it to me with open palms.

I ripped open the wrapping, cracked the cookie, pulled out the strip of paper, and read it to myself. "I love these things. I hope whoever writes them never uses proper English."

"What does it say?"

Something wonderful is about to happy.

He laughed as he stood, reached out, and pulled me in the direction of the stairs.

"Can't argue with that."

Chapter 27

When I stirred the next morning, *joyful* was the word that came to mind. Mick was lying on his side, his back to me. I watched the slow, rhythmic up and down of his shoulders, a warm and welcome contrast to the previous night, when he thrashed in his sleep and jerked awake, sobbing, and screamed Shane's name with such intensity that it stunned me. A full week lay ahead of us, plenty of time to find the right moment for him to open up about his fitful nights that, up until then, he'd insisted were just bad dreams destined to remain incomplete and irretrievable.

I curled up behind him, kissed his back, and breathed in the lingering scent of sex—the scent of us. He reached around and took my hand, cradling it to his chest, and mumbled in his raspy morning voice, "Happy birthday, Rach."

He remembered.

My utter contentment shattered when a powerful wave of nausea grabbed me and refused to let go. I bolted upright, clamped my hand over my mouth, and sprinted from the end of the bed into the bathroom, slamming the door shut. I made it just in time, noisily losing Chinese takeout from the night before. That was the only time I was happy about Mick's irritating habit of leaving the toilet seat up.

He yelled through the closed door, "Rachael? Are you okay?"

"Ugh," I croaked from the other side. "I think that food last night was bad."

"You want some tea or something?"

"Maybe tea."

I heard him jump out of bed, slip on his jeans, and make his way upstairs to the kitchen. I stood to check out my sickly reflection in the mirror—bloodless lips, beads of sweat glistening along my hairline, and my hands shaking like a junkie's in desperate need of a fix. I slinked down onto the bathroom floor.

Shit! Is this how I'm going to spend our time together? Getting over food poisoning?

My anger and disappointment almost drowned out the churning in my stomach. I pulled myself back up and caught another glimpse of my reflection. *Night of the Living Dead* came to mind. I grabbed a washcloth from the rack, soaked it in cold water, and patted my face, lingering on my forehead. I brushed my teeth and swished some mouthwash. My stomach seemed to be settling down, but I was still unsteady. I dressed, clipped my hair up, did a final quality check in the mirror, and shook my head in disgust before making my way upstairs.

Mick was standing in the kitchen, a mug of hot water in one hand and a tea bag in the other, as though clueless how the two fit together.

"How long should the bag stay in the water?"

"Three or four minutes is good."

He dropped it in. "You sure you're okay? You don't look so good."

"It'll pass. I'm sure it's that chicken from last night. I shouldn't have eaten it. It smelled funny."

He shrugged and handed me the mug. "It smelled fine to me, and besides, you hardly ate anything."

My stomach was cramping, and I was tired, like my-bone-marrow-had-been-sucked-dry tired. Once before, I'd had food poisoning that lasted for three godawful days. During the worst of it, I would've welcomed death. I did a quick mental calculation. I still had time for a recovery and a few good days to spare before Mick headed back to the other coast. I wrapped my hands around the mug to soak up its warmth, took a sip, and scrunched my nose.

"More sugar?"

"No. I thought tea might help, but I don't think it's such a good idea right now. Maybe apple juice?"

"I don't see any," he said, poking around in the double-wide refrigerator. "I'll run down to the corner and get some."

"No, it's okay. I'll be fine."

"Go lie down. I'll be back in a few minutes."

He dressed and was out the door in record time. I peeked out the window. He was instructing Bruce to stay put. Mick's hands were shoved into his pockets, and despite the warm weather, a hood covered his bowed head. His shoulders were shrugged to his ears, and sunglasses hid most of the rest of his face. A lone, intrepid paparazzo loitered across the street, snapping shots. *Of what? His nose?* With or without his face in full view, the headline would've been a real grabber: "Mick Sullivan Buys Apple Juice!"

There it was again—the queasiness surging and receding in waves. I dashed back downstairs to the bathroom. *This isn't fair.* My father's words squirmed to the surface from the darkest corners of my brain: *"The key to contentment, Rachael, is accepting the fundamental unfairness of life."*

Thanks, Dad.

When Mick returned, apple juice in hand, I was still hugging the toilet. He tentatively knocked on the door. "Rach, maybe we should go to the doctor. You could get dehydrated."

"No. It's starting to pass."

"Shit, you're stubborn. You don't seem okay to me. If you're still puking by this afternoon, we're going to the emergency room."

I had a clear vision of the circus that would become. "Mick Sullivan in the ER!" Every event, large or small, crystallized into an imagined tabloid headline. When the nausea felt like it had faded for real,

I stood, steadied myself, and opened the door. Mick was sitting on the edge of the bed, anxiously strumming his fingers.

"Whoa, you're chalk white. You should lie down."

For the first time, I didn't want him next to me. Too drained to want to do anything but sleep, I crawled back into bed. He tucked me in and leaned over to kiss my forehead.

"Go away," I muttered, waving him away. "I smell like vomit." And I drifted off into a murky sleep.

The afternoon sun peered through the windows, warming my cheeks. I glanced at the clock. Four hours had passed? I felt better. In fact, aside from the taste of roadkill in my mouth and the gnawing hunger pangs, I felt healed—that feeling of near weightlessness when the veil of illness has lifted. After easing myself up off the pillow, I lowered my bare feet to the floor. The vibrations of music penetrated the floorboards. He was downstairs in his office.

A shower, a change of clothes, something in my stomach, and I would be as good as new. Maybe the week was salvageable after all. After washing away the remnants of the best-if-forgotten morning and getting dressed, I went into the kitchen and opened a can of tomato soup—a get-well culinary custom handed down from my mother. It worked its magic.

Feeling better by the minute, I made my way down the stairs to the basement and found Mick strumming his guitar, his headphones on, singing to himself, his back to the staircase. A lit cigarette maintained a delicate balance on the edge of his desk, the rising stream of smoke encircling his head. He was wonderfully tousled. I came up and tapped him on the shoulder, and he jumped midlyric.

His lips slid into an easy grin as he turned to face me, pulled the earphones down around his neck, and gave me a quick kiss. His five-o'clock shadow prickled my face at two in the afternoon.

"So, you decided to join the land of the living? You've got some color back in your cheeks. Think the worst is over?"

"I hope so. That was nasty." I took a breath and held my hand over my nose. "Mick, maybe it's just me, but it really stinks down here. Is it okay if I open the window and air it out a little?"

He laughed. "You're not the first person to point that out. I'll get it." He removed his earphones, set down his guitar, and walked over to the window to open it. "Better?" He came back, took the last swig of his beer and one last drag on his cigarette, and dropped the butt into the empty bottle.

"It will be," I said. "What are you doing?"

"I might have a chance to write a couple of songs for a movie soundtrack. I was working on some ideas."

"Really? That's amazing!"

"Well, it's not a done deal. The suits have to work out the details, but I'm hoping it'll come through. Don't tell Gracie, but I've actually been thinking that once my current contracts are up, I might toss the acting and focus on music for a while."

"Seriously?"

"It could all disappear right now, and I'd be fine with it. Better than fine. Don't get me wrong. It's been great, and it's made me a stupid amount of money, but... I can't see myself still doing the acting thing ten or twenty years from now."

He'd succumbed to few trappings of the rich, making it easy to overlook his obscene wealth. The yawning gap in our social statuses was clear, but somehow, I hadn't given much weight to the light-years' distance in our financial situations. It felt like another relationship obstacle I'd failed to take into account.

"It's like everybody wants something from me, you know?" he said, continuing the thought. "Randy, Gracie, Steve, and about a dozen other people whose names I can't even remember are always clamoring for my time, for my money, for a piece of me. It's not what I thought I was signing up for. If I stick with it until I'm, like, forty, there seriously won't be anything left of me. And the fucking hilarious part is that they don't give a shit about me. Not really. Okay, maybe Gracie. But that's it. I could croak tomorrow, and they'd mourn the loss of income, but there's a gang of twenty-something guys getting boners just thinking about taking my place on their client lists."

He laughed as he pulled another cigarette out of the box. "Did I just say all that out loud?"

"I... I didn't realize you felt like that."

"Yeah, well, it's not happening anytime soon."

He hastily changed the subject. "Listen, Rach, I read that there's going to be a meteor shower tonight—the Orionid. It shows up every October around this time. I thought we could go up on the roof and try to watch it from there. It's probably a lost cause because of the city lights, but if there's a lot of activity, we might catch a glimpse of a shooting star or two. Maybe bring a little wine? It's supposed to start around midnight. You might even be able to count it as our first date." He winked at me.

At eleven o'clock, we brought blankets, some music, a bottle of wine, and a couple of Styrofoam cups up to the roof. We lay on a blanket, side by side, my head nestled in that sweet spot on his shoulder, looking up at a starless sky. A warm silence settled in.

"Mick?"

"Yes, Ms. Allen?"

"Do you think that woman is still out there, watching us? I mean, there haven't been any threatening messages for a while. Maybe she's moved on to something or someone else?"

"I've been wondering the same thing. But I think it would be a mistake to assume she's done. She could be checking us out every time we walk out the door and just hasn't made contact lately."

"That's a creepy thought, but yeah, I guess you're right."

He kissed me where my shirt had slipped off my shoulder, his breath warm and moist with red wine. I glanced up and spotted a lone shooting star making its way across the midnight sky.

"Mick, look!"

The trail it left behind was visible even through the glare of the city lights, and I wondered how long it would last before it burned itself out.

Chapter 28

I kicked off the next day with another frantic dash to the bathroom and a replay of my ghostly image in the mirror. When Mick insisted on a trip to the emergency room, I didn't argue, though I tried and failed to convince him to stay in the car to avoid the inevitable scene. The shutter click of cameras was the first thing to greet us as we made our way to the ER entrance, with Mick's arm encircling my waist. The intrusion on his private life barely registered with him. Aside from the humiliating video of the two of us, which even he said crossed the line, his philosophy about paparazzi was one of if not acceptance then a fatalistic acknowledgment of his powerlessness to change the situation.

The emergency waiting room was a zoo, noisy and crowded—humanity at its lowest point, all against the backdrop of an outdated and depressing decor. And that uniquely unpleasant hospital smell was making my stomach churn. I took a seat in one of the deceptively welcoming bright-yellow chairs as Mick sauntered up to the counter. Every cell phone in the ER was aimed at him except for the receptionist's. Like Mick, she seemed to have mastered the art of ignoring chaos.

"Excuse me, my girlfriend is sick, and I need someone to take a look at her."

The woman behind the counter never looked up.

"Patient's name?"

"Rachael Allen."

"Your name?"

"Mick Sullivan."

She chuckled and raised her head, clearly expecting someone who had the good fortune—or bad, depending on your perspective—of having the same name as a well-known actor. But the expression on her face when she saw Mick standing there was worth the trip to the ER. He had her undivided attention. Slipping off his sunglasses, he leaned in, gifting her with a lazy smile and chatting her up like he'd bellied up to a bar and was offering to buy her a drink.

"Listen, I would really appreciate it if you could help us. You see the woman over there?" He nodded in my direction.

Everyone else turned on cue to look at me, and I felt my face redden.

"She's really not feeling great. Is there any way someone could see her right away?"

If the woman didn't close her gaping mouth, she would drool all over her shiny gold name tag. "Let me see what I can do." Without stopping to take a breath, she leaned in and whispered, "Do you think I could get your autograph and maybe a picture?"

"Sure. No problem."

She ran over to open the swinging double doors and allowed Mick into the inner sanctum. He gave me the thumbs-up as he went in. In a matter of minutes, she signaled me to follow her, and I was on my way, leaving the huddled masses waiting their turns. Mick was already in the examining room, his arms crossed, all smiles.

"Membership in the famous club does have its privileges," he said.

A nurse marched in; took my temperature and blood pressure; asked some routine questions about my medical history, my allergies, and my symptoms; and left, never glancing in Mick's direction. Another wave of nausea washed over me as a doctor walked in. That time, I was spared the actual retching.

"Hello"—he looked at my chart—"Ms. Allen and...?"

"Sullivan. Mick Sullivan."

Recognition registered in the doctor's eyes, but he said nothing. "I'm Dr. Blevins. What seems to be the problem today?"

"I've been throwing up since yesterday morning. I think it might be food poisoning. We had some takeout a couple of nights ago, and I think it was bad."

"Have you been feeling sick as well?" He turned to Mick.

"No, I'm fine. But we didn't eat the same thing."

"Ms. Allen, if you could describe your symptoms and tell me when they started..."

He scribbled in my chart as I recounted my unpleasant experiences over the previous two days. Mick was strumming his fingers on the arm of his chair, a habit that could be either endearing or aggravating. Right then, it was about to make me jump out of my skin.

"Well, it could be food poisoning. Or a virus," the doctor offered. "Any chance you might be pregnant?"

I laughed. "I hope not. We've never had unprotected sex."

"I'd like to get blood and urine samples so we can run some tests to be sure."

The nurse knocked, entered, and motioned for me to follow her. "We'll only be a minute," she said, smiling in Mick's direction. She escorted me to the bathroom then to the lab.

When I returned, Mick was immersed in his phone, reading messages, texting. "So did you provide bodily fluids?"

"Yeah." I caught my reflection in the paper towel dispenser mounted over the sink. If it were possible, I looked even paler and more drawn than I had that morning.

"Maybe he can give you something for the nausea, and in a couple of days you'll be as good as new. I swear, that's the last time we order takeout from that crappy place," he said, shaking his head.

The doctor knocked and came in. We turned in unison to face him. He looked at Mick.

"I want him to stay," I said.

"It's not food poisoning." He glanced at us both and hesitated, longer that time, as if he were a judge about to read a defendant the anxiously awaited verdict in a trial. "It's morning sickness. You're pregnant."

The blackboard of my brain was wiped clean, devoid of all coherent thought. When Mick had left the time before, condom wrappers were scattered in almost every room in the house, like candy wrappers left behind in the wake of a sugar binge.

He'd stopped drumming his fingers and was sporting an uncharacteristic wide-eyed, slack-jawed expression. *The paparazzi would have a field day with that one.* Mick had become one with the chair and was rubbing his temples in an apparent attempt to make it all go away. That morning, I'd been upset because I thought I might be screwing up our week. Now, I feared I might be screwing up our lives.

So much had happened since his last visit that I hadn't been keeping track. *But the last time I reached for that pink box under the sink was...* I counted backward. *Six weeks.* And I knew my body—every twenty-eight days, never a day more, never a day less. I was unable to take a deep breath, something I desperately needed to do.

"But we were careful."

My naive pronouncement triggered a flashback to sex education class in middle school, when I thought condoms—what the boys called "rubbers"—were made of steel-belted, tire-like material, and I couldn't imagine ever taking part, much less enjoying, what my teacher was so awkwardly describing in front of a class of giggling preadolescents. Jenna, always a step or two ahead of me, had set me straight.

The doctor smiled sympathetically. "Lots of babies are born as a result of 'careful' sex."

I tried to tune in to what the doctor was saying, but the reception was sketchy, his voice breaking up. "You'll need to make an appointment with your gynecologist for prenatal care and get an ultrasound to see how far along you are."

I eked out the words. "Oh, okay."

"Do you have any questions?" he asked.

Yeah, what the hell am I going to do now?

"No questions." I shook my head, and my gaze shifted to my feet dangling from the table like a child.

"Well, your nausea should fade at about thirteen weeks. Until then, eat small meals and stick with bland foods. Here's a prescription for prenatal vitamins to take until you can see your doctor."

He quickly scribbled something on his pad, and I reached out to take it. My hands were surprisingly steady, in contrast to the somersaults taking place in my stomach.

"Good luck."

He turned to Mick and shook his limp hand. "Nice to meet you, Mr. Sullivan."

Mick nodded and grunted in acknowledgment. The doctor left, but neither of us made a move to stand or utter the "P" word. Hospital sounds hummed outside the door, but in our room, with the walls closing in around me, the only sound was the crinkling of the paper on the exam table, amplified a thousand times as I shifted positions. We were each venturing into uncharted territory as we explored our own jumbled, anxious thoughts. I wanted to draw him over to my side of the room, have him put his arms around me, and tell me everything was going to be okay.

Like in the movies.

"Mick, aren't you going to say anything?"

He looked like he was the one who was going to throw up. "What is there to say? This certainly wasn't planned, and it isn't something either one of us wants right now." He took a deep breath. "Let's just go home," he said. "We can talk about it later."

We caught a cab and rode home in unaccustomed silence. When we opened the front door to the building, my foot landed on an envelope. I picked it up, and without speaking a word, Mick grabbed it from my hands, ripped it open, and silently read it.

"Fuck!" he growled as he crumpled the papers, tossed them on the floor, and headed to the fridge for a beer.

I picked up the crumpled papers and gingerly unfolded them. One was another photo—a sonogram of that woman's unborn child. A note read, *You have a perfect soul. He will too. Soulmates never die.*

So, not only was I pregnant, a fact that Mick clearly wasn't ready to deal with, but a crazy stalker believed Mick was the father of *her* baby. *And, oh yeah, she wants me dead.*

Happy belated birthday, Rachael Allen.

Chapter 29

When I reluctantly opened my eyes the next morning, the previous day's trip to the ER didn't feel real. But the fist of anxiety that smacked my chest signaled otherwise. In fact, I felt worse, as if the hurt and confusion had needed to cure overnight to fully form. I performed a quick self-inventory. The nausea was absent, but so was Mick. Maybe the revelation really was too much for him and he'd made a stealthy escape back to LA. If that was true, Mick wasn't who I thought he was, and no way would I go through with the pregnancy alone. I'd just started a new job and didn't have a place of my own. Telling my parents was not an option. They hadn't wanted me moving to Brooklyn in the first place. They would take the opportunity to remind me of my bad decisions where men were concerned. They didn't believe I was a twenty-four—*no, twenty-five*—year-old virgin. At least, I didn't think that's what they believed. No, their disappointment would come from my creation of an impossible-to-undo obstacle to a better life. My father had faced the same obstacle, the one that cost him his bright vision of the future. The obstacle he'd tried to drink away. *Am I recreating the same mess they made of their lives?*

I'd pieced together my family history. Twenty-six years before, my father was in the midst of studying for exams when my mother blurted the news of her pregnancy over a dinner of boxed macaroni and cheese. The plan had been for him to finish his architecture degree, then they would get married, travel, and eventually get a house and have lots of kids. But that plan was shelved because of me.

He had to drop out and take on two jobs. They simply didn't have enough time or money for him to continue his degree. My mother worked part-time at a supermarket until I came along. When they realized that whatever money she made would go to childcare, she ended up staying home with me. He gave up on his dream of becoming an architect, the other kids in their imagined future never materialized, and my father's resentment festered into an emotional boil when he got stuck in a job he hated. Drinking had dulled the sharp edges of his disappointment.

No, I couldn't tell them. I was going to have to take charge and make the hard decisions. And if Mick couldn't muster up support for me, we had no future anyway. As repugnant as the prospect was, I would end the pregnancy. I would have to ask him for money. I didn't have nearly enough squirreled away, and for him, it would be like loose change left on the nightstand. As my decision was made, I let out a single sob, a shudder, a desperate bid for air. I curled up into a ball on the bed and clasped both hands over my mouth to stifle a cry before reclaiming control. The sureness of my choice slowly ushered in a certain degree of calm. Jenna would be my support system. Our rift would be easily forgotten. She would hold my hand to help me through it, just as I'd done for her—more than once.

I forced myself out of bed and into the bathroom to dress, ready to face whatever the day held in store. As I stared at myself in the mirror, my features melted away like wax on a burning candle, creating a messy puddle of emotions.

I heard noises coming from upstairs. So Mick hadn't run away after all.

We would have "the talk." Better to be done with it—quick and exquisitely painful. I washed my face, brushed my teeth, slipped on one of Mick's T-shirts, and made my way up the stairs to the kitchen. Climbing the steps to the gallows would've been easier. When I arrived at the top, Mick was sitting at the kitchen island, wearing only jeans and his glasses, reading the news on his phone and drinking coffee. He flashed a smile as though the previous day's events were long forgotten, divorced from today.

"Good morning! I see you finally decided to drag your lazy ass out of bed." He laughed, put down the phone, removed his glasses, and came over and kissed me. "You want some coffee?"

"No... the thought gets my stomach churning again."

"Oh. Sorry. No coffee. So how are you feeling?"

"I'm fine. Listen, Mick, I think—"

"Rach, let me talk first. Look, I was a real dick yesterday. So I'm apologizing to you"—he gently placed a hand on my stomach—"and whoever is in there for the way I acted. It was a knee-jerk reaction, and I'm sorry. I'm an asshole. Actually," he added with a grin, "I'm sorry I'm an asshole. Yeah, a sorry asshole—that's me."

I was dizzy, trying to adjust to his sudden about-face. "So what are you saying?"

Then he asked the question that was rattling the bars of the cage inside my head. "Do you want to keep the baby? I mean, you're the one who's going to have to go through the whole pregnancy thing."

"I'm not thinking about the pregnancy. I'm thinking about a baby, a child. Is that what you want? Are you really ready for that?"

He hesitated and sat back down. "No, but ready or not, it's here."

I backed off and began pacing. "Look, we haven't even established what our relationship is, exactly, much less if we want a child together." I was addressing the floor. If I met his gaze, my resolve would vanish. Taking a shaky breath, I forged ahead with my hastily prepared speech. "I'm thinking it's not the best thing for either one of us right now. You're crazy busy with your career, and I just got my foot in the door at Houdini. I'm thinking I should end the pregnancy before it's too late. And we can get on with our lives. And, you know, less fodder for the tabloids."

"You seriously think I give a shit about the tabloids?" The flush of anger in his face made it clear I'd chosen the wrong argument to make my case.

"Okay, forget I said that. I think that's Grace's voice in the back of my head. It's kind of hard to drown it out."

He stood. The unibrow was back. "Screw the tabloids. Screw Gracie, and screw that stalker chick. Look, maybe by the time the baby comes, I can fix my schedule to where I would spend most of my time in New York." He shrugged. "Or you could move to LA with me if you'd rather do that."

"Mick, do you even hear what you're saying? Once the baby gets here, there's no turning back. No matter what happens between us, we would always have a kid together. I don't think you've really thought this through."

"Yes, I have. I was planning to ask you to move in for real, make this a permanent arrangement, make our relationship 'official.' It's the reason I came out here—well, that and your birthday—but your head was someplace else that first night. Then you were so sick I thought I should wait." He sighed loudly. "I'll admit I wasn't expecting a baby as a part of the deal. I never thought I even wanted kids, but now that it's happened, I can't imagine getting rid of it. Can you?"

My initial reaction was equal parts astonishment and apprehension. *Live together for real? Have a baby together? Would my parents be able to accept Mick? What's going to happen with the stalker? With my job?* At some point, we would have to deal with them and more.

"I don't know, Mick... This is... Are you sure?"

"No." He laughed, dragging his fingers through his hair as if that would help him think more clearly. "But I would never be sure. Making big, life-altering decisions is not my strong suit. I tend to just fall into things—decisions by default—and it looks like this baby will follow the same pattern. But I am sure of one thing," he said as he reached out to tug on a tendril of my hair, his voice receding to a rumble. "I want us to be together."

"But what if this is a mistake?"

He cradled my face in his hands, tracing my jawline with the fingers he always complained were too long, too slim, too feminine. The calluses from the constant friction of guitar strings against his fingertips felt familiar, reassuring, seductive even. He smiled down at me. "Rach, I told you, I don't believe in mistakes, and even if I did, this—you and me—wouldn't be one of them. You're the opposite of a mistake."

He was saying all the right things, and he clearly wanted us to be together, but he hadn't said, 'I love you.' Maybe his love language didn't include those words. Anyway, actions speak louder than words.

Right?

Chapter 30

We decided to shelve any further discussions about the fuzzy concept of the future until he returned from LA in a few weeks—time oddly unmarred by the stalker's threats. We talked and texted several times a day. Sometimes, it was mundane. *It's pouring rain, so I'm just sitting in my trailer, reading.* Other times, it was deep, pondering life questions. *Our lives are really going to change in ways we haven't even thought of yet.* Clearly, we were both excited and a little scared about what was to come. So when he arrived from the airport a little after midnight one night, we crawled into bed and stayed up talking until three in the morning. I'd stopped trying to crack the code on my life and was going with what felt right. By the time we finally fell asleep, my belief that we could really make a life together work had begun to gel. *Me, a mom, and Mick, a father?* The idea seemed unreal, but it was as real as it could get.

While he was trying to catch up on sleep the next morning before heading into the city for a meeting, his cell phone rang. The caller ID said it was Shane. A ripple of revulsion ran through me. I was in no mood for Shane's egomaniacal tendencies, but I knew he would keep calling until someone answered, and I wanted to spare Mick the annoyance. I grabbed the phone and hurried upstairs to the kitchen.

"Hello, Shane," I said in a monotone. "Mick is asleep."

"Listen, can you just tell him thanks for passing *Pale Whisper* on to me? Supposed to sign the contracts this week."

"What? I thought Mick had that part. He told me he was supposed to start shooting soon."

"He was, but I saw the script, and it was perfect for me. That's why I needed to talk to him when I was there before. I knew he wouldn't give a shit one way or the other, and he hadn't officially signed on yet, so he did me a solid. Anyway, tell him to give me a call. Thanks, Rach."

I hated that he called me Rach, but I loved *Pale Whisper*. Mick had been slated to play that part when I first met him, and he'd been so looking forward to the job. He was being way too generous with his skeevy friend. I couldn't think of anything to say that didn't sound pissy.

"No congratulations?" he goaded. "You're not still holding it against me just because I fucked your friend, are you?"

His self-assured tone was enough to trigger a stroke. It wasn't even worth the effort to conjure up a comeback.

"Goodbye, Shane."

"Wait!" he said. "Okay, so you think I'm a dick. That's fine. But just so you know, Mick is no saint either. I could tell you stories that would make that straight hair of yours kink up in knots."

"Shut up."

"So you think when he comes to LA, he sits around scribbling your name in his notebook? Man, you're naive. I'm sending a video from last week when he was here. Watch it and see if you still think I'm the dick."

I threw the phone down, alternating between fury at Shane and dread over what he was threatening to reveal. The surety of our relationship that I'd experienced the night before softened, becoming more malleable, and that feeling of nauseating uncertainty I thought I'd finally conquered was creeping up yet again, my mind racing with crushing possibilities.

I heard the ding of a message on Mick's phone. If I clicked on the link, would I be detonating a bomb that would blow up our newly laid life plans? Whatever it was, I was certain it was something I didn't want to know. But I *had* to know.

The video was hard to make out at first. A blur of writhing, naked bodies, accompanied by a soundtrack of primal moans. One guy and two girls, trying every combination and position.

When you learn something you don't want to know about someone you love, there's a protective delay, a laying down of insulation, as you reluctantly process the information. I stared at the screen as everything I thought I knew about Mick was stripped away. He was in a nondescript hotel room with two very flexible women, one with water-balloon breasts.

Shane's smoky voice in the background cheered him on. "Fuck her good, Mick."

My stomach was sick, almost as sick as my heart. *Is this Shane's idea of revenge? Are we even now?* It didn't feel like even. It felt like the opposite of even.

Mick suddenly emerged from the bedroom, still sleepy eyed and wrinkled from his nap. "Who was that?"

"Shane."

He looked different to me. The characteristic arch in his eyebrow now appeared arrogant rather than surprised. His seductive half smile had become a dismissive sneer. The realization hit me with a breathtaking force. He was simply a more palatable version of Shane. I was too numb to be devastated. I started the video again and shoved the phone in his face.

At first, he laughed. "What is this?"

He rubbed the sleep from his eyes as he grabbed the phone and held it at arm's length to bring it into focus. I watched as recognition registered on his face.

"What the f—Wait, this is my phone. How did you get this?"

"Does it even matter? I'm exhausted, Mick. No, I'm past exhausted. I can't do this anymore. I thought I was up for it—I *so* wanted to be—but I seriously can't deal with all the crap that goes along with your life."

I'd been delusional to think I could accept the long absences, the adoring fans, his "Gang of Five," the stalker—and now, it would seem, other women. I would have to focus on rebooting my pre-Mick optimism and getting on with my life.

Choking on a slurry of anger and pain, I turned to leave the room.

He seized my arm, holding me in place. "*Jesus*, Rachael, this was before I even met you!"

"Shane said—"

"Fuck. What did he tell you?"

"What do you think? He said this is what you've been doing when you're in LA."

"He knows that's a fucking lie. He took the video, and he went in after me."

I slapped my hands over my ears and squeezed my eyes shut. "I don't want to hear this."

"Look, we were both wasted."

"Oh, well, why didn't you say so? That explains everything." My voice cracked as hot tears ran down my cheeks. "I guess I got upset for nothing."

"Rachael, that was years ago. I swear there's been nobody but you since we hooked up."

"So that's what this has been to you, a hookup?"

"You know that's not what I meant. You're twisting my words."

The video was still running, and I felt a fresh sting of betrayal.

"I don't believe you," I said, shaking my head. "Even if I did, who is this person in the video? I don't know him."

"Look, my past is done, baked, burnt to a crisp, whatever. Was it stupid? Yeah. Colossally stupid. I'm sorry you saw this, but it has nothing to do with me now. It has less than nothing to do with us."

He was pleading "not guilty" to the charges. But "not guilty" doesn't always mean innocent. *This is the father of my child? My future?* I hated myself for loving him, for believing in him. Mick's celebrity status had always come with a get-out-of-jail-free card for his bad behavior. But I had none to offer.

"How would you feel if it were me in the video?" I demanded.

He winced.

"You just proved my point."

I was walking away, and he yelled, "Wait!"

"Wait? For what?"

"Where are you going?"

"I have to think about what's best for me and, now, for the baby. And clearly, you're not it. Not even close."

I felt as if someone else's words had escaped my lips, but as I uttered them, I knew they were true. I'd been walking a tightrope between pleasure and pain for a while, and I was about to take a tumble without a net. I wanted to slap him, spit in his face, make him feel the pain and humiliation I was feeling.

"I can't deal with your life. I... I don't know if I want to. I know I don't have to. I need time to think, and I can't do that here. I'm going to pack and go to my parents.'" I didn't realize the decision was made until the words burned my tongue. "And Bruce is coming with me." It wasn't a request.

"What? For how long?" he asked, pinched panic in his voice.

I was not going to be swayed. Not this time. I had to extricate myself from his life and get on with my own.

"You're leaving me? You can't be fucking serious—over something that happened years ago—that Shane's lying about?"

"Mick, this life—your life—it's not for me. And it's not how I want to raise my child."

"You mean *our* child!" He stopped and raked both hands through his hair. "Shit, Rach, I can't believe you're really doing this." His breath caught as he pleaded with me to stay.

I was breaking his heart before he could break mine—any more than he already had. I needed to get out of there, away from him wanting me.

"Mick, I think you know I'm right. But the main thing is *I* know I'm right. And we've got time to figure out how much you want to be involved with the baby."

"Involved?"

I'd convinced myself that he was more than the sum total of a bunch of bad decisions and irresponsible behaviors touted in the tabloids. A part of me always knew that a part of him was broken—and I couldn't fix him.

My father's sage words of advice popped into my head: "Rachael, don't waste time beating your fist on a wall, hoping it will turn into a door." Words of wisdom had become his undervalued currency since he stopped drinking. But in that moment, they were worth their weight in gold. That was exactly what I'd been doing, and I wasn't going to do it anymore. As I headed to the bedroom to pack my suitcase, Mick grabbed his phone, started dialing, and headed to the kitchen. I heard him twist the top off a beer.

"Shane? You son of a bitch!"

Chapter 31

I took the train to New Jersey, but instead of going home, I hid out at Jenna's, and she soothed my battered soul with Fritos and bean dip, just like when we were fourteen and sat on her bed late into the night, debating the best techniques for French kissing, something neither of us had actually done. We'd both moved way beyond that in experience—as well as its consequences. I spilled the whole sordid story to her in a single breath and cried until I was seized with hiccups.

"Oh, Rachael," she said as she hugged me tightly. "How far along?"

"I think about ten or twelve weeks, but I have to go to the doctor to find out for sure."

"When are you going to tell your parents?"

The depth of my disappointment in Mick and in myself drowned all rational thought.

"I can't even think about that right now. I just want to survive Thanksgiving dinner." I took a breath and looked out the window. From that angle, I could see my parents' house.

"And after that?"

"I don't know. I've decided to keep the baby even though I know how impossible it will be for me to do this on my own. But I can't forgive Mick for cheating. I just can't."

"You sure he's lying? My money's on Shane being the liar in this scenario."

"Maybe they're both liars," I said, my anger building again. "I saw the video. The image is burned into my brain."

"If you weren't knocked up, I'd make us margaritas, and we could drink until he didn't matter anymore. I guess you're going to have to settle for some talk therapy." She hesitated. "Rachael, as long as I've known you, I've never seen you like this. Leaving and coming here hasn't cut the tie with him—just stretched it a bit."

"But I hate the way he makes me feel so out of control. My life is changed forever because of him, and it's going to be so much harder. I'm ashamed to admit it, but I'm struggling with myself every minute not to pick up the phone and call him."

"Yeah, love stinks." She paused a beat. "Rach, look, whatever you decide, I'll hold your hand, but you want some free advice from your flaky friend?" She scooted closer to me and wrapped her arm around my shoulders. One of her stubby pigtails, the blue one, brushed against my cheek.

"Yes, please."

"It's really pretty simple. You have to decide what hurts more, living with him or without him. Don't overthink it. Just go with your gut."

I knew my answer, but in my current state of mind, I couldn't possibly know if it was the right one.

I hid out at Jenna's place for two days until I was ready to face my parents. I wasn't going to tell them just yet, but I wanted to be sure that my pregnancy and my failed almost-relationship weren't written all over my face. I had no grand plan, but at least I no longer burst into tears, wailing each time Jenna mentioned Mick's name.

With my overnight case in tow, I walked to my house and rang the doorbell before using the key. I swung the door open, and Maggie started barking as the Thanksgiving wreath jarred loose from its nail on the door and hit the concrete, sending a tiny pumpkin rolling from the cornucopia into the crisply manicured hedges.

"Crap!" I waded through the bushes until I found it, stuffed the evidence into my purse, and hung the wreath back up.

I opened the door, surprised my mother hadn't beaten me to it, but Maggie was waddling my way. "Hey, Mags. Did you miss me?" The alarm was signaling its two-minute warning, and I entered the code to silence the beeping. The aroma of turkey, dressing, and candied yams floated into the entryway, well on their way to the Thanksgiving table.

"Rachael! You're here! Happy Thanksgiving, sweetie," my mother said as she hurried to the doorway to greet me open-armed. She stopped short as she glanced at the less plentiful cornucopia then at my suitcase. "Are you staying?"

"Yeah, for a while, anyway."

She hugged me then stuck her head into the den, where my dad was watching football. "Don, Rachael's here!"

He emerged from the den, his darkened football cave. "Hey, beautiful! Glad you decided to come see your old dad on Thanksgiving." He gave me a hug that said he'd missed me.

My mother motioned for him to get the suitcase.

"You're staying over?"

"She's going to stay home for a while," my mother announced as though she'd known it all along.

"Has something happened with that crazy woman?" my father asked as he grabbed my bag.

"A weird note or two, but everything's basically fine."

They peered over my shoulder to see Bruce sitting in a parked car in the driveway.

"Why is the driver still there? What's he waiting for?"

"That's... Bruce. He's my... bodyguard."

They both had an almost comical look of confusion and concern.

"So something *has* happened," my father said.

"No. It's just a precaution. Mick hired him a while ago. He's staying at an Airbnb down the street, and he'll come with me if I venture out."

My father shook his head in disbelief. "Jesus, Rachael."

"It's okay, Daddy. Really."

I never thought my parents' house would be the place I'd want to escape *to*, but it *was* good to be home, away from the crushing emotional drama I'd left behind in Brooklyn.

"I hope you're right." My father grabbed my suitcase. "I'll put this up in your room. Let me know when it's time to carve the turkey."

I followed my mother—and my nose—to the warm kitchen. Wrapped in her holiday apron, she bounced back and forth between the oven, the fridge, the cutting board, and the sink like a metal ball in a pinball machine. She turned to me.

"Why didn't you invite Mr. Sullivan to have Thanksgiving dinner with us?" she asked, wiping her hands on her apron.

"Mom, don't call him Mr. Sullivan. He's my age."

"Okay, so why didn't you invite Michael?"

My stomach clenched. *Don't cry, Rachael. Whatever you do, don't cry.*

"He had other plans."

"Well, that's too bad. We have plenty of food." She was giving me the once-over. "Speaking of, you look like you've put on a little weight, sweetie."

"Gee, thanks, Mom."

"Oh, don't take it that way. Maybe you're not getting enough exercise out there in Brooklyn."

"I think it's just a matter of cutting down on trips to the Italian bakery over on Court Street."

Am I going to wait until I walk in with a screaming baby in my arms before I share the news? As that image formed in my head, I willed myself not to run over and puke into the kitchen sink. I tied my own apron, adorned with turkeys carrying picket signs that read, "I'm stuffed," and started cooking up the cranberry sauce and pumpkin pies, my well-established Thanksgiving duties. My mother launched into one of her breaking news flashes, which I somehow looked forward to with equal amounts of curiosity and dread.

"Ms. Richards across the street is going to have surgery soon. Her daughter is in Europe right now, and she just found out she's pregnant," she blurted.

"Who? Diane?"

"Yes. She's not married, you know." She uttered that last sentence in a conspiratorial whisper. "Poor girl."

Maybe my mother could tell. It was probably written in bright-red letters across my forehead, Hester Prynne style, and she was relating this tidbit in an effort to get me to give it up. But she was happily basting, having shifted the conversation to the disgraceful goings-on down the street, and transitioned to the latest scandal involving my Uncle Tommy. I felt a gossip coma coming on. Within a couple of hours, the pies were baking in the oven, and the cranberry sauce was in the fridge, waiting to take its rightful place in the holiday spread. The doorbell rang just as my mother was taking the turkey out of the oven.

"Mom, are you expecting anyone?"

"No, not a soul."

"I'll get it," my father called from the den.

"Don, be sure to look and see who it is before you open the door!"

The door creaked open—then silence. I'd forgotten to reset the alarm.

"Daddy, who is it? Daddy?"

"You have company." He sounded agitated.

I wiped my hands on my apron and made my way to the front door.

"Hey! Surprise! Happy Thanksgiving!" Mick was leaning against the doorframe with one hand and holding a cigarette in the other. The scent of beer and cigarettes wafted into the house.

"He's drunk," my father proclaimed. If looks could indeed kill, Mick would have been flatlining.

"Just a few beers. After all, it's Thanksgiving!" His thick-tongued speech was making the situation worse, much worse.

"Rachael Claire, why the hell is *he* here?"

"I don't know."

"I'm calling a cab to take him back to wherever the hell he came from."

"I've got it. Please. You can go back to your football game. I'll deal with this."

My father hesitated, started to walk away, then turned to give one last devastating look over his shoulder at Mick's unsteady figure in the doorway before he retreated. Wearing only a T-shirt and jeans, Mick was shivering, his warm breath creating a smoke screen in front of his face.

"Don't just stand there! Get in here before you freeze and before someone sees you."

I grabbed the cigarette from his fingers and tossed it into the yard as if it were a live grenade.

"You're a mess," I said, more disappointed than angry. "Please tell me you didn't drive here."

"Nope. Uber. Nice guy. Gave him a fat tip. I mean, he's working Thanksgiving."

He stepped in, grabbed me from behind, and kissed me. The taste of beer was overwhelming. He'd been at it a while.

"Hey, you look kinda sexy in that apron." He gave me a slow-motion wink. "Sort of a French maid thing going on," he slurred.

"Stop it!" I whisper shouted. "My parents are in the next room." I pushed him away then grabbed his T-shirt to reel him back in before he landed flat on his back.

"Did you tell them?" he asked as he reached out to pat my stomach and missed.

"No, I haven't told them."

"Bring your dad back. I'll tell him right now."

"Shhh! Seriously? If there was ever a time *not* to tell them, this is it."

He sniffed the air. "Hey, that smells awesome. When's dinner?"

"*Jesus.* Come lie down."

I wrapped his arm around my shoulders, and we zigzagged to the living room. He sank into the sofa, a deadweight, one leg hanging off the edge of the cushions.

"What are you doing here?"

"Don't be mad," he slurred his plea. "I want you to come home. I need you."

Hearing my mother's footsteps, I pulled the daisy afghan from the back of the sofa and covered Mick with it. I'd crocheted it under my mother's tutelage when she was desperate to have me follow her example as a homemaker. He was out in an instant, already snoring.

"Is he okay?" my mother asked as she appeared in the doorway.

"Do you mind if he just sleeps it off here?"

"He's not going to be sick, is he?" Her lip kinked as she glanced around the room at her spotless wall-to-wall beige carpet.

"No, I think he's fine."

"Well..." She looked at him splayed out on the sofa, shook her head at the scene she'd witnessed time and again with my father, clicked her tongue, and sighed. "I'm going to need you to set the table soon." She returned to the kitchen and her Thanksgiving dinner preparations.

I remembered too many of those drunken nights—my father stumbling up the stairs long after bedtime; bitter, muffled voices; tears; and the morning-after acrimony. The worst memory, the one I wasn't sure I could ever truly forgive him for, was the night I was in the kitchen with Aiden, my high school boyfriend. When he was leaning in to kiss me, my father stumbled in, his breath carrying the familiar sweet stink of bourbon. His dark, bloodshot eyes zeroed in on Aiden.

"Daddy, you remember Aiden," I said in an attempt to normalize the situation.

"Aiden, huh? Well, Aiden, I think you're done here."

I wanted to dissolve into a puddle on the kitchen floor and drip down through the floorboards.

"You should go," I whispered to Aiden.

"Like hell you will!" my father said. He struggled to put one foot in front of the other in Aiden's direction.

Aiden scurried from the kitchen, and I heard the front door slam.

"I hate you," I mumbled under my breath as I turned to leave.

"Don't turn your back on me. I'm your father!"

His thick-tongued demand for respect made my skin crawl. I ran up the stairs to my room and slammed and locked the door.

"Open the goddammed door, Rachael!" He pounded his fists on the door until it ripped from its hinges and crashed to the floor. He was seething. My father had never hit me, but that wasn't my father anymore.

I curled up into a defensive position on the floor next to my bed. Downstairs, Maggie was barking furiously.

I heard my mother's frantic footsteps and her voice in my room, pleading, "Don, no. No!"

In a rare show of strength, she positioned herself between my father and me. "Get away from my daughter!" she shrieked.

There was a stunned silence then the unfamiliar sound of my father sobbing. I peered up to see my father frozen in a defeated slump, his arms slack at his sides. My mother led him away, her face drawn, her expression one of shock, disbelief, and grief.

She glanced back over her shoulder at me and commanded, "Go to Jenna's."

I darted down the stairs, scooping up Maggie along the way, and bolted over to Jenna's in the cold and the dark.

It was an ugly memory.

I sat on the edge of the sofa, looking at Mick—really looking at him. I should've been livid, disgusted, but something in his face swept away the brewing cauldron of negative emotions. He wasn't my father. He seemed far more serene than he ever did when conscious, even more than when he slept. I ran my fingers through his hair, leaned over, kissed the bridge of his nose, and held his hand, which was surprisingly warm. He'd told me that I had surprised him, but so far, my life with Mick had been a string of surprises—not the kind where everyone jumps out and yells, "Surprise!" It was more the kind where someone sneaks up behind you, jams a gun in your back and growls, "This is a stickup."

We sat down for Thanksgiving dinner, serenaded by Mick's snores from the next room.

"What's going on?" my father spat out, his face contorted into a scowl as he nodded in Mick's direction.

"I don't know, Daddy." I shrugged and stared at the fork in my hand. "I invited him and he said no, but I guess he changed his mind."

"And he shows up shit-faced?"

"Don, *really*..." my mother interjected.

"Is there something going on between you two?" my father asked.

"Nothing. Absolutely nothing." I shook my head.

Missed opportunity number two.

"I think maybe the holidays are depressing for him. But he said his mother is coming to visit over Christmas."

"Well, at least he won't be bothering us."

"I feel kind of sorry for him," my mother said.

My father's eyes narrowed as he shot my mother a look of disdain.

"What?" she said. "I'm not saying I approve of him showing up here in that condition, but maybe his life isn't all it seems. Maybe we should be a little more compassionate."

"That guy has a problem." My father hesitated before he continued, "I know what I'm talking about."

"Daddy, I—"

"What is it?" he snapped.

I wanted to tell them, but the jarring truth about my life, about Mick and me, wouldn't come out. The effort triggered a pounding headache.

"I'll fix him some leftovers when he wakes up and call a car to take him back to Brooklyn."

I felt like a snake trying to shed its skin. I wanted to slither out the door and never return.

Chapter 32

After the Thanksgiving debacle, Mick returned to the West Coast, and I took advantage of the time to sort through my tangled feelings about him, about us. If I could just lay them out like color-coded index cards, maybe I could make sense of everything and understand what I was doing. Okay, love belonged over there, lust beside it—the line between them was never very clear—joy somehow fit in there. Ah, but disappointment—it belonged in that other spot. Confusion was there, too, and distrust managed to squeeze in. But my need was the space hog, the bully on the block, pushing everything else into the background, negating all my efforts to think clearly and logically, to do the right thing. No matter how hard I tried, I always started and ended in the same place, powerless to change any of it.

So, Mick was far from perfect. That fact was clearer than ever. But his imperfections were what had ensnared me from the start. When I'd looked at him, I had seen everything I wanted. Now, when I filtered him through recent events and my parents' eyes, he became a blight on the landscape. All I knew was that I couldn't forget Shane's words and the ugly truth he'd revealed to me. And I just didn't want to feel bad anymore.

Mick left a stream of voice messages and texts. I deleted them all. Hearing his voice, seeing his words, would weaken my resolve to face facts and figure things out on my own. Just replaying his voice in my head tested my will.

Meanwhile, my father was being attentive, even solicitous: "Rachael, how about joining your dad for breakfast?" "Want to go for an after-dinner walk with me?" "What say we catch a movie?" He seemed to sense that something was churning inside me that had nothing to do with the stalker situation, which had strangely receded into the background. I appreciated his unspoken concern, but I wasn't ready to share.

Three days a week, Bruce and I were commuting into the city, to my job at Houdini, which I'd grown to love as much for the distraction as for the amazing opportunity it offered. I'd moved beyond just writing blog posts and was a vital part of the music industry, making recommendations that were taken seriously, and I was tasked with scheduling and attending meetings that I was responsible for. I even had a company credit card to use for things like taking a car service to venues and paying for catering when meetings ran long.

Though my morning sickness had faded, I fatigued easily, reminding me that a person was growing inside me and was scheduled to make an appearance in less than six months.

Over the weekend, I met Jenna at Drip for coffee, with Bruce in tow. He sat at the next table to give us space.

Jenna gave him the side eye before she asked, "So? How are you? Have you talked to Mick yet? Told your parents?"

"Screwed up, no, and no."

She sighed an extended breath. "Rachael, the clock is ticking."

"You think I don't know that?" I said, louder and angrier than intended.

Jen's eyes widened, and she opened her mouth as though to say something but then clamped it shut.

"Sorry, I'm seriously stressed out."

"Is he still trying to call you?"

"Yeah. Calling, texting. Like, a hundred times a day, but I haven't read or listened to any of his messages." I took a sip of my coffee. It no longer made me nauseated, but it was giving me heartburn.

"You're stronger willed than me. I would've listened to them and read them out loud a dozen times by now." She leaned across the table and put her hand on mine. "Rach, don't you think you should at least listen to what he has to say?"

Since when is Jenna Mick's defense attorney? I looked at her chipped purple nail polish, and it anchored me. "Maybe... I don't know. I'm afraid if I hear his voice, I'll cave."

"Well, that should tell you something right there. I know I've been in the anti-Mick camp, but the situation has changed. Big time."

After more hand-holding, coffee, and unsolicited advice from Jenna, we wandered over to the book-and-magazine section of the café. I needed something new to read on my commute.

Jenna was perusing the racks and called me over. "Rach, you need to see this."

She shoved a magazine in my face. Mick was on the cover of a glossy weekly—a candid shot of him coming out of a bar alone with the headline, "Mick Sullivan Parties Solo." My chest tightened. His sexy, disheveled look had shifted to abandoned and homeless.

"Talk to him, Rachael. I think you need to. For both of you."

Chapter 33

That afternoon, I opened my laptop. Though I'd been ignoring Mick's emails on my phone, they felt more insistent staring back at me from the computer screen.

"I'm sorry. I'm sorry. I'm sorry. I'm sorry. I'm sorry…" It seemed to go on forever as I scrolled down the page.

I clicked on another one. He'd attached an audio file of Van Morrison singing "Brand New Day." As I listened, I was back in the aisle at Zabar's, and he was slipping his sunglasses down, looking into my eyes for the first time. Then there was this message: "Rachael, I know I said there are no mistakes, but I need you to forgive me and come home." Ignoring his pleas had been so much easier and far less painful.

The ringing of my cell phone felt like an electric shock. Mick was calling for the sixth time that day. I stared at the phone on my desk for three more rings and grabbed it just before it rolled over to voice mail.

"Hey."

"Rachael? Thank God! I've been trying to get in touch with you for forever! Why haven't you answered? I didn't know if you were ignoring me or if something had happened. Are you *trying* to make me crazy?"

"I'm sorry, Mick, but it's easier this way."

"Easier? For who?"

When I didn't respond, he said, "Rach, I have to see you. I'll be back next week. Can we talk—in person?"

I needed to be smart. "Talk about what?"

"Seriously?"

I hesitated. "Okay, so let's talk."

He exhaled. "Good."

The relief in his voice was palpable. It pulled at my heart.

"I'll come and get you."

"No, that's not a good idea. Just let me know when you're back, and we can meet somewhere."

We waited out an uncomfortable silence.

"Rach?"

"Yeah?"

"How are you feeling?"

"Fine. Just tired."

"So everything's good with you and the baby?"

"Yes, everything's fine."

When we hung up, I sobbed, my shoulders heaved, and my mascara streamed down my face, streaking my cheeks. Maybe Mick really didn't believe in mistakes, but I did, and I didn't know if I was making a huge one or if leaving had been my mistake. *Am I doing this for him, for me... for us... for the baby?* My emotions were in a tug-of-war, where the loser would plunge into a swampy pit, dragging the winner in as well.

The next week, Mick called as promised and asked if I could meet him at eight o'clock, anywhere I wanted. At 7:55, I found myself pulling into the nearly empty parking lot of the Madison train station. The commuters were home by then, watching the news and eating dinner with their families, while I sat in the dark parking lot of New Jersey Transit, listening to classic rock and waiting for my ex-boyfriend, my ex-lover, my baby daddy—to do what, I wasn't exactly sure. A Cadillac Escalade pulled into the far end of the lot and stopped. My cell rang.

"Rach, I'm here. Where are you?"

 DENSIE WEBB

"Over near the ticket machine. The green Toyota."

He slowly pulled in beside me, unfolded himself from the car, and reached for the door handle of my Toyota. I felt hope rise in my throat, hope that I could forgive him, hope that he had really changed, hope that we might have a future. As he sat down in the passenger seat, the familiar fragrance of Gitanes tobacco and Ivory soap filled my head, triggering a lusty Pavlovian response and a crushing ache in my heart. Feeling nothing would have been so much easier.

He turned toward me. "Hey."

I detected the faint scent of alcohol and mouthwash, a not-so-subtle reminder of what I was running away from. He ran his fingers through his hair and fidgeted in his seat.

I gave a wan smile. "Did you have any trouble finding it?" My voice sounded foreign to me—flat and deep, as if I'd aged forty years in the past few weeks.

"GPS."

"Oh, yeah, of course." I glanced out the window at the gas-guzzler.

"Sam rented it for me." He stuffed his hands into the pockets of his leather jacket. "I'm really glad you're here. I wanted to—"

"Mick, I just wanted you to see that I'm fine and that I'll *be* fine. I don't want you to worry."

"If you didn't want me to worry, then you should have answered my calls," he said, a sharp edge tainting his voice.

"You're right. From now on, if you want to know how I'm doing, leave a message, and I promise I'll either call or text."

"But I came here because I wanted to talk… about us." He looked confused, concerned, and hurt.

The twisted knot in my stomach tightened.

"Rachael, talk to me."

"I know it's several months away, but we can talk about shared custody if you want. We could—"

"What the fuck? Shared custody? That's where we're at?"

He was so close I could feel his body heat, and I had the urge to reach out and touch him. I wanted to feel the high of being in his arms again. I put my hand on the center console to be closer. He reached out and curled his fingers around mine. His touch was wreaking havoc with my will.

"Mick, don't." I slowly pulled my hand back and gripped the steering wheel. "I'm sorry, but I can't do this."

"Rachael, I miss you. Everything that's happened—it's really messing with my head."

My heart thumped in my chest. I had to convince myself not to jump over the console to him, wrap my arms around his neck, and kiss him hard. Giving in would've been so easy. But the easy thing is seldom the right thing. I had to be the clear thinker in this situation. My baby's future had to be driving my decisions.

"Some things are unforgiveable, and what you've done... I... I think you should go."

"But I just got here, and we haven't even talked about anything."

"I've already told you how I feel, and you've told me how you feel. There's really not much else to say... is there?"

"So, what, we're done? Just like that?" He looked as though he might cry, but I couldn't be sure. I'd only seen him cry in movies.

I swallowed and gave him the most brutal response possible.

"Just like that."

Chapter 34

Insomnia set in. Every time I closed my eyes, I saw Mick. I heard him whisper my name, felt his lips pressed to mine. I was tortured by my longing for him. I sat up, resigned to another sleepless night, when my cell rang. The sound was jarring at two in the morning. I didn't recognize the number.

"Hello?"

"Rachael? It's Grace."

"Grace? What's wrong?" The distressing tabloid image of Mick flashed across my brain.

"It's Mick. He's in the hospital. He's been in an accident."

As soon as Grace uttered the words "accident" and "hospital," my head felt like it was stuffed with bang snaps all hitting the ground at once. *Has the stalker finally made good on her threats? How badly is he hurt? Was he drinking?*

"Rachael, you still there?"

"Yeah. Yeah. Is he okay?" My voice trembled, and my tears were on standby as I waited for her response.

"Broken leg, possible concussion. They're keeping him overnight for observation. I know you two are, um, having some issues, but he asked me to call."

Relief hadn't fully registered.

"What happened?"

"Car accident. Mick wasn't wearing a seat belt."

He's okay... He's okay. I repeated the words to myself like a mantra.

"Was he drinking?"

Grace knew Mick well enough to know that my question was justified. "I don't know, but he wasn't driving. He was in an Uber."

"Which hospital?"

"Rockefeller Medical. Room 405. Oh, and he's registered as Michael Abrams. You'll need clearance, so I put you on the list of approved visitors. But you should wait until morning."

Even in the hospital, with a broken leg and a concussion, he was zigzagging to avoid detection.

If sleep had been just out of reach before, now it was miles away. I checked the news online every few minutes to see if there was any mention of the accident. Nothing. I went downstairs, made coffee, and stared into space. My father's sudden appearance pulled me from my trance.

"What are you doing up?" he asked as he poured himself a cup and took a seat across the table from me, ready for conversation despite the ungodly hour.

My first impulse was to say, "Just couldn't sleep." Instead, I said, "Dad, there's something I need to tell you."

He didn't seem worried. He seemed relieved. "I'm all ears."

I made a rushed mental list of all the things I could say, the things I *should* say. What came out was "Mick is in the hospital. He's been in a car accident, and as soon as it's light out, I'm going to head into the city to see how he's doing."

He frowned and slowly set his coffee cup on the table. "Was he drunk?"

My immediate, visceral reaction was anger, defensiveness, and resentment. I grimaced in annoyance. Then I realized his question was justified. I'd asked Grace the same thing.

"He wasn't driving, but I... I don't know all of the details."

He exhaled loudly. "So why exactly is this *your* problem? I'm sure he's got an entourage to help him with anything he needs."

"Daddy, please..."

"How in the world did you find out?"

"His publicist called me."

"His publicist? Why the hell is his publicist calling you in the middle of the night to tell you he's been in an accident?"

"I think he asked her to."

He stood and stomped to the sink to empty his mug. Instead, he slammed it onto the counter and turned to face me. "Rachael, that makes no sense. What are you not telling me?"

He was backlit by the rising sun shining through the window above the sink. I was relieved that I couldn't make out his expression.

I stood and headed to the stairs. "Not now, Daddy. I can't deal with this right now."

By the time I arrived at the hospital, my anxiety was in full bloom. I was still bruised over what Shane had revealed to me, but that didn't stop me from needing to see that Mick was really okay. The automatic doors to the hospital lobby whooshed open, and a blast of icy air, even colder than the air outside, hit me. I made my way to the elevator, pushed the up button, and waited. When the elevator doors opened, a woman in a wheelchair was being escorted out, a baby in her arms. Her blond hair was askew, and she looked stressed. Understandable. *Babies don't come with instruction manuals.* A dark-haired woman walking beside her, carrying a diaper bag and flowers, looked just as overwhelmed. I was happy for her and smiled at her beautiful new baby. I only hoped that I would have people in my life who would be happy for me in a few months when I would be wheeled out, a precious newborn in my arms.

My name was on "the list," just as Grace had promised, and I made it through the protective bubble that Mick's presence required. As soon as the elevator doors opened to the fourth floor, I spotted a bodyguard standing outside Mick's room, his beefy arms crossed, scowling as if readying himself for a wrestling match. He saw me, smiled, and waved me over.

"I'm Rachael Allen."

He nodded. "Yes, Ms. Allen. I know who you are."

"How's he doing?"

"I think he's driving everyone crazy, so that's a good sign. I heard he might be released later today."

"Can I go in?"

He cocked his thick neck like I'd said something odd. "Of course."

I pushed open the door, and Mick was intently scrolling through his phone. He glanced up, and the moment he saw me, his face brightened, but he looked worn out, and not just because of the several days of scruff on his face or his unwashed hair. He was gaunt, and the dark-purple circles under his eyes suggested sleepless nights predating the accident.

"Rachael!" He tried in vain to sit up, but his casted leg was cumbersome and kept him stuck in place. "Grace told me you might be coming. Come here," he said, patting a spot on the bed beside him.

Our reunion was somehow both awkward and effortless. "How are you feeling?" I asked.

"Leg hurts, and my head has definitely felt better. Doc says mild concussion."

His phone dinged repeatedly. He ignored it.

"More importantly, how are *you* feeling?" he said.

"Good, actually." I placed my hands on my stomach. "The morning sickness has gotten much better. But my pants are getting tighter." I chuckled.

He jumped right in. "Rach, listen, we have to fix this. I swear to you Shane is lying. I can prove it to you."

He tapped on his phone and turned the screen toward me. The video started up. *He's actually going to show me that video again? He's insane.* I leapt off the bed and hugged myself, ready to bolt.

"Wait, wait. Look at my chest."

"What?" I shook my head in disbelief. "Why?"

"Look closer. There's no tattoo."

I tried to zero in on his chest and put blinders on to everything else happening on the screen.

"Remember? I told you I got that tattoo several years ago. There's no way this could be recent."

I glanced at it again before slowly turning the phone facedown on his bed as I searched for the reset button in my brain. So Shane was the liar. *Then why do I still feel sick?*

"So, then explain to me why he would do this to me, to us."

He shook his head as though trying to break loose the right words. "My relationship with Shane is complicated. No doubt, he can be an asshole. Maybe he was pissed because you didn't fall for his 'charms.' I don't know. All I know is that nothing he told you is true."

He reached for my hand. "You're it for me, Rachael. I thought you understood that."

My head believed him, but despite clear proof of his truth telling, my heart was dragging its heels. I wasn't sure which one to listen to. Mick had never done anything to suggest he was the person Shane made him out to be or that he was anything like he was portrayed in the media. And he'd tried his best to protect me from the woman who wanted me out of his life. But doubts, like weeds, can pop up even when you think you've yanked them out by the roots.

He raised my hand to his lips and kissed my palm. "Rach, please. Come back home with me."

I needed to be pragmatic and to ask for—no, demand—what I wanted. I pulled back. I cleared my throat and stood straighter. "If we're going to do this, I have one request—it's actually a non-negotiable condition."

"Anything."

"I want you to stop drinking."

He cocked his head in surprise. "What? You think I'm an alcoholic?" he asked, almost in a whisper.

"I think you drink too much, and you have a high tolerance, which is a sign you could be headed in that direction. I've seen what alcohol can do to a person, to a family, and it's not good."

He was thinking—hard.

"No drinking? At all?"

"As I said, non-negotiable."

"Wow, I've never thought about it." He placed his hands on my stomach and looked at me with such hope that my heart broke all over again. "But if that's what you want, if that's what you need to make this happen, I think I can do that."

Chapter 35

That afternoon, a cab dropped us off in front of Mick's building, with Bruce following close behind. The steps leading to the front door looked like a climb to the peak of Mt. Everest.

"You sure you can do this?" I asked.

"Sure," he said, not looking at all sure.

"Let Bruce help you."

"I got it." He handed me one crutch, and to a soundtrack of grunts, groans, and a few choice profanities, he managed to grab the railing with one hand while using his good leg, a single crutch, and his casted leg to make his way up to the top.

Winded and perspiring despite the cool temperature, he fumbled in his pocket for the key.

"It's okay. I have a key." I reached into my purse and pulled out the key, a reminder that we'd never completely severed the tie.

We went inside, and he stood by the sofa, balancing himself on crutches not quite tall enough to accommodate all six-foot-two of him.

"Are you hungry? Want something to drink?" he asked as if he were in any shape to be waiting on me. "No alcohol, I guess—for either of us." He smiled and gestured toward my stomach.

"I'm good."

"So how are your parents? Jenna?"

"They're fine. Sit down, Mick. You're going to wear yourself out."

He sat, and a few seconds passed while he caught his breath. "Have you told your parents... about the baby?"

"No. Jenna knows, though."

He exhaled. "God," he whispered, "I've missed you. You have no idea."

I sat on the sofa next to him and wrapped my arms around his neck, all the while questioning if I was doing the right thing. He pulled me in and kissed me. I rested my hand on top of his, and my body fully relaxed for the first time since I'd walked out the door, headed to New Jersey.

"So, we're good?" he asked.

I wrapped my hand around his and squeezed. "We will be."

We quickly settled into a warm, familiar routine.

A few days after my return, Mick was downstairs in his office, and I heard the sound of guitar chords. I went down and strolled over to his desk, where he was sitting, his casted leg propped on an open drawer.

The drama of the previous weeks had so consumed me that Shane's supplanting of Mick in *Pale Whisper* had slipped into the background. I still didn't understand how Mick put up with him and let him get away with everything, including almost destroying our relationship.

"Hello, mother of my child. What's up?"

"I've been wanting to ask you something. Why did you let Shane have that part?"

"*Pale Whisper?*" He gave a noncommittal shrug. "He needed it more than me."

"Don't you think he should be doing *you* favors instead of the other way around? Have you already forgotten what he tried to do to us?"

"No. I haven't, and I won't," he said evenly. "I don't expect you to understand."

"How can I understand if you won't tell me? You say he's your friend, that he's helped you out so much in the past, but he does nothing but try to sabotage you now. I don't get it."

The color drained from his face, and his breath stuttered. "Rachael, I really don't want to get into it right now."

"But I want to understand. It feels like there's something eating away at you, and I want to help," I said, determined to know the truth.

He looked up at me, his eyes darker than their usual shade of chocolate, inviting me in but at the same time issuing a warning. My heart pounded against my rib cage.

I placed my hand on his chest, taking in his thunderous heartbeat. "Mick, what is it?"

"Look," he said, struggling to lower his casted leg to the floor. With some effort, he stood and whispered, "I'm going to tell you something I've never told anyone." He sighed, and his expression slackened. "It's the only way for you to understand my connection with Shane—why I let him get away with all this shit."

His shoulders sank, and with trembling fingers, he lit another cigarette. "Okay. Here goes." He exhaled slowly, watching the smoke rise from his lips like hazy tendrils escaping a burning building. "Five years ago, Shane took the blame for something I did so I wouldn't go to jail."

"What? Drugs?"

"I wish. It was worse. Much worse." He shook his head and stared at the floor.

"How bad could it be?"

He looked up at me. I saw something unreadable in his eyes, something frightening, something I wasn't sure I wanted to understand. He blurted, "I killed someone."

The impact of his confession felt like someone had punched me in the stomach and sent me sailing across the room, bruised and gasping for air.

"Rachael, did you hear me?"

"I... I don't understand. You would never hurt anyone."

"It was an accident." His voice was small, weakened by guilt. He sank his head into his hands, grabbing fistfuls of hair as if he might yank it all out by the roots, taking the memory with it. Regret radiated off his slumped shoulders and filled the room. "I had just bought this new Porsche with the money from my first big contract. I was racing around, testing the limits like an idiot. The twisted part is I wasn't even speeding when it happened. The road made a sharp turn, I hit a patch of ice, the car fishtailed, and I had a head-on with a woman in another car." He stopped talking and stared off into space. "It happened so fast. I don't remember much." He took another drag and seemed to notice a bloodstain on the cigarette that resembled lipstick marks. He'd bitten his lip.

"She died?" I whispered.

"They said it was on impact."

"Oh my God... Oh my God. So Shane was in the car with you?"

He hesitated then nodded.

"Rachael, there's something else. I—"

"But why would he need to take the blame if it was an accident and you weren't speeding?"

"Rachael," he mumbled, not looking at me, "I was drunk. The accident probably would've happened, drunk or sober, but I'd already racked up two DUIs. I could've spent the next twenty years in prison." He raised his head, his voice more frantic with each word. "My life would have been over. I would have killed myself before I went to prison."

That wasn't hyperbole. I felt the fear in his voice. His face reddened, bloated with the effort of holding back tears. My mind raced as I tried to absorb the information, to rationalize, to deny the facts, to devise a plan.

"Shane wasn't drinking?"

He shook his head as he watched ashes float to the floor from his cigarette stub, now little more than a filter. "The whole thing was his idea. He yanked me over and got in the driver's seat before the police showed up. I was too tanked to even realize what was happening. He told them he was driving me home."

"He wasn't charged with anything?"

"A misdemeanor. No jail time. I basically owe everything to him."

"So, what, now he can treat you—and me—however he wants?"

His eyes were swimming in self-loathing, his teeth clenched, the muscles in his jaw visibly tightening. "Rach, don't you get it? I killed someone." His words dissolved into tortured sobs, echoing the sounds he made when he woke during the night.

He was confessing to an event that had permanently scarred his soul. And I could feel it cutting into my own. I wrapped my arms around him. *Is he expecting me to absolve him of his sins?*

I'd spent a lot of time over the past several months missing him, but now he was so close that I could feel the rise and fall of his chest with each sob, yet I missed him more than ever.

Chapter 36

Grace and Randy didn't try to hide their exasperation at Mick's generosity toward Shane with *Pale Whisper*.

"What the hell were you thinking, Mick?" Randy asked. "Do you have any idea how you've screwed with our connections at the studio? *Shit*, what is it with you lately?"

He mumbled something about needing time off and being happy for Shane, saying he would be great in the role. He hung up the phone and said to no one in particular, "Can't please all of the people all of the fucking time." He wandered over to the window in the bedroom and pressed his forehead against the pane, watching as his breath fogged the glass in fluid, ever-changing patterns. With his confession to me, he'd exposed to the sunlight something that was much more comfortable hiding in the dark. And like a creature of the night thrown into the light, he sometimes seemed about to self-destruct.

"Are you okay?" I asked.

He simply shrugged.

I kissed him softly on the cheek and retreated. Mick was best left alone as he crawled back to that space in his head that kept him safe, kept him sane. I went upstairs to the kitchen to scrounge for something to take the edge off the insistent hunger that had become my constant companion.

My cell rang, and the caller ID said "Unknown." I answered tentatively. It was Shane. He hadn't even called when Mick was in the hospital or in the weeks since. I didn't know how he got my number, but I knew I had to come to grips with the fact that if Shane was going to have a recurring role in Mick's life, he would be a fixture in mine as well. I swallowed hard.

"Hello, Shane."

"Rachael... long time, no speak. How's Mick's baby mama?" His smirk was audible. Maybe he thought he'd gotten rid of me for good with his attempt to rip apart my happiness. He wasn't going to apologize for almost setting my future on fire. But if Mick was willing to let it go, I had to do the same.

"I'm fine, Shane," I said in the most civil tone I could muster.

"Well, maybe you're the one I should talk to anyway. You started all this crazy shit."

I counted to five before speaking. "What are you talking about?"

"That sicko stalker—she somehow got my cell number and address. She's been leaving messages, sending letters to my place, threatening me because I got the part in *Pale Whisper*."

"How do you know it's her?"

"Mick showed me some of those cards and letters and told me the shit she was doing. This is definitely her."

"Wait. How would she know that Mick was supposed to be cast?"

"It was in all the trades. Easy to find."

He was silent for a second or two, then in a vulnerable voice—as vulnerable as Shane could ever be—he asked, "You think she'd really follow through on her threats?"

"I have no idea, Shane. What exactly is she doing?"

"Only threatening to slit my throat from ear to ear if I go ahead with it. Said she'd ruin my 'pretty face' with acid. She's leaving messages on my cell, saying all kinds of weird shit about Mick being her husband and that he's the father of her kid. Oh, and you'll appreciate this—she thinks you and I are plotting against Mick to blow up his career."

That last part was almost funny—almost.

"Well," I said, "Randy, Grace, and Steve have all gotten calls, letters, and e-mails and turned them over to the police. You should too. I'm just surprised she waited this long to start contacting you."

"How did she get our contact info, anyway? It's not like we're in a central celebrity database somewhere."

"Don't know. But the odds of her becoming violent are pretty slim. At least, that's what the police say."

"I sure hope you're right. She's one crazy bitch."

"So are you going ahead with it?" I asked.

"With what?"

"*Pale Whisper*?"

"Fuck, yeah! This could be a breakout role for me. I just wanted to know if I should beef up my security, maybe get another bodyguard."

"If it would make you feel better..." I said, ready for the conversation to be done.

"Hey, thanks. That's super helpful," he said, oozing sarcasm. "I'll talk to Mick. Is he there?"

"Nope. Anything else I can help you with, Shane?"

He hung up. I stared at the phone then closed my eyes to compose myself before standing at the top of the stairs. "Mick!"

He stuck his head out of the bedroom. He was dressed in pants ripped to accommodate his cast and was barefoot. He was gripping a hairbrush like a weapon.

"You going somewhere?" I asked.

"I have a meeting in the city tonight with Gracie. I thought I told you. She's leaving for the holidays and insists we meet before she takes off. Wanna come with?"

He'd once again managed to filter out the craziness surrounding him.

"I'll pass. Grace is not exactly my BFF." I was about to go back to the kitchen, but I needed to tell him. "Listen, that was Shane on the phone."

Mick's shoulders slumped. "What did he want?" he asked, his voice flat.

"Seems as though our friendly neighborhood stalker is now harassing and threatening him. He's freaking out. He wanted to talk to you, but I told him you weren't here."

"Good. How the hell did she get everyone's contact info, anyway?"

"Maybe she hacked into someone's account?"

"Yeah, maybe. We've all changed ours. Is Shane going to change his?"

"I don't know, and I don't care. What are you meeting with Grace about?"

"I think she wants to read me the riot act about *Pale Whisper*, maybe kick me around the block a few times, put my balls in a vise."

"Seems to me Shane is the only one who's good with this whole thing," I said. "He was, anyway, until he started getting threats."

"Yeah, well... It's done," he said, sounding defeated. "Randy's going to be there. Said he might have something else for me. We'll see. Wait up for me?"

"I'll try."

Later that night, I'd dozed off but woke when I heard Mick's voice then Shane's. They were headed downstairs to Mick's office. I got up to get something to drink and overheard them arguing over whether Mick would intervene on Shane's behalf and finance his defense team for his second paternity suit that year.

"I'm done, Shane!" Mick yelled. "No more."

If I hadn't heard what came next, I wouldn't have believed that even Shane could be so manipulative and cruel.

"Fuck you, man!" he shouted back at Mick, letting out a forced, drunken laugh. "I guess this is the end of the road. It's been a hell of a ride, dude. Lasted longer than I thought it would. I knew I could play that fat conscience of yours."

"What the fuck are you talking about?"

"You were so shit-faced. I can't believe you still don't remember." Shane's laugh sickened me. "You weren't even driving the fucking car! It was *me*. I'm the one who killed that chick."

The silence that followed was agonizing. I stood at the top of the stairs, frozen in place, struggling to embrace the purifying relief that all Mick's guilt and self-recrimination was based on a grisly lie. This was Shane's desperate, drunken attempt to make Mick feel small, having drained all the payback Mick was willing to give. I wanted to go to him, but he had to absorb the impact of Shane's confession alone.

I heard glass shattering and a prolonged scuffle. I imagined bones cracking and weapons being drawn.

"Get the fuck out of here, Shane. Now! And don't come back, or I swear to God you'll wish you hadn't."

Shane stumbled up the basement stairs and, without acknowledging my presence, scurried out the door, mumbling an impressive string of profanities. Mick hobbled up the stairs and slammed and locked the front door behind him.

He paused, his back still to me, placed a palm against the door, and hung his head, shaking it in disgust. I came up behind him and wrapped my arms around his waist, my cheek resting on his back. It was wet with perspiration. I listened to his frantic heartbeat. He slowly turned to face me, and I gasped. His face was a mess—a swollen, bruised eye; a busted, bleeding lip; and a scrape on his cheek that was going to morph into an impressive scab.

"As if the cast wasn't enough. How bad is it? I'm supposed to start production on a new job next week. This is going to fuck with the scheduling. And the budget."

When I didn't respond, he said, "The studio is going to kill me."

Chapter 37

No one was happy about the delay, but the movie was going to be shot around Mick until he was completely healed and the cast was off. In the meantime, his mother was on her way from the airport to meet the mother-to-be of her first grandchild, and according to Mick, she was "beside herself." The three of us were going to celebrate Christmas together. I still hadn't told my parents that I'd be MIA on Christmas Day, and I wasn't looking forward to that last-minute conversation. Mick had apologized repeatedly to me and to my parents for his drunken appearance on Thanksgiving, but I wasn't sure if my father would ever accept his apology, despite the fact that Mick had stopped drinking—for good, he'd sworn to me.

"Rachael, I think you should know something about my mom. She doesn't have a mean bone in her body, but she just might hug you to death if she doesn't talk you to death first."

"We'll get along fine," I assured him, though I wasn't really sure what to expect.

His stories about his mother, though always told with implicit affection, ranged from hard to believe to just plain weird. There was the time she'd decided to can her own vegetables, and she spent a week's paycheck buying up canning jars, a pressure cooker, and the less-than-perfect produce from a neighbor's crop. She canned everything in a single weekend, proud of her ingenuity and ability to scrape by. One night shortly after, they woke to gunshots. His mother grabbed the shotgun she kept by the bed and ran to the trailer door in a granny nightgown, her hair in pink foam curlers, a mask of Noxema covering her face, ready to disembowel anyone who crossed her path. Another gunshot rang out—from inside the trailer. She whipped around and found all her hard work exploding in the pantry, her lovingly canned vegetables detonating. She spent days cleaning up the slimy mess. Recouping from the financial loss took far longer. According to Mick, she took it in stride, as she did every disaster in her life.

"Just be yourself, Rachael, and she'll be crazy about you. Just one favor. Let's not mention anything about the stalker. She's got high blood pressure. I haven't told her anything, and I'm afraid if she knows what's been happening, she would literally have a stroke."

His concern for his mother's well-being was further confirmation of the core of goodness in him.

"Not a word, but what do we tell her about Bruce?" I motioned in the direction where Bruce was stationed out front.

"She knows I sometimes have bodyguards. Maybe I'll tell her he needed the overtime or something."

While we waited for her arrival, Mick retreated to the garden to smoke, still puffing away despite his promise to quit before the baby came. *One vice at a time.* I looked out the kitchen window to see him lighting a second cigarette off the first. When he wandered in, the door buzzed. I stayed in the parlor while he answered. The butterflies in my stomach kept me company.

His mother's voice preceded her—all singsongy Southern loudness. And in she came—floral print dress, orange-red lipstick, suitcase-size straw purse, raven-black hair plastered in place with enough hair spray to singlehandedly destroy the ozone layer, and a bright, toothy smile. The past fifteen years in Los Angeles hadn't made a dent. She was all sunflowers, Dixie beer, and freshly picked cotton.

She hugged her son, backed up, glanced at his cast, and grabbed him by the chin, turning his head back and forth. "What happened, Mickey? Get in a dog fight?"

"Something like that," Mick said, laughing.

"Who started it?"

"He did."

"Did you win?"

"Actually, yeah, I did."

"Well, it's all good then." She unceremoniously pushed him aside and floated in. "And you must be Rachael! Don't just stand there, hon. Come give your baby's grandmama a hug!" And she rocked me back and forth to some unidentifiable tune she was humming. She backed up, still holding me by the arms. His mother had the same soulful brown eyes and long black lashes, the same not-quite-right nose, the same rich, unrestrained laugh.

She gave me a quick once-over. "Honey, you don't look pregnant to me. You're skinny as a rail." She didn't hesitate or ask permission when she patted my stomach.

"Well, I'm only about fourteen weeks. It's just a pooch right now."

"Has the morning sickness passed?"

"Yes, ma'am. I was sick for a while, but I'm feeling fine now."

"Bless your heart. Has Mickey been taking good care of you? He means well, but he's not great with sick people." She turned toward Mick, hands planted on her hips. "Mickey, you remember when I had that operation? I was in a bad way, and you—"

"Mom, please, not that story again. Rachael isn't interested."

"Are you kidding?" I said, grinning. "Ms. Sullivan—I mean *Ms. Abrams*—that sounds like the best story ever. Sit down and let me fix you something to drink."

"Call me Cora, hon, and I'll take a gin and tonic on the rocks. With lime, if you got it." She turned to Mick. "Mickey, she's just as sweet as she can be. And pretty as a picture. You'd better take good care of her, you hear?"

"Yes, ma'am. That's the plan." Mick's countenance changed around his mother—a little less self-confident, a lot more little boy. He uttered "Yes, ma'am" and "No, ma'am" a lot, and there were occasional lapses in which his final *g*'s were left dangling as he uttered unfamiliar pronunciations. He was no longer Mick Sullivan, successful actor. He was little Mickey Abrams from the Lake Pines Trailer Park. Their history—just the two of them all those years—showed. Clearly, he knew what she wanted before she asked and was there with it—another drink, the remote, a blanket, her pills, some conversation.

An easy, undemanding houseguest, Cora settled into one of the extra bedrooms, quietly rising each morning to make her own coffee—instant was just fine. But as soon as Mick or I opened the bedroom door, she stood at the top of the stairs and began to talk. "Good morning, boys and girls! I'm so glad I came to your party! What's on today's to-do list?" She talked about everything from the weather—"Too cold"—to the NYC subways—"Too crowded"—to Mick's childhood—"Too poor"—to our future together—"Too many good things to count." And of course, she shared her plans for her first grandbaby. "Maybe that child is going to be an actor like his daddy!" She wound down only when Mick and I shut the bedroom door for the night.

She was so proud of her famous son that she was always about to "bust a gut," to quote a phrase she was fond of using. Mick was constantly removing perfectly shaped orange-red lipstick marks from his forehead, his cheeks, his chin. "Just a little sugar," she would say as she pinched his stubbly cheeks as if he were still a cherub-faced three-year-old. But he didn't seem to mind. And by association, Cora Sullivan was proud of me. Her pride was automatic, no questions asked. As far as Mick's mother was concerned, I was already part of the family.

I was on my tiptoes, reaching for a bottle of lotion on the top shelf of the storage cabinet in the bathroom, when Mick came up behind me. "Need some help, shorty?" He reached up, grabbed the bottle, and handed it to me. Then in a single motion, he pulled me toward him, swept my hair back, and kissed my neck. I breathed him in as that familiar wrenching desire rose inside me, and I leaned back against his chest and closed my eyes. I was about to turn around to face him when he pressed me against the sink, his breath quickening on my skin. I reached back, and Cora appeared out of nowhere, standing in the bathroom doorway, sharing our intimate space. Mick was plastered up against me, his head buried in my neck as if about to take a bite, his hands somewhere between socially acceptable and "get a room, why don't ya?" I let out a barely audible squeak and stiffened. He lifted his head to look at Cora but evidently didn't think it necessary to disengage.

"Mickey, do you think we could watch one of your movies tonight? I never get to watch them with you."

"Sure, Mom. I'll show you where they are in a minute."

"Rachael, honey, have you been to one of his premieres?"

I cleared my throat. "No, ma'am."

Mick hadn't budged, and I wanted to disappear down the drain.

"I went to a couple. Not for me. Too many people—too much screaming. Gave me a headache. I prefer to see it on CD, sitting in my chair."

"It's a DVD, Mom. But I think we can catch one on streaming."

"Well, you know what I mean. When you're done in there, come point me in the right direction." She turned to go, but just when I started to breathe again, she stopped to face Mick once more. "You got any popcorn, hon?"

"Rach?" he asked.

I searched for my voice. "Um, yeah, it's in the cabinet above the refrigerator."

"I'll get it for you later, Mom."

Cora walked away as though it were nothing out of the ordinary to find her son pressed up against a woman's backside, her eyes closed in passion. Maybe it wasn't.

"God, that was embarrassing," I said.

"Why? It's not like you had your purple panties down around your ankles and we were doing it doggy style." He laughed. "She didn't care."

My parents wouldn't have been so cavalier about such an open display, even behind a half-closed door in our own bathroom. I could almost hear my mother clicking her tongue in disapproval. The very thought intensified my blush from rose pink to pomegranate red.

One thing was certain—being around Cora O'Sullivan Abrams was a monster reality check. She had both feet planted firmly on the ground, and if, in the past, Mick had let his head fill with the helium of fame, she had punctured it, releasing just enough to bring him down to earth. She never cut him any slack.

"Michael Christopher Abrams," she said once, "get your butt off that sofa and pick up those clothes! There's no reason why Rachael has to do it. And it's not like you can't afford help."

Each time she issued her orders like a Louisiana drill sergeant, he reluctantly stood and, shaking his head, muttered, "Yes, ma'am," and did as he was told. When he would go to the garden and light up, she often followed him, and when they returned, they'd be laughing in stereo.

Once when Mick was in the city for a meeting with Grace and I was loading the dishwasher after lunch with Cora, I looked out the kitchen window to see her standing in the snow-covered garden, her arms folded against her body, shoulders shrugged up to her ears. I opened the window, and a snowy breeze blew in.

"Cora, you're going to freeze. Come on in, and I'll make you some hot chocolate."

She waved at me. "I was fixin' to, but why don't you come out here and join me, hon? I don't get a chance to see snow at home."

I stepped out onto the small concrete slab we called a patio and threw one of Mick's jackets over Cora's shoulders. "It is nice, isn't it?"

She leaned over and gave me a squeeze. "Makes everything quieter, more peaceful. Don't know if I could put up with a whole winter of it, but this is pretty."

We were watching the dry dusting of snow dwindle. Everything felt crisp, clean, and sharply defined.

Cora turned uncharacteristically serious. "Rachael, honey, can I ask you something?"

"Sure, Cora." I hoped it wasn't going to be about the bathroom incident.

She took a breath and paused as though reconsidering whether to ask. "I noticed Mickey isn't drinking. Did you have something to do with that?"

I was surprised by her question but more than willing to share. "Yes, ma'am. When I found out I was pregnant, I gave him an ultimatum: stop drinking or... Well, anyway, he's kept to his promise to stop."

Cora closed her eyes, her long lashes gathering snowflakes, her reddened cheeks deepening their blush, and she whispered as if reciting a prayer, "That's a damn good thing. His daddy was a drunk, you know."

Her comment stung like a giant rubber band snapping back onto my chest. "No, ma'am. He never told me."

I'd been aware of Mick's fondness for booze ever since our first encounter in Zabar's, when I detected the lingering scent of alcohol.

And from the first day I walked into his house, I'd witnessed first-hand his ability to knock back large quantities, usually on a daily basis, though he rarely got sloppy drunk, Thanksgiving being a regrettable exception. My willful denial of his drinking had been a salve on an old wound. While my father transformed into a sadistic bully when he drank, alcohol softened Mick, making his drinking far easier to overlook.

Cora sighed. "Well, can't say as I'm surprised Mickey hasn't talked about his daddy. He was a mean drunk. Put me in the hospital twice."

"I didn't know," I said again, trying to rein in my swelling panic. My father's dad had died long before I was born, but I knew he was an alcoholic too. *Will Mick eventually follow in his father's footsteps, just as my father had followed his? Is Mick's fate sealed despite his promise to me to quit?*

"The worst was the day he left for good." Cora stared out at the falling snow, which had picked up again. "Mickey was only five. It was Thanksgiving. He was so excited, waiting for his daddy to get home. When Ira finally walked in the door two and a half hours late, the food was cold, and he was two sheets to the wind and madder than a junkyard dog. When he took his fists to me, I heard Mickey crying, gagging, choking under the table, where he hid." She shook her head as if recalling the tragic story of someone else's life.

"I think Ira rolled up all the disappointments in his life into that one beating. He left me bloodied and black-and-blue, with a broken jaw, three cracked ribs, two missing teeth, and a nasty gash on my forehead. Mickey was a smart kid, knew to call 911. Probably saved my life." She lifted up her poufy bangs to reveal a faded scar that started on her forehead and disappeared into her hairline. "I went around snaggletoothed for years. Couldn't afford to get 'em fixed until Mickey made enough money to pay for it. Anyhow, we never saw or heard from his daddy again. Though we did hear he was in prison a while back. Probably dead by now."

"I... I can't believe he never told me," I said, my voice quivering.

But then, I hadn't told him about my father—not in any detail, anyway. We shared the same shame but were reluctant to share it with each other.

"I think it left him with a permanent bruise, one he'd rather not mess with to see if it still hurts."

My eyes welled up with tears.

"It's fine, sweetheart." She took my hand and patted it. "He's got a baby on the way now. I'm so happy to see him being responsible. He saw how it turned out for his daddy. And I know he doesn't want to follow in those footsteps. He's got a hell of a lot to lose."

So do I, I thought.

Chapter 38

I wormed my way out of Christmas with my parents by feigning illness. Continuing to withhold the truth from them made everything seem sordid.

Cora advised me to "fess up" to them sooner rather than later. "From everything you told me about your daddy, the longer you wait, the harder it'll be. I know Mickey can be tough to take sometimes, but once they get to know him, they'll love him just as much as you do—*because* you do." Her unbridled optimism was as infectious as a virus and just as hard to eradicate.

Christmas in Brooklyn was understated. Money had been in short supply when Mick was growing up. "We didn't have a pot to piss in," as Cora said. She and Mick had no extravagant holiday traditions. And he seemed to have no interest in attending any of the countless holiday parties he'd been invited to on both coasts. Cora was leaving in three days, and he wanted to stick close to home. We had a small tree with a few red and green balls and icicles that Cora and I hung. We decided to exchange one gift each.

What exactly do you get someone who can buy anything? I fretted over my choice before settling on a ukulele, Mick's latest musical obsession, and a playlist I created to go with it that included "Somewhere over the Rainbow" by IZ, "I'm Yours" by Jason Mraz, and "Banana Pancakes" by Jack Johnson. His unbridled enthusiasm over my gift surprised me. It provided me with a mental snapshot of a five-year-old Mickey Abrams opening a present and finding something he couldn't even allow himself to wish for.

"This is so cool, Rach," he said as he started strumming.

His gift to me was small, the exact dimensions of a ring box. It reminded me of my hopes for the future, which had once seemed so crystal-clear but now felt like I was trying to make out my reflection in a fogged mirror. I wasn't ready for this—not yet.

"Let your mother open hers first. Here, Cora." I handed the red shoebox-sized present to her, and she clapped in excitement.

No one would guess she could get whatever her heart desired by simply mentioning to her son that something had caught her eye. She ripped open the package in one swift motion. It was a first-class, round-trip, open-ended ticket from Los Angeles to New York. "It's so you can help when the baby comes. I know it's not much of a present. I would have bought you a ticket anyway. But you didn't exactly give me a Christmas list," Mick said, smiling.

She surrounded Mick in a mama bear hug. "This is perfect. I'll be here come hell or high water."

I couldn't procrastinate any longer. I didn't want to disappoint Mick or Cora, and I could feel them watching me. I held my breath, mentally rehearsing my reaction. *What can I say? "Uh, can I get back to you on that?"* My heart thumped in my chest as I cracked open the box and dared to take a peek.

It wasn't a ring. It was a necklace—his necklace, the one with the Ten Commandments. Since he'd confessed his sins, maybe he no longer needed their protection. Then I remembered his words: *"It meant something to my mom, so it means something to me."*

Mick was giving me one of his most valued possessions. I could barely eke out the words before my throat closed. "Are you sure?"

He took it from me and put it around my neck. I clasped it in my hand. It was now *my* amulet to protect me from harm.

For Cora's last evening in Brooklyn, I was preparing a rare home-cooked meal, putting together traditional Southern fare—fried chicken, mashed potatoes and gravy, green beans seasoned with bacon and onions, and steaming hot corn bread. Cora was sitting on a barstool next to the island, snapping beans. The conversation shifted from recipes to babies.

"Doesn't make a lick of difference to me if it's a boy or a girl," she said.

I wanted this baby, but I hadn't given much thought to whether it would be a boy or a girl. The idea made it seem so much more real, more tangible. Pregnancy is a state, a condition. But a boy or a girl—that would be another human being living, breathing, eating, crying in the middle of the night, occupying space, and depending on me for everything. The thought brought on an avalanche of worry.

"Let's just be happy if that child is healthy," Cora added before coming around to where I was standing to envelop me in a hug. Her jasmine perfume surrounded me as she whispered in my ear, "Hon, don't you worry. Everything may not turn out exactly like you planned—life has a way of surprising the dickens out of you—but everything's gonna be just fine."

I had full-throttle faith that somehow, Mick's mother just knew.

Chapter 39

"Come here, Rach." Mick was perched on the edge of the bed, his hands on his knees, fingers tapping impatiently, brow furrowed.

I brushed the back of my hand across his smooth skin. He'd shaved for the occasion.

"Don't worry about my father," I said. "He'll be pissed, but he won't pull out a shotgun. I promise." I heard myself giggle.

I was in a giggly mood. Mick's mother had returned to Los Angeles, but her welcoming embrace convinced me that I was underestimating my parents' capacity for acceptance. I was hoping they would be just as excited as Cora about their first grandchild.

He tugged on the towel wrapped around my body. As it slid down around my ankles, he placed his warm hands on the small, firm roundness of my belly and kissed it. He looked up at me as though searching for the answer to a question he hadn't yet asked. His Adam's apple bobbed up and down as he swallowed hard.

"Marry me, Rach."

He'd given no hints, nothing to make me think marriage was on his mind. The Christmas-present panic had been my own doing. His eyes widened, unblinking.

"Rach?"

Yes. The word formed on my lips, but I stopped myself. "No," I said more harshly than I'd intended. "Not like this."

He looked surprised then hurt and angry.

"Like what? What the hell are you talking about?"

That was not the way I'd envisioned it. If it was going to happen, I needed a sign, some reassurance that Cora's prediction would come true. And rattling around in the back of my mind was the distracting certainty that his lawyer, his manager, his agent, and his publicist would all think my pregnancy had been a strategic move to trap him into marriage and take a deep dive into his bank account. Unpleasant talks of prenuptial agreements, divorce settlements, and child support would likely take place before we would even say, "I do." Maybe I wasn't in the strongest bargaining position, but marrying Mick was going to happen on my terms or not at all.

I picked up the towel and covered myself again. "You're only asking because I'm pregnant."

"That's not true," he insisted.

"Mick, seriously. Would you want to get married right now if I weren't pregnant? Moving in together is one thing, but getting married?"

"Don't you want our son to have a father?" He was using new information from a sonogram as leverage to sway me.

"What? All of a sudden, you're Mr. Provincial? You sound like *my* father now. You'll be the baby's father. You just won't be my husband."

"I thought that's what you wanted." He sighed.

"Just give me some time," I whispered.

His response was flat. "Okay. I'll drop it... for now."

Mick rented a car to drive to New Jersey so that we could announce the news to my parents. If we waited much longer, my appearance was going to be announcement enough. We decided to leave Bruce behind for the day. Three would definitely be a crowd in that situation. Little conversation passed between us as we cruised down the New Jersey Turnpike, though my thoughts were in overdrive.

We were just a few exits from the Madison city limits when Mick turned down the music and glanced at me. "You sure he's not going to pull a shotgun on me, Rach? This marriage decision may be out of your hands." He chuckled nervously.

"He can sound really intense, but he's a softie on the inside. I just hope they'll take the news like your mother. She was giddy over the idea of being a grandmother."

"She's just happy I'm settling down. And she likes you—a lot. You're a Louisiana girl." He smiled and winked at me. "To my mom, this is just more good news in my life." He leaned into the steering wheel, beating his thumbs in time to the song playing softly on the radio. "But I do wish you'd told your parents we were together before now. It would make this a hell of a lot easier."

He was right, of course. But it was too late to second-guess my decision not to tell them at Thanksgiving. "I really thought about it when I was staying with them, but it just seemed like too much for them to handle. And then when you showed up trashed, well... And my father was sure from the beginning you were going to take advantage of his innocent little girl."

"Oh, this is just great. He had visions of me twirling my mustache and unzipping my fly, and now I'm bringing you home pregnant?" He turned to me, incredulous. "So what exactly made you think waiting until now was going to make it any easier for them to take?"

"Relax, Mick. I think it'll be fine."

"Then why do I feel like I knocked up my high school girlfriend and her dad's about to beat the holy crap out of me?"

He pulled into the driveway, and we could see my parents through the window, sitting on the sofa in the family room, laughing at the television screen.

"Let's do this," I said.

"Wait." He took my face in his hands and kissed me.

I gave him a quick kiss and reached for the car door, but he pulled me back and drew me close, pressing his body against mine. That time, I kissed him in earnest, and I felt his anxiety dissipate.

"*Now* let's go inside," he said.

My mother was pleased as punch to have the famous Mick Sullivan pay them another visit—sober this time. Unlike my father, she had easily forgiven his indiscretion at Thanksgiving. She'd had lots of practice. And, in his honor, she was playing the role of the perfect Southern hostess—coffee, pound cake, the good china, and linen napkins in the formal living room.

I went in and sat in the chair next to my father. My mother followed and sat next to me, leaving Mick and me facing each other in our socially awkward semicircle. She served coffee from the silver set that was always on display atop the antique bookshelf, waiting for the right opportunity to be put into service. She polished it once a month, just in case.

Like any good hostess, my mother tried to keep the conversation going, peppering Mick with polite questions about his exciting career: "What are you working on now?" "When is your next movie coming out?" "Are you going to be at the Academy Awards?" She wasn't going to wind down anytime soon. My father's silence, however, was prickly and foreboding. Mick glanced over at me and gave an almost imperceptible nod. The moment didn't feel right, but I cleared my throat, shifted in my seat, and set my coffee cup on the edge of the table.

"Mom, Daddy, there's something important I need to tell you, and..."

My father's thin-lipped glare directed at Mick wasn't making it any easier. It seemed to make no difference that Mick had shaved, beaten his hair into submission, and chosen a dress shirt to wear instead of a T-shirt that displayed a band logo or said "fuck" on the back. And his breath was minty fresh.

"Is it about the stalker?" My mother's voice was weighted with maternal concern.

"No, it's something more personal I need to talk to you both about."

"Now, Rachael, honey," she interrupted, "I'm sure it can wait. If it's something of a personal nature, Michael may feel uncomfortable."

"Mom, it involves Mick."

"Oh?"

I was far more nervous than I realized. *Better to just spit it out.* "I came to tell you that... I'm pregnant."

I forced a smile as I surveyed the facial landscape. My father looked like he'd taken a bite out of a lemon and the juice had squirted into his eyes, temporarily blinding him. My mother had assumed the horrified look of someone who just learned her daughter was a five-dollar-a-trick hooker with a heroin habit. She glanced at Mick then back at me and back at Mick.

"Oh, honey, no," she sputtered.

My father's face was getting redder by the second. His ears were about to emit a high-pitched steam whistle.

"I knew it!" he yelled as he jumped up and pointed an accusatory finger at Mick. "I knew it all along, you son of a bitch!"

I sprang from my seat, knocking the untouched contents of my coffee cup onto the spotless beige carpet. The slow-motion trajectory of the dark brew distracted me as I fought the urge to clean it up before it set into a stain.

"Daddy! Stop it!"

"Don, don't!" my mother joined in.

"Mr. Allen, wait—" Mick interrupted, trying to rein in the unfolding disaster.

"You shut your mouth. You think I don't know what you're all about? I don't give a shit how rich and famous you are. You're nothing but a selfish, self-centered lush. You think you can just snap your fingers and whatever the hell you want becomes yours? This is my house, and this is my daughter—"

I scooted closer to Mick to form a united front. "I'm not your baby girl. I'm a grown woman, and I can make my own decisions about my life." I turned to look at Mick. "About *our* life."

My mother stood in front of my father, holding his face in her hands. "Don, look at me. It's done. This isn't helping anything. Please don't make it worse."

I had the fleeting thought that my father might actually be capable of reaching for a shotgun or, at the very least, that two-ton crystal swan on the coffee table, to clobber Mick over the head with it. I could almost feel the impact and see the blood and the shattered glass on the carpet. This was not how the scene had played out in my head—not even close. Nobody could talk my father down when he got like that. Time and distance would allow him to cool off, to think more clearly. We needed to get out of there. I grabbed Mick's arm to make our exit before things were said and done that could never be stricken from the record. But he was inching toward my father with a look of composed determination. My father gently pushed my mother aside, but she held tight to his arm. Mick was half a head taller and almost twenty years younger. If the confrontation turned physical, the odds were not in my father's favor.

"Mr. Allen, look, I know you think this is just one more thing I've done to hurt Rachael. But we talked it over, and she's going to move in with me permanently. I love her. I hope you'll eventually be able to accept that."

As I absorbed the impact of Mick using the *L* word for the first time, I realized my father was trembling, his face a miserable mix of frustration, disappointment, and rage.

"You can't try to charm your way out of this!" he yelled. "Everything that's happened to her in the last few months is because of you. She had a future full of possibilities, which you have now taken away.

If you really cared about her, we'd be talking marriage right now. What's going to happen to her when you move on to the next one? Huh?"

"Jesus Christ! Daddy, you don't know what you're talking about."

He glared at Mick. "You took advantage of the situation—of her!" He shook his fist at Mick. "You think all that money gives you permission to do whatever the hell you want, anytime you want, no matter who gets hurt."

Mick's resolve transitioned into irritation then rage. "I'm not saying I haven't made some ugly mistakes, Thanksgiving being one of them. I apologized for that. It was stupid. But you're acting like I forced myself on her!" He took a deep breath, winding himself up for the punch line. "I've got news for you, *Don*. She doesn't need you to protect her from me—or anyone else!"

My father vibrated with pent-up fury. "It's no secret where you came from, and you haven't changed. You're still nothing but poor white trash!"

Mick turned away, his face ruddy, hesitated, and faced my father again. "Oh, and by the way, if you think our not being married is a problem, you're going to have to take that one up with Rachael. I asked her, and she said, 'Thanks, but no thanks.'"

I'd never spoken to my father that way—not when he was sober, anyway. I'd fantasized about it, sure. But the imagined repercussions of unleashing my opinions on him unedited always stopped me cold. Trying to undo a lifetime of fearful paternal compliance was next to impossible. Mick had erupted, and I felt the tectonic plates of the earth shifting. I was frozen in place, waiting for the aftershock.

With a jerk of his head toward the door, Mick issued a pointed directive: "Come on. Let's get the hell out of here."

I was at that fork in the road, the one I'd always heard about but hoped never to encounter.

"Rach?" Mick reached for my hand.

My choice, the choice I made when I went back to Brooklyn, took my hand, put his arm around my shoulder, and guided me to the door. We marched out without looking back, hurried to the car, and slammed the doors. The stillness and sudden silence created a sanctuary for me to review the devastating turn of events. The sounds of irregular breathing filled the car. I'd been crazy to think my father would be okay with this. I'd somehow convinced myself that his life's history would have no bearing on my own.

"Are you okay, Rach?"

"No," I sobbed. "What the hell just happened in there? That was awful!"

"I'm sorry, but I couldn't deal with the crap your father was dishing out. He acts like I raped you... *Jesus*. He was prepared to hate me before he even met me, and I know I screwed things up royally at Thanksgiving." He tightened his grip on the steering wheel. "I expected them to be pissed, but it was worse than I thought it would be. So much worse."

"They'll come around... eventually," I said as my breathing returned to normal.

"Are they really going to get over this? To get over me?" He sounded not so much angry as dejected.

"What are they going to do? Shun me? They may be old-fashioned, but they're not primitive." I closed my eyes and took a deep, calming breath. "Honestly, I don't even want to think about it right now. Let's just go home."

He reached for my hand. "Rachael, you do know I love you, right? I'm sorry I haven't said it until now."

I leaned in, kissed him softly, and whispered, "I love you too."

As we backed out of the driveway, I glanced in the window to see my mother shaking her head and my father comforting her. I'd been lulled into a false sense of comfort and security by Cora's reaction to our news. My parents had different ideas about what was acceptable behavior for their daughter. Getting knocked up by a famous actor was not on the list—a wrecked reputation and a black hole of a future. It made no difference that I was a grown woman or that Mick made it clear he wasn't going anywhere anytime soon. Or even that he said he loved me.

They hadn't even asked if I was okay. Although we hadn't heard a peep in a while, I just knew that woman was out there, watching, waiting. I hadn't stopped looking over my shoulder.

I began to think that maybe I should've taken Mick up on his marriage proposal, to smooth things over, keep the peace. But then my marriage would be on my parents' terms. *No. This has to be just between the two of us. If I weren't pregnant, if my parents weren't there with their theatrics, what would I want?* I wasn't going to say yes until I had the answer.

Chapter 40

Mick was back in LA for a week, and I was carrying on with my own routine, working, sharing tea with Heloise, talking to Jenna, and easing into conversations with my mother while somehow avoiding the baby elephant in the room.

I was in the bedroom on my laptop, messaging back and forth with Houdini. They'd sent me a demo of a new group they wanted my input on. I was more focused than I'd been in months and was choosing not to dwell on the complications a new baby would present with a full-time job. I had to believe everything would work out. Breaking the news of my pregnancy to my parents and saying no to Mick's marriage proposal had somehow empowered me to decide on my own what I wanted, what I needed.

I was lost in the music, evaluating the band's potential, when the strong smell of gasoline wafted into the room. I sniffed a couple of times, hit Stop on the music file, removed my headphones, grabbed my phone, and followed the trail upstairs. I slowly made my way through the kitchen and into the parlor, the odor intensifying as I neared the front door. I stopped to listen—just the sound of my own shallow breathing. With one hand clamped over my mouth and nose, I rounded the corner to the vestibule. Lying on the floor, just under the mail slot, was a small pile of filthy gasoline-soaked rags. As I stared in horror, waiting for them to burst into flames, I heard a car engine start up out front. I stumbled over the rags and pressed my face to the glass pane next to the front door. A blue Buick was driving off. Bruce was nowhere in sight. I turned back to the grimy pile resting on the rug. Atop the rags was a box of matches and a folded sheet of stationery. I pinched the paper between my forefinger and thumb, and it fell open.

The handwriting, now familiar, spelled out, "Get rid of her, or next time, it will come with a lighted match. Now, you'll be thinking of me. They may not be sweet thoughts, but you'll be thinking of me."

My phone dinged with a text from Bruce: *Just ran down to the corner for something to drink. Be back in two minutes.*

She'd been lying in wait.

Chapter 41

The next week was free of scrawled threats, angry e-mails, and desperate handwritten love notes. The time had come to end my self-imposed house arrest. I needed provisions. Breathing fresh air felt good. Bruce accompanied me, of course. He wasn't much of a conversationalist, but he wouldn't stop apologizing for his brief absence the day she managed to sneak by and not so subtly threaten to burn the house down with me in it. He asked how I was feeling.

"Pretty good, all things considered." I was in my pregnancy honeymoon, after morning sickness but before my body would become unrecognizable, belonging to someone else, someone I was increasingly anxious to meet.

Bags of groceries in hand, I entered the lower level, then I left them at the bottom of the stairs. With newly acquired weight, I became winded easily, so I decided to put everything away later. In the bedroom, I stripped down and slipped on one of Mick's T-shirts. I was about to collapse on the bed when I caught my reflection in the mirror. I was fascinated by my profile, which seemed to have changed overnight. Turning to the side, I stretched the T-shirt over my belly and examined it. The last time Mick was there, he said he couldn't see much difference. My pumped-up breasts, on the other hand, he commented on and caressed often. But now it was undeniable—that hard-as-a-rock protrusion between my hips. I wondered what his reaction would be when I looked like I'd swallowed a basketball.

I went to the bathroom and splashed cold water on my face. I was reaching for a towel when I heard the distinctive creak of hardwood giving way to someone's weight on the floor above. I quickly shut off the water and cocked my head. *There it is again.*

"Bruce?"

Silence.

Fear creeped under me. My heart was beating in my throat, and the artery in my neck pulsated. I checked the alarm control on the bedroom wall. Still set. It couldn't be Shane. He had relinquished his keys after Mick kicked him out, and we'd put him on a "do not enter" list with Bruce and had even changed the locks and the alarm code.

Someone was definitely walking the length of the parlor, heading to the stairs that led down to our bedroom. I grabbed my robe, my phone, and my keys from the dresser and inched the bedroom door open, surveying the staircase up to the kitchen. It was empty, except for the groceries at the bottom, waiting to be put away. I sprinted out the door.

"Bruce, there's someone in the house!"

He yelled at me to go next door and barked into his radio, alerting the security firm. I ran down the sidewalk, almost tripping on my robe tie twice, and I stood on Heloise's stoop, shivering and hopping up and down on the frozen concrete.

I pounded on the door. "Heloise, it's Rachael. Let me in, please! Heloise! Open the door!"

Heloise's crisp, distinctive steps approached, and she opened the door casually, cordially.

"Well, hello, Rachael. You're going to freeze to death like that. Come in! Come in!"

Soiled kitty litter had never smelled so good.

"Someone broke into the house!"

"Have you called the police?"

"The security people are on their way, and they'll call it in."

"Can I make you some tea?"

"Uh... sure. Thanks." In Heloise's universe, tea made everything better. She headed for the kitchen.

"I don't know how she could have gotten in!" I yelled into the kitchen.

"She?" Heloise responded, her curiosity piqued.

"I didn't see her, but I know who it is. It's some crazy girl who's obsessed with Mick, and she thinks I'm getting in the way of their relationship."

"I thought you and Mick were just friends."

"Well, yeah, we were. It's more than that now. And that's making the situation worse. She drops menacing notes in the mail slot. That package on our stoop was from her. She's even threatened a friend of Mick's."

"Do you know what she looks like?"

I turned from the window to take the cup of tea from Heloise and sipped the scalding brew. "No. Why?"

"I was going to tell you I saw a young woman digging through your garbage out front last week. I thought she was looking for food. But she didn't look homeless. A full-figured girl, blond hair."

George and Tony pulled up and jumped out of the car. I dropped my teacup on the saucer and left it rattling. I ran out onto the stoop, clutching my robe shut with one hand and waving frantically with the other.

Tony yelled at me, "Get back inside!"

The minutes passed, unbearably protracted, and I worried about their safety until they reappeared at the front door, their guns again resting in their holsters. Neighbors had begun to congregate outside.

As Tony and George approached her door, Heloise offered, "Would you boys like some tea?"

"No thanks, ma'am," Tony said.

"So?" I asked, fearful of the response to my open-ended question.

"It's all clear. But I can tell you how she got in. Through the basement window. It was open. The welcome mat was really laid out for whoever it was. I figure she somehow scaled that fence and got access through the garden in the back without being spotted."

I clearly remembered the day Mick opened the window for me. Neither of us had given it another thought.

"You sure she's not still in there, hiding somewhere?"

"We checked every closet, every corner. You're good. Doesn't look like anything was taken, and no obvious damage. The police'll come to take a report. We closed and locked the basement window for you, but you really need to speak to Mr. Sullivan about getting alarm contact points on that window and any other openings in the place," George said, genuine concern in his voice.

"Thanks, guys. Would you mind walking me back in?"

"Sure. No problem."

I gave Heloise a hug. "If you see that woman again, could you call me on my cell?"

"Absolutely. And listen," Heloise whispered, "I still have my Colt .45 if you want to borrow it. You can't be too careful in a situation like this."

"Thanks, Heloise, but I'm good."

George and Tony walked with me through the house to allay my fears and reassure me that it was all clear. After they left, I sat on the edge of the bed and watched through the window as they drove away.

"It's okay. It's over," I said to the room.

I leaned back on the bed and reached for my pillow to prop myself up before pressing "Mick" on speed dial. But instead of the give of fluffy down, I felt a bricklike hardness underneath. I lifted the pillow to find a box wrapped in brown paper, similar to the "suicide basket," with Mick's name scribbled on the outside. A stranglehold of fear tightened my throat. His number-one fan had left another gift. Maybe in her warped mind, breaking and entering was the proper way to deliver gifts to her beloved. The thought of her being in the bedroom, touching our things, and lifting my pillow left me feeling queasy. As I picked up the box, the sickeningly sweet smell of wisteria wafted up. I opened the nightstand drawer, pulled out Detective Melnitsky's card, and dialed the number.

"Yes, I'm calling for Detective Melnitsky."

"Hold, please."

I waited and waited and waited.

The woman came back on the line. "Who were you holding for?"

"Detective Melnitsky."

"Hold, please."

I obediently waited several more minutes until I was disconnected.

I dialed again and was put through to his line but got his voice mail. I left a message then called back a third time to ask if I could talk to anyone else on the case. I was placed on hold again and waited, until I finally said, "Forget it," and I tossed the phone on the bed.

I picked up the heavy package and shook it, stirring up the scent, which was stronger now, overpowering. I held the box to my ear and listened. It wasn't ticking, but maybe that just happened in the movies.

I dialed Mick's number.

"Hey, it's me."

"Hold on a sec, Rach." He was talking on another phone, telling whomever it was that he would call them back.

"Sorry. That was Randy. Some weird shit about product placement in my last movie. Not important. How's my favorite pregnant girlfriend?"

"I'm fine, but listen, we've had another close encounter."

"*Jesus*. What happened?"

"She got in through the basement window. We left it open."

"She was actually in the house? *Shit*... Are you okay?"

"Yeah. Bruce, George, and Tony checked out every square inch to make sure it was safe for me to come back in. But she left a package they didn't see. I haven't opened it yet. I thought I'd do it while you're on the phone... moral support."

"Rach, are you nuts? Forget it. No telling what's in there. Wait for the cops!"

"Supposedly, they're on their way. The security guys called, and I called, but they put me on hold for about twenty minutes and then disconnected me. I called back and got voice mail. Who knows when they'll show up. Anyway, you opened the last one. Maybe it has some clue as to what her next move will be or something for the cops to be able to trace her. It reeks. Probably just more weirdo crap she's doused in cheap perfume. Besides, you said it yourself-—the police haven't done anything so far."

"Call the security people back. Let them handle it!"

"No. I want to see what's inside. Maybe it'll help me understand what's going on in that demented head of hers."

"I already know what's going on in her head. Crazy shit. Throw the fucking thing away!"

I hesitated. "Nope, I'm opening it. Hold on," I said. "I'll put you on speakerphone."

I set the phone down on the bed and, bit by bit, peeled back the brown paper wrapping, cut the tape, and shook the lid of the box until the bottom fell out. I gasped, choked on my own saliva as I jerked back, and fell off the edge of the bed and onto the floor. I backed crablike toward the bathroom as I scrambled to create distance.

"Oh my God! Oh God! Shit! Jesus! I'm going to be sick."

"Rachael? Rachael? What is it? What happened?'

I was already kneeling over the toilet.

I cried into the bedroom, "Come home! You have to come home! Now!"

"Rachael," he shouted, "go to Heloise's! I'll catch the next flight out."

I was frozen in place by a toxic blend of terror and disgust—a glassy-eyed rodent carcass stared back at me. It was the size of a cat, its throat slashed, stuffed inside a bloody plastic bag and doused in perfume to hide the stench.

I knew all the drama couldn't be good for the baby. Most people sing lullabies and read stories to their unborn children. My baby was developing in a bath of adrenaline and nightmares of mutilated rodents, serenaded by the sounds of my terrified screams.

When I stopped trembling, I carried the box out front to the garbage.

Bruce dogged my every step. "I wouldn't throw that away. It's evidence."

"I am not keeping this thing with me in the house."

"Give it to me. I'll hang on to it until the police get here."

Relieved to have it out of my hands and out of my sight, I was passing it over to his outstretched hands when I noticed an envelope tucked inside, next to the plastic bag. It was the same stationery as the notes that had come with the suicide basket and the gasoline-soaked rags. The handwritten note read *You're the father of the most amazing little boy in the whole world. Your baby needs you. Get rid of your whore girlfriend. I belong in your bed, not her. If I can't be with you and fulfill our perfect destiny, no one will. You live inside me.* Pasted onto the note was a picture of a mutilated, bloody body. A cutout of Mick's head was carelessly glued onto the image.

After half a dozen more unsuccessful tries, I finally got Detective Melnitsky on the phone.

"She's back, Detective."

"Tell me exactly what happened, Ms. Allen."

"Well, she broke into the house and—"

"Did a squad car come?"

"The security firm got here quickly, checked everything out, and reported to the station before they realized that she'd left a package. But no police yet."

"You should have let me know, Ms. Allen."

Through clenched teeth, I said, "I tried! I got put on hold and was disconnected. I left you a voice message."

"Oh. Sorry, I was out on another case. Did you get a look at her this time?" he asked.

"No, but a neighbor saw a blond woman digging through our garbage earlier."

I heard him typing.

"She left some really sick stuff behind."

"What kind of stuff?"

"A shoebox wrapped in brown paper, with the biggest rat in it I've ever seen, its throat slashed, and a note."

He cleared his throat and paused before asking, "What does the note say?"

I pulled the note from the drawer and read it to him as calmly as if I were reading a postage-due notice—until I got to the part that said, "Get rid of your whore girlfriend." My voice cracked as a rush of heat seized my chest, raced up my neck, and grabbed my throat.

"Ms. Allen, I'll need to come by and dust for fingerprints and get the note. Is now a good time?"

"A good time?" I snorted. "Yeah."

The next day, Melnitsky called back. "Same fingerprints as before—no hair fibers, no evidence."

No progress in the case.

Chapter 42

It was Ladies' Night, half price. The place was loud and crowded but far different than I'd envisioned—cleaner. The smell wasn't unpleasant, but it wasn't something I would dab behind my ears. Still, I couldn't have felt more out of place if I had stepped into a guys' locker room after a game. But I had been outnumbered. Though Mick and my father agreed on nothing, they each, unaware of the other's position, gave me the you-have-to-be-prepared speech. And after the gasoline-and-match incident and the dead rat under my pillow, still with no solid clues for the police to follow up on, I caved.

The firing range was populated by camo-outfitted, macho hunting types; a few men who looked like they should be banned from owning firearms; and a handful of frightened women, like myself, each of whom I was certain must have her own horror story that had brought her there.

Mick had said he was around guns as a kid—the unlicensed variety. He'd never done much with them except shoot beer cans off a fence in the woods behind his trailer park. My dad was more the gun-club variety. I'd never understood the appeal. But now I viewed that angry hunk of metal as a security blanket, a last resort in case the unthinkable happened. I couldn't deny that things were getting worse.

I was twelve the first and only time I'd held a gun—at my father's insistence. He hadn't gotten the male hunting partner he longed for, and I was the next-best thing. I hated everything about it. I hated aiming at unsuspecting turtles basking on rocks in the sun and at sparrows flying to who knows where—maybe to nests where un-hatched eggs awaited the warmth of their mothers' bodies. But I did as I was told. It was only a BB gun, but to me it felt like an AK-47. My father was a good teacher, and I was a good student, but when a bird fell from the sky and hit the ground with a thud, I couldn't stop crying. He couldn't teach me how not to feel that. That was the first and last shooting lesson for father and daughter.

Now, almost fourteen years later, Ed, a guy sporting a seventies-era mustache and decked out in camo from head to toe, was regaling me with the pros and cons of a .22 versus a .45.

He pointed at the .22-caliber pistol he'd placed on the counter while scratching his thick mustache with the other hand. "If this is for self-defense, you might have to shoot 'em three or four times before you'd do any real damage." Then he lovingly picked up the .45 and held it out with both hands as if ready to genuflect and bow his head. "With a .45, all it takes is one shot, and you're done."

Any gun was a weapon of mass destruction, as far as I was concerned.

Ed continued, "Try this. A Kimber .45." He paused for effect and straightened the bill of his cap. "The Cadillac of .45s."

I picked it up. It was heavier than I'd thought it would be. I didn't even know enough to ask questions, but Ed was patient with my complete lack of gun know-how, showing me how to load, how to lock and unlock the safety, how to hold it, aim, and shoot. I wasn't nervous until he started a list of *dos* and *don'ts*. "Don't do this, or you could lose part of your little finger. If you do this, I promise you, you'll only do it once. Don't stand like this, or you'll feel it in your back tomorrow. Hold it like this because it's going to kick back into your chest." He handed me earplugs, headphones, and a box of fifty bullets.

"Enjoy," he said as if sending me off for a facial and a mani-pedi. "Just let the guy in the orange vest know if you need anything."

I walked through double glass doors and onto the firing range. The noise of gunfire penetrated even the earplugs and headphones, the shots resonating in my chest.

The detailed instructions Ed had provided seemed to vaporize. I picked up the heavy chunk of metal and examined it. I had to admit it was sleek and elegant in a rough, masculine sort of way. But it felt as foreign in my hand as if I'd just reached down and discovered I'd sprouted a penis.

If I pulled the trigger, I would be crossing a line. But a strong survival instinct had kicked in. I had to be prepared to defend myself and protect my baby.

As I squeezed the trigger, the sound reverberated through my earplugs, my arms jerked up uncontrollably, my shoulders kicked back, and my feet, which I thought were firmly planted, stumbled. The raw power contained in the machine I held in my hands was greater and infinitely more frightening than anything I'd imagined.

The next day, Mick and I headed to the police station. He sat crumpled on a bench in the corner, sunglasses on, a hood over his head, his one uncasted knee bouncing up and down, up and down. He looked like a meth dealer awaiting booking instead of a celebrity seeking protection. The forms said in bold, capital lettering that the applicant had to appear in person, no exceptions. I had no official address in New York, which meant Mick had to apply for the permit and buy the gun himself. I handed him a clipboard with the forms, and he began scribbling his information. His presence in the station triggered the usual rubbernecking then a trickle of autograph seekers and people wanting photographs with him. Before long, the paps would appear. Mick Sullivan getting a gun permit in a Brooklyn police station would be a great story.

"Come with me, Mr. Sullivan. You can finish the paperwork back here." An officer escorted us to what looked like an interrogation room and shut the door.

"That was nice of him," I said.

Mick glanced at the two-way mirror on the wall. "Yeah. Let's get this over with and get the hell out of here."

Once the application was approved, Mick walked out of a gun store on New Utrecht Avenue in Brooklyn, sporting a $1,500 Kimber .45 with a rosewood grip. He brought it home, loaded it, and ceremoniously placed it in a drawer next to the sofa. Rather than making me feel safer, more secure, the weapon's presence only amplified my growing dread.

The next day, Melnitsky called. "Good news, Ms. Allen."

I frantically motioned to Mick to come closer, and I put the phone on speaker.

"We've got her. She confessed. We're holding her for questioning. I'll keep you in the loop."

"Are you sure?" I shook with excitement.

"As I said, we're questioning her now, and we'll do a fingerprint match to be sure."

I hung up and cried with relief. Mick held me, and for the first time in a long time, I felt safe. The nightmare was over.

Chapter 43

The door buzzer went off. I jumped at the sound and slapped my hands over my heart as the espresso pod flew across the room. Pregnancy had heightened my senses, and the dead rodent and gasoline-and-match incidents had left me incredibly skittish. The smell of gasoline fumes had taken up permanent residence in my brain. I unconsciously held my breath as I walked over to the intercom, pressed the video button, and stared at the screen.

"Grace? I didn't recognize you at first—with the hair. Just a sec. The buzzer hasn't been working right. I'll come open the door." I turned and yelled into the house, "Mick! Grace is here!"

As I opened the front door, he walked up behind me, sliding his arm around my disappearing waistline.

She handed me a steel-gray envelope. "Here, this was stuck in your mail drop. Looks like it didn't quite make it through." It had a typed address and a postmark on it, so I folded it in half and stuffed it in my pocket. "What's the bodyguard's name?" she whispered, glancing in Bruce's direction.

"Bruce."

She snickered.

"Yeah, I know."

"Randy sent over a ton of scripts for you to read, Mick. They're in the car. Why don't you just run right out and get them?" she said, making running motions with her fingers.

"Yes, ma'am, Miss Woodelson," he said with a mock salute.

She tossed him the keys.

"Be careful, Mick," I warned. "There's still ice on the steps. Let's not break the other leg."

Ignoring my warning, he hobbled down the steps to retrieve the box from Grace's car. I stepped out onto the stoop. Most of the snow and ice had melted, but I could still see my breath. I rubbed my arms to remove the chill. The air was crisp and fresh, and the breeze made the clouds look like shifting white sands on a pristine beach of blue. It was midday. The street was vacant, the older kids in school, the little ones napping. And the paps? *Who knows and who cares.* Right then, in that moment, I could stand on the stoop, enjoy the spectacular weather, and pretend my life was normal. *Maybe now it will be.*

Mick stopped to talk to Bruce and gestured down the street, clearly giving him permission to take a well-deserved break now that the stalker was in custody. Bruce surveilled the area one more time before he reluctantly jogged down to the corner bodega, ever vigilant despite our break from worry.

Grace turned toward me. "So, Rachael, I understand congratulations are in order." She said it casually, as though we were friends getting together for chai lattes and girl talk.

"Thanks, Grace." I was never quite sure whether she was being genuine or condescending.

"You know, when we first met, you and Mick as a couple wasn't something I would have predicted. But," she continued, "he's a good guy. Not too many of them, especially in this business, and for him, being with someone who's not a part of all this crazy shit might be what he needs. Maybe you can help keep him on track."

I laughed and shook my head. "Thanks. But I don't know how much influence I have on him."

Mick approached the stairs, lugging the box of scripts, and Grace surprised me when she leaned forward to hug me. The two of us had gotten off to a rocky start, but she was making unexpected overtures of friendship. Maybe this was a clean slate. Perhaps a détente-like friendship was in our future.

I heard a car backfire in the distance and watched nearby pigeons take off in flight. No, not a car. A popping sound. I heard it again and cocked my head to listen. Firecrackers? In January? And again. Grace jerked, and hugged me more tightly.

"Grace? You're going to knock me over. What are you doing? Grace?"

Her body went limp, and she slipped out of my arms and down onto the stoop.

"Grace!"

She lay there in an unnaturally contorted pile, blood trickling down the steps, creating small, delicately designed crimson puddles in the patches of leftover ice and snow.

I jerked my head up. Papers were everywhere, some still floating gracefully in midair, butterflies in flight looking for just the right spot to alight. Mick was standing in the midst of the swarm, gripping one arm . . . blood oozing through his fingers and a look of mute incomprehension on his face. I had the urge to scream, but nothing about the scene felt real enough to warrant a scream. I wanted to rush down the stairs to him, but my movements were two beats behind my brain. Another popping sound was followed by a searing pain in my shoulder and the shocking sight of my own blood.

Heloise opened her door and stuck her head out to survey the chaos.

"Heloise, go back inside. Now!" I yelled.

Mick stumbled, backing away from the stoop. He seemed in shock, unable to make the rational decision to take two steps forward and climb the stoop to safety. Knocked sideways with terror, I wanted to run to him. I screamed his name, but he didn't seem to hear. I felt the rush of another bullet whiz by. The porch light shattered, and shards of glass rained down on my head. My body was pumping out adrenaline like an uncapped fire hydrant.

I whipped around to run inside and call 911.

For the first time, my pregnant belly felt cumbersome as I scurried up the steps. My blood smeared over the rug in the vestibule—the rug I'd noticed the first time I entered his place, the one we made love on, the one that the first frightening letter and later the gasoline-soaked rags were dropped onto. I collapsed onto my knees and scrambled into the parlor. My bleeding arm gave way, and I fell face-first onto the hardwood floor. As I righted myself, blood dribbled into my eye. I grabbed my phone and dialed 911.

I screamed the address before the operator even had a chance to speak. "Someone's outside with a gun, and she's going to kill us. Hurry! Please!"

I dropped the phone, crawled over to the end table by the sofa, jerked open the drawer, and reached inside. The gun was right where we left it. The rosewood handle felt smooth and reassuring in my hand this time. I scrambled to the window, pulled myself up on the windowsill, and saw Mick on his knees, hunched over. A blond woman hovered, pointing a gun at his head, her finger on the trigger. Mick was shielding his face with his hands, looking up at her every few seconds, wild-eyed. One shot at close range, and his life would be over.

I managed to raise the window a couple of inches, perch the pistol on the windowsill, and aim as best I could. The gun was even heavier than I remembered. My hands trembled and my body pulsated with fear as I tried to conjure up the lesson—how to hold the gun, how to aim, how to steady my hand, how to prepare for the kickback. But no one had prepared me for the level of panic I was experiencing, or the torturous feeling of aiming at a living, breathing person. Sweat trickled down my forehead, lingered on my brow, and mixed with blood before it slipped into my eye, blurring my vision. This was a universe away from the shooting range, where I let out a celebratory yelp when I hit the bull's-eye. I would have nothing to celebrate if I hit the target this time. Even less if I missed. *Focus, Rachael. Focus!* This was it. Everything depended on the accuracy of my aim.

The pain in my shoulder sizzled. Blood dripped from my sleeve to the floor, and the sight made me weak, nauseated, unsure. I had to focus. *One shot.* I would have a single shot to hit the target. That woman was so close to him. I closed one eye and looked down the sight as the instructor had showed me. *One shot.* Release the safety. *One shot.* The hammering of my heart drowned out all sound. The woman suddenly turned her face toward the sun, the gun still pointed at Mick's head, and closed her eyes. For a single flicker in time, she looked positively beatific, as if patiently awaiting the rapture. I prayed along with her as I pulled the trigger and squeezed my eyes shut.

I felt it.

Deep inside.

My throat tightened, and I gasped for air, but it was like breathing in reverse. All the blood left my face, and the burning, throbbing pain in my arm was magnified a thousandfold. Outside the window was a jumble of a never-before-imagined scene, and inside, a fire pit of my scorched emotions. Ejecting the gun from my fingers, I stared in disbelief. Mick lay on the ground, his head smeared with blood, the woman lying motionless next to him.

"I killed him," I said out loud, choking on my words.

My sense of loss, of grief, was immediate, blinding and bottomless, as if someone had reached into my chest and ripped out all my vital organs. The hideous realization of what I'd done and the thought of my life without Mick sliced through me, and I cried out as I doubled over, clutching my heart, and the pain vomited out of me.

They say it's your past that flashes before your eyes, but I saw my future, the one that would never be. I was left with half a life, my future a gaping, ugly wound. I glanced at the gun on the floor and, for a nanosecond of mindless grief, considered stopping my pain with a single shot.

The police rushed in and raised my sagging form from the floor as my body shook in violent surges. I hungrily took in gulps of air between sobs.

The officers guided what was left of me to the front door, and I inhaled the crisp air I'd been enjoying just a few life-altering minutes before. I scanned the insanity of the scene. The street was flooded with flashing lights and sirens and people scurrying around. As they helped me into the back of an ambulance, what I saw made me doubt my sanity.

Chapter 44

Mick was crumpled against the door of the ambulance, clutching his arm against his blood-soaked shirt.

I was astonished I didn't hear, didn't see the events unfold. Heloise had run back inside and returned to the stoop, gripping her old Colt .45 pistol. Startled by Heloise's appearance on her stoop, the woman shook her gun in Mick's face, shouting at him that they would now be together forever.

I'd always thought Heloise was embellishing her story when she said she was a good shot, but she'd assumed the position, aimed, and squeezed the trigger without hesitation. At the exact moment Heloise hit her target, I had fired and missed. I didn't even come close—the bullet embedded itself in the trunk of an old red maple across the street. But the gunshot, Mick's collapse, and the blood smeared on his temples convinced me that I'd delivered a kill shot, not to that deluded woman, but to the person I loved most in this world.

Grace was declared dead at the scene. A bullet had entered her back and pierced her heart. I couldn't help but wonder if I might've been the one carted off to the mortuary if she hadn't dyed her hair to look like mine.

The police cars, the security detail, and the ambulances buzzed. Reporters and paparazzi would descend any minute. Mick was ashen and shaken, his easygoing demeanor replaced with a look of childlike shock, betrayal, and pain. He and Gracie always went head-to-head, and obscenities flew whenever they talked, but they'd been together for ten years, starting long before his career took off. She'd been like a sister you always fought with but loved anyway.

As the police led me down the front steps, Mick looked up and shivered in relief. When I reached the ambulance, his words spilled out, jagged with unrealized grief. "I heard the shots. I saw Gracie fall, and I saw you crawl inside. *Jesus*, there was so much blood... I thought..." He leaned over, pulling me in so tightly with his uninjured arm that I expected my ribs to crack. I ignored the stabbing pain in my shoulder. His next words were almost lost as he murmured into the nape of my neck and his erratic breathing echoed in my ear. "But you're okay. Thank God. I don't know what I would've done..."

We rode to the hospital in a protective bubble, stubbornly huddled together while the paramedics checked our vitals and tended to our wounds. The deafening sirens, the crackling voices over two-way radios, the cheap-gin smell of rubbing alcohol, the tinny scent of blood, and the flashing red lights—my senses were overwhelmed, and I was in a narrow tunnel, unsure of how long it would take to get to the end. Or whether there would even be an exit. Police followed close behind us, while another squad car drove to the Lower East Side address listed on the would-be assassin's driver's license.

A pack of hungry paparazzi lay in wait at the ER entrance. Mick refused to be carried in on a stretcher, and he stood in front of me as a shield from the unrelenting flashes and shutter clicks, but he never let go of my hand. A chorus of voices shot from the crowd:

"Mick, what happened?"

"Mick, over here!"

"Mick, how bad are you hurt?"

"Mick, to your left!"

The black spots in my eyes from the flashes made it hard to maintain my balance. Mick swung at the camera closest to him, knocking it to the ground. I heard it shatter. "Get the fuck out of her face!" His grip on my hand tightened.

We made our way inside, and everyone—nurses, doctors, attendants, people waiting for medical attention—rubbernecked to catch a glimpse of our tabloid tragedy. Mick's grip was a vise around my fingers, but we were forced to unlock hands when the nurse instructed us to lie down on the examining tables and he separated us with a curtain. Our bloody but mostly superficial wounds were checked out by an ER doctor. I flinched when he placed a cold sonogram wand on my belly, and I nervously watched the screen until I heard the reassuringly rapid heartbeat. He bandaged my wounds and was working on Mick when I pulled the curtain back and mentally replayed the events from every angle imaginable.

"Rach, maybe you should sit down. Did they check to see if the baby is okay?"

"Don't move!" the nurse snapped at Mick as he attempted to sit up.

"They did a sonogram. The baby's fine," I said as I patted my stomach.

"Does it hurt?"

"Not too much. They gave me some painkillers they said would be safe for the baby."

An officer, dressed in a suit and tie that made him look like he was dropping by on his way to a funeral, hovered outside. He entered the room, flashing his badge just as the nurse left. "Detective Buckley." He zeroed in on me. "And your name is?" He had his notebook at the ready.

I took a step back. "Rachael Allen."

"Ms. Allen, could you tell me what your connection is to Mr. Sullivan and the incident today?"

Mick jumped in. "Just wait a fucking minute! I thought you guys had that crazy woman in custody. What the fuck happened?"

"After questioning, it became clear that it was a false confession."

"She confessed to something she didn't do?" Mick asked, incredulous.

"It happens," the detective said, shrugging.

"Shit. We've been telling you for months something like this was going to happen! You had us believing we were safe!"

The detective's cell rang. He turned away without excusing himself and stepped outside the room to answer. "Buckley here... Did you find anything? Deceased?... What else?... No shit... What does it say?... You sure it's him?... Okay, send it to me. I'll see what I can find out."

He came back into the room. "Mr. Sullivan, I need to ask you a few questions." He glanced at me. "Alone."

"Why?"

"Alone would be best for now, Mr. Sullivan."

That was my cue. "I'll go see if I can find something to drink." I leaned over to give Mick a peck on the cheek.

In time, I would hear the events told to the police and the lawyers, and Mick and I would rehash it so many times, trying to make sense of it all, that I began to feel as though I'd witnessed the exchange firsthand.

The detective dove in. "So, you two are in a relationship?"

"Yeah. Wait," Mick said, "I heard you say someone else was dead?"

"The woman's sister."

Mick stared dully into space. He'd bitten his lip hard and was licking off the blood.

"Mr. Sullivan?"

"Huh?"

"How long?"

"How long what?"

"How long have you and Ms. Allen been in a relationship?"

"What the hell does that have to do with anything?" Mick asked, irritated and confused, too weary to try to make sense of the question.

"Please, Mr. Sullivan. Just answer the question."

Mick sighed and raked his fingers through his hair. "I've known Rachael for about eight months, when all this shit started, but we've been together for maybe six."

"Did I hear correctly that she's pregnant?"

"Yeah."

"Do you know the woman who attacked you?"

"No. But it's gotta be the one who's been stalking and harassing Rachael and me over most of the last year, sending crazy letters, e-mails, and weird photos."

"You never had any personal contact with her?"

"Not that I know of." He shrugged. "I see thousands of people when I'm doing promotional tours. I only remember the ones I have regular contact with."

"Were you in Austin at a film festival earlier this year?"

"Yeah, but what does that have to do with anything?" he asked, his voice raised in irritation again.

"Did you meet a woman while you were there?" Buckley asked, his pen and notepad ready.

"I met lots of women..." He shook his head as he corrected himself. "I met lots of *people*."

"I'm specifically interested in the women you might have met."

"Okay..."

"Did you have sexual relations with any of the women you met while you were there?"

"Listen, Mister—" Mick started as he sat straighter.

"Detective Buckley."

"Listen, *Detective Buckley*, maybe you're getting off on this conversation, but it's starting to piss me off. Big-time."

"Believe me, Mr. Sullivan, it's relevant to the case. The sooner you answer my questions, the sooner you can get out of here. I don't give a shit if you pitched tents in every state from here to California. All I care about right now is what happened today and whether a woman you met in Austin might be related to the case. I'll ask again... Did you have sexual relations with any of the women you met in Austin at the film festival while you were there?"

He emptied his lungs of air. "Yeah," he said. He took a resigned breath and shook his head. "There was this one chick."

"Do you remember when and where?"

"I was staying at a hotel downtown . . . I forget the name . . . and I picked her up in the hotel bar. Or she picked me up. I was trashed. I wouldn't be able to ID her in a lineup."

"Did you see her again?"

"No. I left the next morning to catch a flight. That was it."

"Does the name Brenda Benton mean anything to you?"

"No...Wait. That's the name Melnitsky mentioned, but he said you couldn't find her." He glanced at the doorway, worried that I would be walking through at any moment. "Is that who this was?"

"It would seem so. Do you remember anything about the woman in Austin?"

"I think she was blond. That's all I remember. Are we done yet?"

"Not quite, Mr. Sullivan. The officers are in the shooter's apartment," the detective said. "There is a male infant there. And her deceased sister. She left a note. In it, she accused her sister of trying to take her baby away, to get custody—And she provided details about an alleged sexual encounter with you in Austin. And it says that you are the baby's father."

"Jesus! She's been saying that crazy shit for months." Mick jumped off the examining table, ready to make his exit.

"Mr. Sullivan, there's a photo of the two of you. Together. In bed."

Blood rushed to his face, pounded in his temples. He couldn't swallow. Buckley flipped his phone around and shoved it into Mick's line of vision.

"I can't see shit. I don't have my glasses."

Buckley pulled a pair of reading glasses out of a pocket and handed them to Mick. He slipped on the drugstore frames and took the phone from Buckley's hand. There he was. There she was. In bed together. His mouth gaped in a drunken sleep as she spooned his unconscious form, smiling, her breasts pressed up against his back, holding the phone at arm's length, gathering proof of their encounter—the same woman whose brains he'd just watched splatter all over the street outside his place.

As Mick stared at the photo, Buckley delivered the punch line. "The timing of the festival and the approximate age of the infant fit with her claims that you are the father. We will, of course, need a DNA swab to verify."

The image on the phone jump-started the right neurons. Snatches of memory that had been tickling the back of his brain for months came into focus, and he powered through the drunken fog of that night and the morning after. He later told me that the memory felt like an assault.

After forcing down vending-machine coffee and waiting for what I thought was a respectable amount of time, I reentered the ER. The smell of burnt coffee wafted in with me. The envelope Gracie had pulled from the mail slot and handed to me was clasped in my hand. It had survived the whole ordeal, pristine, unmarred.

"Mick, that woman really believed the two of you were getting married." The oversized steel-gray envelope was engraved with raised lettering scripted in robin's egg–blue ink. Fatigue and shock pummeled me as I handed him the invitation. He glanced at the elaborate script announcing his upcoming nuptials.

We invite you to join us in our celebration of love. The pleasure of your company is requested at the marriage of Mallory Brenda Benton to Michael Christopher Sullivan on February 25, 2023, at half past four in the afternoon.

His shoulders sank. He looked back up at me, cleared his throat, and wiped his nose with the back of his hand.

The nurse came in and swabbed the inside of Mick's cheek.

"What's that for?" I asked, confused and concerned.

"Rach," he whispered as he reached out for me, his voice hoarse with defeat. "Come here. There's something I have to tell you."

Epilogue
Twenty years later

"Are we grilling the steaks tonight?" my husband yells from his office.

"I'm mixing up the marinade now," I shout as I frantically whisk olive oil, fresh basil, and lemon juice together. "My parents will be here soon."

Our son is home from college for the summer, and they're anxious to see him. Right now, he's sequestered in his bedroom, and I hear the familiar hum of music coming from his room. My husband's own brand of music drifts up from his office into the kitchen, blending in, creating a kind of musical porridge that sounds just right.

The door buzzer goes off, and Chili, our ten-year-old labradoodle, begins barking her head off. Once again, I yell toward the bedrooms, "Guys, they're here!"

My husband comes bounding up the stairs two at a time, guitar in hand, and for a second, I don't see the man I've shared my life with, raised our son with, and slept next to for twenty years. I see the twenty-something celebrity who bought an espresso machine in Zabar's with me and sent my life down an impossible-to-predict path. He stands in front of me and looks down at his faded T-shirt then back at me. He still has the ability to give me that look, and in a flash I'm twenty-four again, standing in the parlor, drowning in desire as he leans in to kiss me for the first time. I can almost taste the brandy and tobacco on his lips, though he's long since stopped smoking, and he hasn't tasted like brandy in years, not since he joined AA almost twenty years ago. He has a few more laugh lines, and that famous head of hair has specks of silver, but he's still heartbreakingly handsome.

He hangs the guitar on the wall next to a plaque from last year that recognized our talent agency, Serendipity Tunes, for its accomplishments.

"Should I change?" he asks.

"You look fine."

I hear the door buzzer again. "I'll get it," I say, but I pause, my hand pressed against his chest, absorbing his reassuring heartbeat, before I turn and head to the front door with Chili leading the way, her tail wagging like a metronome to a silent tune.

"Hi, sweetheart!" my mother chirps as she steps in. Barely pausing to take a breath, she says, "You're missing a light bulb out there. You need to replace it. It's not safe at night." She's still trying to create order where none exists.

"Okay, Mom. I will."

"Where is everybody?" she asks, craning her neck to peek around the corner into the parlor. She bends to give Chili an obligatory head scratching.

"They're here. Come on in."

"Your father insisted we take a car service," she leans in and whispers as they step into the vestibule. "He's just not up for trains and subways. You know how it is."

Mick appears from the kitchen, and my father is the first to greet him with a brusque, almost comically masculine embrace and a pat on the back. "Hey, son! How's the music business these days?"

"Good, good. Can't complain. Have a seat, Don."

Against all odds, the two of them now have a warm, amiable relationship. Sometimes, they even attend AA meetings together.

Mick all but gave up acting after the shooting and turned to music, his true passion. It's one we've shared all these years as we worked together at Serendipity Tunes, the agency we established together. He still does the occasional cameo role, and the media takes the inevitable stroll down memory lane, but I'm thankful it never lasts long.

"Can I fix either of you something to drink?" Mick offers.

"Michael, honey, do you have any iced tea?" my mother asks in her sweetest Southern drawl.

"That works for me too," my father chimes in.

We are now a family of hard-core teetotalers.

"Coming right up," Mick says and disappears into the kitchen.

He returns with their drinks just as my cell rings. I glance at the name.

"Sorry. I need to get this." I step into the kitchen, out of earshot.

"Well, if it isn't my favorite movie mogul," I greet Jenna.

"Rachael, brace yourself. You're not going to freakin' believe who called me today, asking for a favor."

"Who?"

"Just guess."

"Jen, I don't have a clue. Just tell me."

She pauses dramatically then blurts it out like a kid who's been sworn to secrecy but it's just too juicy not to share. "Shane Dwyer!"

"Nooo," I say, sinking onto a bar stool at the kitchen island.

We haven't kept tabs on Shane. In fact, he and Mick haven't spoken in years. "What the hell did he want?"

"Oh, that's the best part. He called because he needed me—*me*—to green-light a project for him. His career is in Titanic mode, and he's trying to salvage what he can. I've waited twenty years to screw that guy over, and it felt so freakin' good!" She's giddy, flushed with revenge, and as much as I hate to admit it, the news warms me to my core.

"Rach, have you *seen* him lately? He looks like a freaky Michael Jackson 'after' photo. That pretty face of his wasn't holding up too well even before the plastic surgery, but now . . ." She bursts into laughter. "I'm sending you a pic."

My phone dings, and I glance at his image. "Jesus. Thanks a lot, Jen. Now I won't be able to get that out of my head."

I hear a young man's impatient voice in the background. One of the many perks of Jenna's job is a constant parade of preternaturally attractive young actors. She couldn't be happier.

"Sounds like you're busy, Jen, and my parents are here, so I need to go anyway. Can I call you later?"

"Oh, sure. Tell Don and Sarah I said hi. And be sure and tell Mick about his douchebag of an ex-friend."

"Will do," I say, nodding to myself.

"I miss you. When are you and hubs coming to visit?"

"Soon," I promise. "Love ya, Jen."

"You too."

Our son walks into the kitchen, and as happens more and more these days, I'm thrown off balance for a split second as my brain processes the vision before me. He's the "spittin' image of Mick," as Cora would say. And I adore how much he looks like his father.

He ambles into the parlor. "Hi, Gran, Papa. How's it going?" His baritone voice is the genetic icing on the cake.

My parents rise in unison from the sofa, groaning softly, and they reach out to greet him as if he's just returned from a tour of duty. I feel oddly guilty that my parents are here and Cora isn't. She passed away last year, and it almost destroyed Mick. The three of us traveled to Louisiana to take her home and say good-bye, but we haven't gone back. It's too hard. I planted jasmine in the garden to remind us of her, of the perfume she wore, and each time a breeze drifts in, she's standing right here beside me, wrapping me in a hug, promising, "Everything's gonna be just fine." She never questioned our decision. Not for a second.

"You look more like your father every day," my father says without a trace of resentment. He has surprised me the most. His love for his grandson and his affection for Mick are now deep and genuine.

"Yeah, I get that a lot," he says. "My friends' moms are always"—he transitions to a strained falsetto—"'Has anyone ever told you that you look like that actor Mick Sullivan?' When I tell them he's my dad, they go all fangirl on me. It's actually kind of creepy."

My son. I couldn't love him more if I'd carried him for nine months. We already had custody of Christopher when I learned my pregnancy was no longer viable. I cried—a lot. And I consoled myself with the certainty that we would have other chances. But there would be no other pregnancies, no other children. I couldn't help but wonder whether our unborn son would've looked as much like Mick as Christopher does. They would've been only a few months apart in age. Maybe they would have been mistaken for twins.

Christopher is a part of me now, and I can't imagine my life without him. I came to realize that as devastating as the whole Brenda Benton episode was, it's what led me to the love of my life and made this family of ours possible.

"Tell them about your grades, Christopher," Mick says.

"Oh, yeah, Gran, I got a three-point-eight GPA. Not too shabby."

"We're so proud of you, Chris." My mother glances at me before zeroing in on Christopher again.

I tense up because I know what's coming.

"Have you decided yet what you want to do when you graduate?" she asks.

That's a touchy subject in our house.

"Mom, he doesn't have to decide right now. He's still got another year of business school."

"I'm just concerned for his future. It never hurts to start planning ahead." She turns toward Christopher.

His lemon-tinted hair—the only clue to the other half of his biological heritage—falls in his face as he fidgets with the hamsa hanging around his neck, blissfully unaware of its chain of custody. "I'm thinking about the acting thing—if Dad will help me." He glances over at Mick, who's sticking to his noncommittal stance.

"We'll see," Mick says. "Just graduate first. Then we'll talk."

I couldn't have concocted a more painfully absurd irony. If Christopher succeeds, Mick will have to guide him through the disorienting maze of fame, and I'll do my best to stand back, let him find his own way, and pray he'll be safe.

I return to my kitchen detail, make the salad, check the potatoes baking in the oven, and then I see Mick, Christopher, and my parents making their way to the garden in its full watercolor bloom. I peer out the kitchen window as Mick and my father "discuss" the best way to grill the steaks, my mother patting my father's arm, acting as mediator. Christopher is looking on, shaking his head at the predictability of the scene. And I'm comforted by the perfect mundaneness of it all.

My life is not what I envisioned the day I asked Mick Sullivan for his photo in Zabar's, and it's certainly not a typical tale of finding love and creating a family, but I'm wrapped in muddled wonderment that it's mine. At times like this, Cora's prophetic words come back to me: "Hon, life has a way of surprising the dickens out of you."

Yes, it does.

Acknowledgements

A special thank-you to Sita Romero, Trish Parker-Knight, and Elise Schiller, for critiquing pages and pages and pages of rewrites. And to Lidija Kljenak Hilje and the Writers Book Club for the many enlightening group discussions on what makes a story sing. A special shout out to Wila Phillips, who critiqued my pages ad nauseam for longer than I care to admit, as I worked my way through the story and for being such a good friend and confidante. Thank you to my editor, Sara Gardiner, who let me see I needed to cut a chunk of the story and write it anew, as well as my line editor, Kelly Reed, who forced me to justify every word. And an immense thank-you to Dana Walker, my sister from another mother, who has been my rock and main cheerleader for as long as I can remember. I would be remiss if I didn't thank the Women's Fiction Writers Association, an amazing group of writers who have answered questions and provided feedback for everything from the book's title to very specific questions about whether a character's actions made sense. A flashback shoutout to the Austin Writers Meetup Group, where this story started several years ago, and to Chris Hernandez, whom I met in the Meetup Group, and who gave me insight into the police procedures. A special note of gratitude to Dr. Reid Meloy, who graciously took time out of his busy schedule to talk to me about the psychology of stalking. And, last, but not least, a bucket of appreciation to Lynn McNamee, the publisher at Red Adept Publishing, who agreed to take on the story and whose team provided me with a knockout cover.